THE PROTECTOR

THE BENEFACTOR

THE PROTECTOR

Jenifer A. Ruth

Five Star • Waterville, Maine

Copyright © 2003 by Jenifer Ruth

First Edition
First Printing: October 2003

Set in 11 pt. Plantin.

Printed in the United States on permanent paper.

Library of Congress Cataloging-in-Publication Data

Ruth, Jenifer.
    The protector / Jenifer Ruth.—1st ed.
      p. cm.
    "Five Star first edition titles"—T.p. verso.
    ISBN 1-59414-027-8 (hc : alk. paper)
    1. Police—Nevada—Las Vegas—Fiction. 2. Las Vegas (Nev.)—Fiction. 3. Serial murders—Fiction. I. Title.
PS3618.U777P75 2003
    813'.6—dc21   2003052870

To Kathy, my inspiration.
And a special thanks to Sherri and Melisa for all your
support and advice. I couldn't have done it without you.

Chapter One

Shrieks and gasps filled the darkened room as a frame of glittering, medieval blades plunged with a resounding thud into the silk-covered body of the young woman lying on the table.

The heavy beat of drums pounded through the room like a heartbeat. The delicate scent of wildflowers wafted through the air-conditioned breeze, bringing to mind afternoons spent in peaceful meadows.

As the swords pierced the cloth, rainbow colored confetti exploded outward from the cloaked figure, sparkling in the bright stage lights and dusting a few people sitting in the front row.

For a moment, complete silence echoed in the darkness.

Laughter and applause trickled down from the back of the room, fanning forward. Heads craned to watch the tall, willowy redhead being lead down the aisle by her toga-clad assistant. With a single hand against her back, the man guided her past the rows of tables and seats, grinning and nodding at the dazed patrons. As she climbed the stage steps, the woman who'd just avoided certain death smiled down into the astonished faces of her audience. The two glided past the lethal rack of swords still quivering in the table on which the woman had lain. Standing center stage, they turned as one. The man stepped back and kneeled at the woman's feet. With a flourish, sending wispy red and silver scarves dancing around the sparkling blue of her body suit, she bowed.

Haunting Celtic music blazed to life, bringing the audience to their feet. Her assistant joined the general applause as he backed off the stage. The spotlight narrowed, centering on the woman, who eased forward with a serene smile gracing her delicate face while her raised hands commanded silent attention.

The velvet caress of her husky voice slid over the audience as she addressed them one final time. "I hope you have enjoyed the magic and mystery that you've witnessed here tonight. It has been a true pleasure performing for you. If you take one thing home this evening I would like it to be this: Magic exists all around you, every day of your lives. If you remember that, your life will always be filled with miracles. You need only to reach out and embrace the wonder of it."

With that said, she spread her arms wide. Mist bubbled up around her, swirling about her ankles, fluttering the scarves that formed her skirt.

Then, without warning, she was gone.

Staring into the large mirror framed with a line of naked light bulbs, Alana sighed and rubbed more cold cream from her face. Most of her skin was clean, but no matter how hard she wiped, her eyeliner clung above her lashes, making her jade green eyes look garish. At times, she couldn't believe that what appeared so beautiful and glamorous under the stage lighting somehow managed to make her look like a two-bit hooker under normal circumstances. But as much as she hated the stage makeup, she had to wear it. Stage lights wiped out every bit of color on her face, leaving her a washed-out ghost with flame-red hair, sharing a striking resemblance to a banshee. And the only alternative she had to wearing the goop would raise far too many questions, ones that she was not prepared to answer.

Without even a knock for warning, the door to her small dressing room swung open, sending a gust of cool air into the miniscule room. Rick sauntered in, still clad in the toga but with a short, terry cloth robe covering his sweat soaked chest. "Good show tonight, Alana."

Alana grinned at the ritual words. Rick always ended the evening with the same sentence. She swore she could stand on stage for hours on end pulling rabbits out of a hat and asking people to pick-a-card-any-card, and he'd say the exact same thing. "I don't know, Rick," she muttered, scrubbing again at her lashes. "There's still something missing from the ending of the second show. And unlike our esteemed manager, I don't think it's topless female assistants."

"Tom giving you a hard time about that again, eh?" Rick asked, flopping into the chair next to her and snagging a towel from a hook beside her mirror.

"Yeah. Just because it's the late show and this is Las Vegas does *not* mean I have to surround myself with half-naked women." Alana began dabbing in vain at her eyeliner with a cream covered Q-tip, gnawing on her bottom lip.

Rick rubbed the towel across his chest and the back of his neck below his sweat-plastered, toffee brown hair while stealing a gulp of the diet soda Alana always drank after the show. "No, just half-naked men. I never took you for the type to perpetrate a double standard. I feel so used."

Alana gave an exaggerated wince at the dramatic whine in Rick's voice. Staring into the mirror again, she threw the Q-tip down with a disgusted growl and grabbed her soda from him. "You know what I mean. If I gave him half a chance, Tom would have *me* up there, prancing around nude. I get enough flack from the family as it is, just being a stage magician. I'm sure *that* would go over real well with Dad."

Rick smirked and leaned back, arms and ankles crossed. "Well, you'd certainly get a different reaction from the men in the audience when you disappeared, that's for sure—less amazement, and much more disappointment."

Alana rolled her eyes as she put her soda down as far from Rick as possible. "Very funny. I'm just shaking with laughter. But seriously, what do you think of the last bit, with me vanishing in the mist? Is it dramatic enough? I feel like it's almost anticlimactic after the swords, but what else could I do?"

Rick rocked on the back legs of his chair, a rhythmic squeak filling the air, and thought about it for a moment. "I guess it *is* a bit of a let down. But if we want to change it, you'll have to rework the whole thing—do a new illusion entirely. If you get any more blatant with your vanishing act, dropping the mist or something, some of the *real* magicians will start wondering exactly how you did it. At least this way, they can blame it on misdirection, mirrors, or God knows what else."

Alana sighed and leaned back in her own chair, picking up the can again and holding the cool soda can against her temple. "I guess you're right, and notice I'm ignoring that real magician crack. I'm more of a real magician than they are, and you know it. They're illusionists, amateurs and imitators. I'm the real thing."

Rick heaved a mock sigh. "Yeah, yeah. Let's go out and start the first faerie pride parade. Create a new Rainbow Coalition. I don't think you want to be the first fey to come out of the closet in front of non-believing humans. You hate the fact that your photo is on billboards advertising the show. You refused to do the TV spot. I can't imagine how you'd deal with the *Enquirer* crowd hounding your every step. Not to mention what your family would say. It's bad enough that you use your powers as entertainment for the norms."

"Hey, a girl's got to earn a living."

Rick cast his gaze skyward, appealing to the heavens for understanding. "Tell it to your dad. Or mine for that matter. They're the ones giving me crap for not stopping you. I keep telling them that I'm just the hired help, but they don't buy it."

Alana smiled at the thought of big, strong Carrick Murphy brought to his knees by two men in their mid-fifties living a continent away. "I appreciate you sticking up for me, Rick. I know that they can both be a pain. But as long as I keep up with my other duties, there's not a whole lot Dad can say about it. I wish he'd realize that I'm an adult and can make my own decisions. I *am* twenty-seven years old, you know."

"Yeah, but you're still daddy's little girl. It's the curse of being the first daughter."

Alana shrugged and began brushing some of the mousse from her flame-red curls. It was an old argument, one that wouldn't change any time soon, if ever. "But you'd think he'd be more fixated on Adain. He's the one off on a wandering spree, with no direction and not following in the family footsteps."

Rick reached forward, dropping a single hand to her shoulder, giving it a light squeeze. "True, but I think your dad's given your twin up as a lost cause. At least you're *trying* to do your duty."

Alana dropped her brush, crossing her arms against her

chest. An angry shade of red crept up her pale cheeks as her lips pursed. "That's right. I *am* doing that, whether I like it or not. How many other women spend all their free time defending the people of a city from witches, warlocks, demons, and God knows what else? Instead of spending my evenings going out on dates, I risk my life for little or no reward. If my dad or yours gives you any more problems about my degrading choice of professions, remind them of that."

Rick shook his head, not the least bit intimidated by her ire. "It's not so much your dad as mine. He doesn't think I'm doing a proper job as your Helper. He says I'm a disgrace to the family, a complete disappointment—that I need to put my foot down with you, guide you back in the proper direction."

Alana snorted. "You wish. You're my Helper, Rick, not my husband."

At that, Rick leaned back, laughing, his eyes dancing. "Too right, even if you were my type, I'd not wish that job on myself."

"Thanks a lot. I really needed the ego boost."

Rick patted her slumped shoulders, then stood with a wink. "Any time, love. Any time. For now, put a shake in it. I hate waiting at the bar alone. All those poor women throwing themselves at me, and no one there to protect me, or at least to weed out the undesirables. You wouldn't want me paired up with some brainless bimbo, or worse yet, a boring matronly-type." Rick gave her his best "I'm a poor, pitiful waif" look.

She laughed.

"Go on, get out of here and get dressed, already. I'll be there to defend your honor as much as you want it defended, I promise. I just need a shower first. I've got to get this gunk out of my hair. But we're not going overboard to-night. The show may be dark tomorrow, but we have other work to do. I think I've got a handle on what's bothering that woman you brought me." Alana smiled at Rick's down-cast expression. "I know you were hoping to squeeze in a date with her before we tied this one up, but if I get no so-cial life, neither do you, Helper."

"You're such a slave driver. Why I decided to stick with you instead of going off with Adain or Fiona I'll never know."

Alana shoved him out of the room. "Because I can put up with more of your insanity than my sister, and your dad would disown you if you hung around my ne'er-do-well brother."

Rick shook his head and grinned as the door snapped shut in his face.

Shadows lurked in the corners of the empty employee parking lot. The low heels of Alana's one true extravagance, Italian leather shoes, clicked sharply against the asphalt. In the distance, she could hear the cars speeding along Fla-mingo Road. The heat absorbed in the pavement still radi-ated through her soles, warming her feet.

Just another night in Las Vegas, and they call New York the city that never sleeps, she thought with a half-smile.

Alana stared into space as she walked, running images from the show through her mind and fixating on the ending. There *had* to be something she could do that wouldn't draw too many questions from the professional magic commu-nity, something dramatic, something memorable, but not too showy.

She hummed one of the livelier tunes from the show as she rummaged through her purse for her keys. Rick always gave her a hard time about all the junk she carried around. He said he couldn't believe she ever found anything in the bottomless pit she schlepped around. He kept threatening to get one of those rolling suitcases for her, so she'd have more room to spread out. According to him, the only reason he didn't was for fear that she'd find a way to fill that up, too.

As she got closer to where she remembered parking, Alana began pushing the button on her key ring. A shrill beep echoed through the garage and her headlights flashed. *I don't know how I ever found my car before they invented these things.*

As Alana reached her car, she caught sight of a faint glimmer of gold shining on the ground. She leaned down and saw a delicate golden claddagh charm lying there, hands clasped around a tiny heart wearing a crown. Someone would miss the little charm when they got home that evening. She decided to hold onto it for now and ask around about it in the morning. Someone would report it missing. It was too expensive a piece of jewelry for someone to give it up for lost without at least calling about it. Lost-and-found would have a report on it. She bent down to pick it up

This act alone saved her life.

As she reached down, a large, heavy object whizzed over her head, tearing several strands of her hair out along with it. The sound of metal smashing against metal rang in her ears. Instinct kicked in, dropping Alana to her knees, mindless of the ground tearing through her hose and scraping her knees and palms.

Without thought, she rolled to the side, focusing and chanting, heat shooting up her arms, gathering in her hands. Her fingers twisted in rapid patterns, rainbow colored lights sparkling at their tips. The scent of wildflowers overpowered the smell of pent-up exhaust fumes that permeated the garage. The faint chiming of tiny bells rose from nowhere. A human shape coalesced in front of her.

A perfect copy of Alana stood up, turned to face her attacker, and then cowered against the side of her car.

Her attacker, masked, with his shape disguised by a long coat, followed the illusionary Alana, slamming a crowbar through her. The metal door crunched, and glass exploded outward from the driver side window.

Panting and grunting, he savagely swung at the replica again and again.

Stunned by the total brutality of the attack, Alana froze, fingernails digging into the pavement. Pure terror closed her throat and sent adrenaline surging through her body. Every muscle shook, demanding that she do something, anything but simply sit and watch the madness unfolding in front of her. A small part of her mind screamed for her to run.

Fighting down her fear, Alana scrambled to her feet, racing back to the employee entrance. The sound of her footsteps drew her attacker's attention out of the red haze of rage and back to his fake target. He stared for a moment at the illusion still crouched in front of him, realizing she suffered no damage. Sensing the trick, if not understanding it, he spun around to hunt for his true target.

As soon as she realized her glamour no longer occupied him, Alana began screaming for help. There was little chance that she could defend herself against her attacker. Her powers were illusionary, not physical. She had never faced a physical, mortal attacker before. She had no training, no time to put together an appropriate spell, no way to stop him.

Time slowed and her labored breath burned her lungs as she raced for safety. She watched as the employee door opened, flooding the shadows with light, noise, and laughter. She called out again, and heard voices responding to her screams. The panic began fading as she realized that rescue was close at hand. She felt tears of relief welling up in her eyes, and she allowed herself a silent prayer of thanks.

A sharp, crackling pain exploded in the back of her head. Everything went dark.

At the shrill ring of the phone, Max whimpered and pawed his master lying beside him. Detective Leo Grady sent out a creative spurt of curses at whoever had the balls to be calling him this late. Not bothering to turn on the lights, he grabbed the receiver with one hand and gave his golden retriever a comforting scratch behind the ears with the other.

"This had better be good," he growled, steel-gray eyes opened to slits, a dull ache pressing through his temples. "I haven't slept in over thirty hours, and I've already met my quota of dead bodies for the week. I'd hate to waste the time it would take to kill you and hide the evidence."

"Leo," the voice boomed in his ear, causing him to flinch and hold the receiver a short distance away. "It's Joe from the 22nd. Sorry to wake ya, buddy, but I think we've got one of yours down here."

Leo ran a hand against his whisker roughened cheek and yawned, trying to pull himself together enough to understand what Joe was talking about. "One of my what?"

"Claddagh."

Leo sat straight up, mindless of the white cotton sheet falling away from bare skin. The cool of the air conditioner blasted his chest, sending goose bumps up and down his arms, causing the scar on his shoulder to ache with the sudden change of temperature, but nothing matched the chill running through his blood at the mere mention of that word. "Damn, are you sure?"

"It was a little gold charm this time, but definitely a claddagh."

Leo's mouth thinned to a grim line, teeth gritting. Too late again, damn it. Sometimes he hated his job. "Have you identified the victim yet?"

"Yeah, Alana Devlin, that female magician who works down at the Golden Dreams Casino. He jumped her with a crowbar in the employee parking lot. We picked her up about twenty minutes ago."

Leo's knuckles turned white as his grip on the receiver tightened, rage at another needless death filling him. Sensing his owner's anger, Max whimpered and licked Leo's arm. "Have the coroners finished with the body yet?"

"Nope, even better." Joe paused for a moment, relishing his friend's reaction to his next words. "She's alive."

Leo cursed again as he nearly dropped the phone, causing Max to whine and jump to his feet. "You're kidding? That's two in a row now. Is she in a coma, like Violet Johnson?"

"Nope, awake and talking, if a little worse for the wear. They took her down to Mercy General. We've got two uniforms with her now, and I thought I'd stick around for the time being, considering what happened to Johnson. I called you right away, thought you might like to know."

For the first time in days, Leo Grady smiled. Things were starting to look up. "Damn straight. This is the best break we've had. Listen, do me a favor and call Gabe. Have him meet me there. And thanks for the heads up,

Joe. I'll remember this."

"Yeah, just remember to pay up that twenty you owe me from the Nicks' game, and we'll call it even."

Leo gripped the phone with his chin as he leapt out of bed and began scouring the floor for his pants. "You'll have it by morning. Just make sure she's still breathing by the time I get there."

"You've got it. With any luck, you've got this bastard nailed."

Leo pulled an already looped tie around his neck before noticing he hadn't put his shirt on yet. He needed to stop and pick up some coffee on the way in. "I'm not betting on luck with this one, Joe. He's had far too much of his own."

"Yeah, but I think that might be changing. Now get your butt down here while I see if I can pull your partner out of whatever bed he's in."

Leo pulled his wrinkled, and now hairy, requisite brown sports coat out from under his dog. Max whined and thumped his tail against the pillows. "I'll be there in fifteen, twenty tops."

Patting Max's head one last time, Leo raced out the door.

Chapter Two

The hum of fluorescent lights droned beneath the groans and complaints of the late night mob crowding the first floor lobby of Mercy General. Leo pushed past the unwashed masses, flashing his badge at one visitor carrying flowers to claim an empty elevator. His foot tapped as the elevator started its jerky crawl up five floors.

The doors slid open to a long, empty hallway, blessedly free of people. Leo flinched at the squeak of his shoes against the linoleum and shoved back the memories of his own agonizing months spent here. A private room paid for by department insurance might be nicer than what the average person could afford, but a hospital was still a hospital. Nothing could change the cold, antiseptic feel of the place.

Turning a corner, he saw the two uniformed officers standing ramrod straight in front of a closed door. Not bothering with the preliminaries, he flashed his badge at the officers. "Detective Grady. Detective Miller called me in. How is she?"

After giving the badge a close inspection, the older of the two stood a fraction straighter. The officer's voice was clipped and concise as he answered. "The doc's finishing up with her, now. Got a pretty nasty head wound, but she's conscious. That's all we know. Detective Miller is waiting inside for you. Detective Hunter hasn't arrived yet."

Leo nodded while pocketing the badge. It was better

news than he expected. Hopefully the Devlin woman could give him something that he could use to catch this bastard. "No one else hanging around or asking any questions?"

Grim-faced, the officer shook his head. "No, sir. Detective Miller told us about what happened to the last victim. We've stuck close and kept a sharp eye out, but nothing suspicious so far."

"Good," Leo replied, glad that Joe had put an experienced officer on the door. "From here on out no one but Detective Hunter is allowed near this room without clearing it with me first, not even medical personnel. I want a complete lock down on this room until I say otherwise. Understand?"

The officer was quick to answer. "Yes, sir. Don't worry. I don't want anything like what happened before put on *my* record."

"Good," Leo replied, reaching for the door. "Let's keep it that way."

Leo eased into the tiny, white room, bracing himself for the image of a vulnerable, beaten woman lying prone in an oversized hospital bed. He hated it when the victims were women. Knowing that they had less of a chance to defend themselves against their attackers than a man did made the attack somehow worse, more of a violation—not as bad as when it was a kid, but bad enough. There were times when he considered transferring out of homicide, if it weren't for the fact that he was so good at what he did. He was one of the best detectives on the squad with a spotless record, at least until this case.

The last victim would haunt him, lying so fragile in her hospital bed, tubes and wires running everywhere, bruised and battered beyond recognition. Violet Johnson had been little more than a kid, barely twenty years old, and he had failed her. If he'd done his job right, she'd still be alive, and this woman would be home sleeping or watching the late show.

With guilt gnawing at his gut, Leo faced the bed. She was pale, but considering the hair, he'd bet the milky white tint of her skin was her natural complexion, not the result of shock. Instead of a frail creature, clinging to life, the only vulnerable thing he saw in this woman was the cute little smattering of freckles across her nose. From the top of her vibrant red hair, to the tips of her scarlet-painted, tapping toes, this woman radiated barely contained energy.

For a woman recovering from a vicious attack, Leo had to give her points for sheer guts as he listened to her ream Joe. With a small smirk, he leaned against the doorframe to enjoy the show.

Her green eyes flashed and her lush lips pursed as she continued her tirade. "I still don't understand, Detective Miller. I've told you all I know, which, granted, isn't much. The mugger was wearing a mask. I have no idea what he looks like. Thanks to the people finding me so quickly, he didn't take anything. But I've got twenty-three stitches in my head and a slight concussion to show for it. The doctor says I'm fine to go home, as long as someone stays with me. Why won't you let me call my friend? I should have been there to meet him an hour ago. He has to be worried, and I want to go home."

Joe tucked the crisp white sheets around her, as one would a sulking child, and shook his head. "I'm sorry, Ms. Devlin, but I need you to wait and speak with someone else first. He'll explain the situation, I promise."

"That's right, leave the tough stuff to me," Leo joked, pushing away from the door. He tried to lighten the atmosphere and establish a rapport with the victim. She didn't look like the type who'd do what she was told. That red hair looked real—with a temper to match, he'd bet. Leo kept an uncharacteristic smile plastered to his face as he approached the bed.

Alana glared up at this new interrogator. It looked like they'd brought out the big guns. Detective Miller was a pale shadow compared to this new arrival. The man had to be at least six foot four, and built like a linebacker, with the slight dent in his nose to prove it. He was the epitome of disheveled, with a mane of black finger-combed hair and wearing a wrinkled suit in desperate need of a dry cleaning. She hoped that they had dragged him out of bed. Otherwise, he needed a fashion consultant in a bad way.

But it was his eyes that caught her. They held her riveted, unable to look away. They were a light, piercing, metallic gray. Surrounded by dark lashes and brows, in a darkly tanned face, they seemed unnatural, as though they could slice through you and see to your very soul. But Alana found them to be almost comforting, given the situation.

Still, she crossed her arms and glared at the detective. No way was she sticking around this hideous place one minute longer. Hospitals gave her the creeps, with their weird machines and tubes, buzzing fluorescent lights, sharp objects, and complete absence of smell. That was the worst. Even evil had a smell, as she knew full well. You couldn't trust anything that had no smell. A full-frontal attack seemed the best option for her release. "Since you seem to be the one in charge, when do I get to leave? I thought you people held the criminals against their will, not the victims."

"I'm Detective Leo Grady, and I am in charge of your

case," the man said as he stepped closer. "I'm sorry for the inconvenience, Ms. Devlin, but given the circumstances, I'm sure you'll understand."

Skepticism filled the look Alana shot him as she shoved the sheets off again and pushed to swing her legs off the bed. She'd had enough double talk from the other detective to last her a lifetime. Even if her butt hung out in the breeze, she was leaving. She didn't care how big and intimidating he was, even if he was trying to act all "good cop", this new guy was going to give her a straight answer and get out of her way. "Well, that really depends on those *mythical* circumstances, now doesn't it? Let me put it plainly. I've been mugged. I've been poked at and prodded by doctors. Now, I want to go home. Seems pretty cut and dry to me."

Alana was annoyed when her legs folded beneath her, sitting her back down on the bed, after one fierce glare from the detective. She strained her neck, trying to look up at him as he replied, "No, it is not that cut and dry. Tell me about the claddagh you found."

Alana's brow wrinkled in confusion. That was the last question she had expected. She didn't see any connection. "The claddagh? You mean that little Irish charm—that's what all this is about? I told the officers that I leaned over to pick it up, that's why the mugger missed me."

The silence greeting her comment smothered the room. Alana could hear the faint whirs and beeps of lifesaving, if creepy, equipment in neighboring rooms. She continued, trying for some hint of a reaction. "It's tiny. It can't be that valuable. Certainly not valuable enough for the Gestapo treatment."

Leo ignored the growing irritation in her voice and turned to Joe. "Do you have it?"

Joe pulled a small, marked baggy from his pocket and

tossed it to Leo. "I didn't think you'd want anyone else to handle it."

Alana leaned forward, trying to get a better look at the miniscule object that seemed so important to the two men. "What's this all about? I'm the one he left bleeding on the ground, I think I have a right to know."

Leo glanced over at Joe, and motioned him to leave. Joe gave Alana a comforting smile before turning. Leo waited to speak until the door clicked shut behind the other detective before speaking again. "What I'm about to tell you, Ms. Devlin, is to be kept in strict confidence. No one else is to know. We've worked hard to keep this situation under wraps, avoiding possible panic."

He paused a moment for obvious dramatic affect.

Her attention caught in spite of herself, Alana urged, "Go on."

Leo measured each clipped word, purposely standing over her, using his size for intimidation. "We've had five murders committed in the last month, each victim being found with some sort of claddagh on their person. Because of this, we think your attacker may be the one responsible."

Leo braced himself for her reaction, knowing that now would be the moment she would break.

Denial came first. "No way. My life is not a made-for-TV movie. Why would I be a target of a serial killer? Is he one of those women-hating perverts? Has he got something against redheads?"

Leo kept his expression impassive. "No, just people in your occupation."

Alana shook her head, flinching as her action pulled at the tight stitches in her scalp. She twisted the edge of her sheets between unfeeling fingers. She'd been in danger many times before, soul rending danger, but never because of her occupation. It made no sense to her. "You're saying that he's killing off magicians. That's impossible. It's a small community. I would have heard if *one* local magician had been killed, much less *five*. Try pulling the other leg."

"Not *magicians*," Leo continued, his patience strained, "but those who deal with magic in some way."

Alana's brow furrowed, which again pulled at her stitches. This time she ignored the sharp twinge of pain. "Come again?"

Leo held up his fingers as he ticked off each of the victims. "So far, we have two wicca practitioners, one palm reader working out of a casino amusement park, one magic store owner, and one psychic book shop employee. All were found beaten to death with some type of claddagh clutched in their hands."

"And now me," Alana whispered, sinking back into the bed and closing her eyes, hands falling to her side. She never imagined that she'd be happy to find herself in a hospital, but it beat the morgue. Alana feared that she was beginning to get a clear picture of why the other detective had kept her in the hospital for so long. And she didn't like what she was seeing.

Leo's mouth tightened, hating frightening her, but knowing that she had to understand the situation she was in. Her life depended on it. "And now you," he agreed, his voice filled with regret. "You can see why it's important that we kept you for questioning."

Alana nodded, her head beginning to pound. As if dealing with supernatural threats weren't enough, now she had a crazed *mortal* after her. She didn't need this. Still, Rick had to be told. He'd be going insane by now, picturing what might have happened to her and what their respected fathers would do to him for not being there to help her. "If

I'm the only survivor, the only witness you have, I can understand the need to keep me here, but I still want a phone call, even criminals get that much."

Leo reached out and squeezed her hand, offering what little support he could at such a difficult time. He needed to keep her on his side. He was the one who intimidated the witnesses; Gabe handled the finesse. But something about this woman pulled at him, made him want to be the one she turned to for comfort, not his partner. "And you'll get that call. I just need to ask you a few questions first."

For a moment, Alana allowed herself to sink into the rough warmth of Leo's hand on her own, to draw strength from him. It had been so long since she had allowed herself to cling to a man, any man. It felt good to imagine for a moment that he cared about her and not how she could help with his case.

Suddenly the door swung open, causing Alana to gasp and jerk forward, pulling her hand from Leo's grasp. The tall, well-dressed, lanky blond stopped in the doorway and gave her a wry smile, blue eyes twinkling. His playboy handsome face lit up with chagrin. "Sorry, didn't mean to scare you. I'm Detective Hunter, Grady's partner."

He stepped in, letting the door close behind him. Leo gave him a warning look, tilting his head towards Alana. Gabe raised his eyebrows, but then shrugged and leaned against the wall. He stood there, allowing his partner to take the lead.

Alana wrinkled her nose as she caught a powerful whiff of the man's cheap cologne, but laid back again in the bed, seeing that Leo was undisturbed by the man. "Ask away, I'll tell you everything I know. But I didn't see much. I don't know how much of a help I can be."

Leo reached into his jacket and pulled out a mini-recorder. He clicked it on, placing it on the side-table. He then pulled one of the guest chairs closer to the bed, putting the two of them on equal footing. He wanted her to feel comfortable talking to him. "Let me worry about that. Let's run through the attack again, one step at a time. What exactly *do* you remember?"

Alana looked over at Gabe, still lurking by the door, then forced her gaze back to Leo. For what felt like the hundredth time, she describe what happened to her. She stuck to the story that she'd come up with when she regained consciousness in the ambulance. After the first couple of swings missed her, she managed to break away and run for the employee entrance.

"But, obviously, I didn't make it," she said, rubbing the bandage covering the stitches on the back of her head, a half-hearted smile sliding across her face.

Leo grinned in return at her attempt at humor. He respected any woman who could make the most of a terrifying situation, having seen too many people, male and female, fall apart when faced with less dire circumstances. Here she lay, faced with the idea of a heartless killer targeting her. Unlike many people, she held herself steady and even found the strength to laugh.

He had to admit, Alana impressed him.

Still, he had a job to do. Impressed or not, he needed more information, something he could work with, something to put an end to this nightmare. "Alright then, let's talk about *before* the attack. You're an entertainer. Have you noticed anyone acting strangely at your shows, a person coming more times than normal, reacting differently? Anyone stick out in your mind for any reason whatsoever?"

Alana took a moment to think about it, and then shook her head, her expression filled with remorse. "No, not really. Not that it means that much. We do our shows in an intimate setting, not an auditorium like some of the bigger names. But I can't guarantee that I would have noticed anyone unusual."

Leo reached out for her hand again, giving it a sympathetic squeeze before continuing. "What about threatening mail? Did you receive anything like that before the attack?"

"To be honest, I wouldn't know," Alana replied, her face chagrin. "I hate to admit it, but I rarely look at my mail. Rick handles all of that. He's my assistant, Carrick Murphy. He goes through the mail, pulls out what I need to deal with or things he knows would interest me, and then takes care of the rest. If I got any threats, unless he felt they were serious and not some kook, he probably tossed them."

Leo nodded, disconcerted by a sudden stab of disappointment at the mention of her assistant. In his experience, beautiful women always had a man willing to take care of them. It shouldn't come as a surprise that she had someone waiting in the wings for her. But the thought of her with this man shook him. "Carrick Murphy, we'll need to bring him in for questioning as well."

Alana laughed, the musical sound jolting Leo and sending tingles shivering down to his toes. "That's what I've been trying to do since they brought me here. He's the one I was supposed to meet. We usually go out for drinks after our last show on Sundays."

Leo nodded, then waved to his partner. "Tell me where he is, and I'll have Gabe bring him here."

Alana tilted her head, studying Leo. It bothered her that she couldn't quite read his expression. "How about I just call him myself? I have his cell phone number, and I'd really like to be the one to tell him what happened."

"Give me the number, and I'll call him." When she tried

to interrupt, he held up his hand and shook his head. "I can understand you wanting to break the news, but I would rather have a chance to talk to him before you do."

Alana stared at Leo, eyes widening with dawning shock. The thought was so ludicrous; she struggled not to laugh aloud. "You can't believe that *Rick* has anything to do with this."

Leo's face turned grim, his lightning eyes flashing. Alana could see dark memories lurking below the surface. "You'd be surprised at what I can believe of people, Ms. Devlin. The number please."

He reached for his cell phone while she rattled off the number. After punching it in, he looked down at the face of his phone, and cursed at the poor signal. He turned to his partner, still leaning against the far wall. "Stay here with her. Don't leave, no matter what. She's *not* to be left alone." He then stalked out of the room, searching for better cell phone reception.

Gabe walked over to sit in the orange, butt-numbing chair by Alana's bed, his clear blue eyes filled with sympathy. He patted her arm. His voice held a soft, compassionate tone as he began. "You'll have to excuse my partner. This case has been hard on him."

Alana's lips turned up into a half-smile, reflecting dark humor. While she didn't trust his pity one bit, this one looked more gullible than his partner, easier to push. She needed to know more about what was happening if she was to protect herself. She hated doing things this way, hated forcing a man to do something against his will, but didn't see that she had much of a choice.

She closed her eyes, letting a simple chant run through her mind. Whatever killed all smell in the hospital also deadened the light floral scent that arose from her, the soft glow at her fingertips hidden by the sheet. Suddenly, she seemed to be more trustworthy, more compelling, more open to listening than before. "Oh really? Well, Detective Grady should try it from my side. It's a lot harder, believe me."

Gabe sighed and squirmed a bit. She watched him fight against the compulsion to talk. He felt obliged to confide in her, no matter what the consequences. Too bad she couldn't blank out the experience for him, taking any guilty feelings from him. "Well, you'll have to give him a little slack. You don't seem to be the type of person who likes to be coddled, but he just wants to be certain that nothing happens to you. And I warn you, he'll be a real hard-nose until he's sure of that."

Alana scratched at the bandage on the back of her head, feeling dejected at the thought that this was the only reason the tall, gray-eyed detective was interested in her welfare. It had been a while since anyone but her family cared what happened to her in the least. Imagining that he felt some attraction to her gave her a warm feeling. But then again, she had been smacked in the back of the head with a crowbar, glancing blow or not. That could be the concussion talking. "I'm his only witness, even if I didn't see anything."

Gabe nodded in response. From the expression he gave, she knew he wanted to stop there, but Alana's spell forced more from him. "That, and he feels guilty."

"What for?" Alana asked as she began rolling her head, trying to ease the aching muscles in her neck. Her little spell had taken more out of her than she thought, the drugs making the casting difficult. To make matters worse, the painkillers were wearing off, and every nerve screamed at her for another dose.

By morning she knew she'd feel like she'd been hit by a truck.

Gabe fidgeted with his tie and smoothed back his hair. He twisted in the chair as the words flew out of his mouth. "The last victim survived the initial attack too."

"What?" Alana stopped all movement and pinned him with a piercing glare.

Gabe paused for a moment before continuing, frozen by that single glance. Still, Alana's magic wouldn't allow him to stop. "The girl was unconscious, but alive when she was found. She slipped into a coma shortly after arriving at the hospital."

Alana tilted her head to the side, one finger tapping her lip. She hadn't considered the possibility that Leo had lied to her. If there was another survivor, Alana's story wasn't quite as necessary as he had led her to believe. "Has she come out of it yet? Maybe she'll be able to tell you more than I can."

Gabe leaned closer to Alana. She felt him gauging her reaction to his words, even compelled from him as they were. "She'll never be able to tell us anything. The guard we left at her door was drugged. She was found dead with a claddagh clenched in her fist. He injected anti-freeze into her IV."

Alana's stomach twisted, her throat tightening. "Dear God."

Gabe nodded. "Exactly, so don't be surprised if Leo goes a little overboard with you. He has his reasons. It was his decision to leave her with one guard. Neither of us ever expected the killer would try to finish what he started while she was still in the hospital, but Leo still feels responsible for her death. He won't make that same mistake with you."

Silence filled the room as Alana absorbed what she'd been told.

"The killer's not done with me, is he?" she asked, fighting against the rising panic. "He'll be back."

Gabe's face hardened as he nodded. "With you not seeing anything that we can use to find him, we *have* to count on it. It's the only way we'll find the murderer before he kills anyone else."

The chuckle that sprang from Alana held no humor at all. Anger and fear warred within her as she fought to accept the place she now found herself in. "So, to you guys, I'm just . . . bait. Is that what you're telling me?"

Gabe wouldn't meet her eyes. "No, not bait. But you'll have to be watched, protected. And if we happen to catch the killer while doing so, all the better."

Alana had to clear her tightening throat before replying. "Yeah, all the better."

Chapter Three

Leo paced the lobby, his mouth set in a grim line. The people around him gave him a wide berth, scurrying further and further away. Even the talking faded within a few feet of his path in front of the information desk. His head jerked forward with every swish of the automatic doors, his expression dark.

Going against the trend, a man rushed towards the information desk, pushing past hospital personnel and visitors with little regard, disregarding Leo completely. He was tall, with long, wavy brown hair. His well-muscled body glowed with a deep tan, even with the pallor of fear underlying it. Just the kind of man to make women's hearts swoon.

Leo felt a quick stab of sickening envy. Some guys have all the luck.

And this is her friend. *No wonder she wanted to call him right away. Probably afraid he'd take off with some babe at the bar. Lord knows he must have plenty of opportunities.*

Leo grimaced at his harsh thoughts, then walked over to meet Carrick.

"Mr. Murphy?" he asked, holding out a hand, an offering that was ignored.

When the man nodded, Leo let his arm drop without comment and continued. "I'm Detective Grady, the one who spoke to you on the phone. If you'd come with me for a moment, there are a few questions I need to ask you be-

33

fore you see Ms. Devlin."

Leo watched as Rick took several deep, calming breaths. Sheer panic etched his face, but Rick visibly took hold of himself. Leo felt pity for the man as his eyes pleaded with Leo for some type of comfort. But he suppressed the sympathy. He'd seen too many killers use that same worried look. "Alana's okay, right? That's what you told me, she's okay. God, I knew I should have waited for her. It's never safe for a woman to walk alone in the dark, not in a city this big. Any idiot knows that. But I left her alone. If anything happens to her, how will I tell her family?"

Leo took the babbling Rick by the arm and herded him into an empty waiting room, closing and locking the door behind them. Leo eased Rick into a chair and poured him some coffee. "She's fine," he said, trying to put Rick at ease. "She has a slight concussion and some stitches, but she's fine otherwise. I've spoken to her myself. But now, I need you to answer my questions. The quicker we're done here, the quicker I can let you go see her."

Rick nodded, clutching his fingers around the warm Styrofoam cup like a lifeline. "Anything, anything at all you need to know. If it can help you catch the bastard who did this, I'm more than willing to talk to you."

Leo smiled as he sat down in the chair facing Rick, the metal legs scratching linoleum as he dragged it closer. "Alright. Let's start with the basics." Leo pulled out his recorder again, sliding the tape with Alana's words into his jacket pocket and replacing it with a new one. "What's your name and relationship to the victim?"

"My name is Carrick Murphy." Rick took a fortifying gulp of the steaming liquid. He stared into the cup for a long moment, as if the caffeine held some answers to what happened. "I've known Alana all my life. Our families moved to America from Ireland together over two hundred years ago. They've always stayed close. We're practically family, all but raised together. I've had my own spare room at their house for as long as I can remember." Rick looked down at his trembling hands as the scalding coffee sloshed over his fingers. "God, she's like a sister—the only family I have in this country. I've worked with her for the past two years as her assistant, both on and off stage. I can't believe something like this could happen to her."

Upon hearing Rick compare Alana to a sister, an inappropriate moment of relief filled Leo. He fought to keep his feelings from reflecting on his face. He had no right to feel anything for a woman he barely knew. "And when did you see Alana last?" he pushed Rick, trying to banish all the strange emotions raging through him.

Rick paused, taking another sip from his cup. "Sometime around midnight, after our ten o'clock show was over. I stopped by her dressing room to discuss the show. We talked for a few minutes, and then I left. I went down to the Emerald Isle Pub, on Flamingo and Jones, and waited for her. We meet there after our last show on Sundays, since we don't work the next day."

"So it's a habit that anyone could pick up on," Leo replied.

Rick shrugged, hunching down over his coffee and gritting his teeth. "Yeah, it's probably the only night of the week that we don't necessarily leave the casino together."

This answer didn't surprise Leo. The killer must be watching his victims, waiting to find just the right time for his attacks, times when they were most vulnerable. He was a hunter, an organized killer who methodically planned each move he made.

"Okay then, have you noticed anyone hanging around

Ms. Devlin, anyone who made you uneasy?" Leo asked.

Rick shook his head in disgust. "No one that stands out."

Still, Leo leaned in and kept probing. "What about threats? Alana mentioned that you took care of all the mail. Has she received anything you would consider worth mentioning?"

Rick grew silent and grim, guilt spreading across his face. His gaze fell to the gleaming floor. "Yes, I did. I never thought anything of it until now. But she did receive a couple of threatening letters."

Leo struggled to keep his own face blank and his voice nonchalant. The answer to his next question could give him another link to his only suspect. "Really? Do you still have them?"

Again, Rick shook his head. "No, damn it. I didn't take them seriously. But I do remember who they were from. That Burke character, the one with that religious public access show on Channel 1."

Jackpot, Leo thought, smiling as he leaned back in his chair, stretching his long legs out in front of him. *That makes three victims with a connection to him.* "Charles Burke, founder of the Hands of Brotherhood Mission and self-proclaimed savior of the sinners of Las Vegas."

Rick stared at Leo, eyebrows raised in question. "That's the one. He's a religious guy, so I didn't take the threats seriously. I mean, I never even considered that he might be violent, just a fruitcake. I didn't think it was worth worrying Alana about."

Leo nodded while switching off the recorder. "Tell it to the hundreds who died in the crusades. Religion fanatics can be some of the most violent people of all. Didn't you study your history?"

Rick's jaw clenched, his brown eyes narrowing to slits. He stood, hurling his empty cup in the nearest trashcan. "I've answered your questions. I want to see Alana now."

Leo ignored Rick's flash of temper and led him up the elevator to Alana's room. Rick started when he saw the guards posted at her door, but remained silent. As the door opened, Gabe stood in front of Alana, blocking her from view. At the sight of Leo, his body relaxed. Leo smiled at the reaction. Gabe hated being left with a victim for so long. It made him antsy.

Leo gestured for Gabe to follow him out the door. "Detective Hunter and I have a few things we need to discuss. I'll leave you two alone for a moment, but we'll be right outside if you need anything."

Rick rushed forward, taking Alana's hand. Leo glanced back at the attractive tableau made by Rick hovering above Alana, before slamming the door behind him.

"I don't think he trusts me very much," Rick said, wincing as the booming sound of the closing door ricocheted through the Spartan room.

Alana chuckled, happy to have someone she knew by her side. She reached up to give him a quick hug, pulling him down to sit on the side of her bed. "Don't take it hard. Detective Grady strikes me as the type who doesn't trust anyone."

"So why don't you tell me what happened?" Rick urged, his voice deceptively calm.

Alana shrugged, sliding her fingers through her tangled curls. "I got jumped in the parking lot. What more is there to say?"

At her indifferent reply, Rick exploded. Hands flying in the air, he leaped off his perch to pace in front of her. "What more is there to say? You're a Protector, for crying out loud. You are supposed to be in the first line of defense against any supernatural attack on human beings. It's what your family has been doing for centuries. Yet you nearly get killed in a parking lot and by a mortal no less!"

Alana's body tightened at the sudden attack, justified though it was. Rick's face glowed a livid red, but she could see the worry hiding behind the anger. "He was human, alright! I didn't sense him coming."

Rick continued pacing at the foot of her bed, the war to control his fear driven anger etched in his every movement. "That's no real excuse, and you know it. Even if you had no warning, you should have been able to take care of yourself better."

Alana watched him, understanding his feelings of helplessness and rage, but not knowing how to defuse them. She kept her voice calm and soothing. "I got away, didn't I? I cast a glamour, distracted him, and got away. What more do you want?"

Rick stopped all movement, shoulders slumping as his hands clutched the metal bar at the foot of Alana's bed, knuckles turning white. "You know what more I want, what more your whole family wants. You should have been able to defend yourself. What if he *had* been supernatural? How the hell do you expect to do your duty if you can't fight physically? Magic only goes so far. Twelve years of dancing didn't help you a bit, like I've told you time and again, did it? I'm not always going to be there to help you, *obviously*. What happens the next time? Do I get a call in the middle of the night from the morgue?"

Stomach clenching, Alana wiped her face of all expression as Rick's barb hit home. "Okay, okay. I get it. You told me so. I need to train, take some form of martial arts or something, otherwise I'm all but worthless. You and Dad have been after me forever about it."

Rick returned to her side, the bed dipping as he sat and took her hand once more. Seeing the sheen of tears forming in her eyes, his voice softened. "And now you see why." With his thumb, he wiped away the single tear that rolled down her cheek.

Alana swallowed, fighting back the lump that threatened to choke her. Her teeth chattered and her hands shook in delayed reaction. "And now I see why. I just never wanted it to be necessary."

"You mean, you never wanted to come back and take over for your father," Rick chided.

"Okay, you're right," Alana admitted, looking down at her trembling hands—not wanting to see the disappointment in Rick's eyes. "I'm more like my brother than I want to admit. I don't *want* to be the first line of defense for anyone. I want to be normal. I want a normal life with normal friends and maybe even a normal relationship. Instead, I'm stuck being part faerie with an ancient imperative, a geis placed on one of my distant ancestors, that I have to follow. I get it, okay? I'm stuck and I need to do what I have to in order to deal with it."

Rick sighed in long pent-up relief. "Maybe you do now. So, as soon as the doctors give you the okay, I'm teaching you self-defense. I'm also taking you out to get a gun, and you're going to learn to shoot it. I will not be the first Helper in my family to have my Protector die on him from lack of training, understand?"

Alana squeezed his hand, calming him while calming herself. "Aye, aye captain. We'll train, as soon as this new mess blows over that is. I somehow doubt Detective Grady's going to let me out of his sight any time soon."

Rick flashed her a half-smile in agreement. "Which

won't be good. We still have to finish with whatever is after Amber."

"Don't worry. There's no way I'm staying here for the rest of the night. We won't be leaving her alone. When we get home, I'll try a little something that I think will reveal what is tormenting her. Then we'll pull together what we need for the ritual and wrap it up. Amber will be fine."

Rick nodded, his trust easy to read. Still, he asked, "What about the attack on you? I get the feeling there's more going on than Grady told me."

Alana sank back into her bed, pulling away from his grasp. "There's more going on, alright—try a serial killer, with me the only surviving victim. It's kinda funny when you think about it. I'm supposed to protect normal people from the supernatural. Now, I have a normal person after me who's killing people he associates with the super-natural."

Rick's face became stone, the only movement a slight tic by his eye. "No, somehow I don't find it very funny at all."

"I didn't think you would. So, we'll have to figure out a plan, once I know what Grady's up to."

Rick stared down at her, worry marring his perfect brow. "Hopefully, he'll come clean soon. We need to get you home. Amber's probably catatonic by now, and it won't be long until your brother or sister calls to find out what's up."

Alana grimaced at the thought of her family. Her stomach started churning, and she was glad for the frigid air conditioning. It was the only thing keeping her clear headed. Pushing Gabe had taken its toll. "Yeah, it sucks being related to a couple of psychics. With Adain and our twin thing or Fiona and her visions, I never get to keep any secrets. I'm just lucky Dad uses psychometry, not pure clairvoyance. At least I don't have to worry about *him* calling tonight."

Rick turned a lighter shade of pale before giving a dramatic shutter. "No, you mean at least *I* don't have to worry about him calling. If I thought he and my dad were bad at nagging me before, I'd be better off dead when they find out what happened to you tonight."

Alana's smile lit the room, chuckling at her old friend's obvious discomfort. "Don't worry, I'll protect you," she winked and promised.

She reached out to pull him into a comforting bear hug, happy to be alive. This attack rattled her, being so unexpected. She'd come to terms with the thought of an early death by some Otherworldly boogie, but not by random mortal violence.

The door swung open, noiseless. Leo froze at the sight of the embrace, so cozy, and then forced himself to move into the room. Carrick Murphy and Alana Devlin's relationship was none of his business. His job was to keep her alive, that's all.

But don't they just look so perfect *together.*

Leo's voice sounded cold, even to his own ears, when he addressed the two. "I've finished speaking with my partner. We've come to an agreement. Ms. Devlin, for your own safety, we'll be taking you into protective custody. You'll be coming with me as soon as the doctor finishes your paperwork."

Alana's eyes widened. No way was she going to be put in a glorified cage. She hadn't escaped her attacker to be locked away for her own good. She'd never be able to prove herself worthy of the title of Protector by allowing others to take all the risks. Not to mention, if she was right about what was stalking Amber, she needed to get on with the business of being the Protector soon. Amber didn't have much time left. She hoped that she had enough strength to start her work tonight, maybe even finish it. "Oh, I *really* don't think so."

Leo's eyebrows arched at the steely look coming over her features. His own face hardened as he watched her partner smirk. "You *really* have no choice in the matter." He walked forward to tower over her, hands clutching her bedrail. "We're dealing with a serial killer, in case you haven't noticed, and your life is in danger. I have the authority to take you in for your own good."

"I don't doubt that you have the *authority*, but it's not happening," Alana replied, her voice sounding reasonable, if a bit icy. "I will not be a prisoner because of what some nutcase has decided to do."

Rick settled into one of the bedside chairs with the aspect of a man watching a train wreck about to happen.

"But it's not your choice," Leo continued, surprised by her refusal to listen to reason. She should be happy that the police were willing to give her such protection. Under normal circumstance, they wouldn't even offer, being spread as thin as they were. But this killer had taken top priority with the powers that be. Catching him before the tourists caught wind of the situation had become mandatory.

Alana smiled, folding her arms as she sat back on the bed. "But it is my choice. My family has lived in Las Vegas for a very long time, Detective Grady. And I'm one of the few members not involved with politics or the legal system. This may be a big city, but it hasn't always been. It was a small town only thirty years ago. And you must know it's got an ingrained good-old-boy system. I just have to make a few phone calls, and you'll be forced to back off, maybe from the entire case. I don't think that's what you want."

Leo's eyes turned glacial as he considered what she was telling him. "You're bluffing."

Alana lowered her head, peering out of eyes gone to slits, her smile turning grim. "Just try me, Detective. I don't think you'll like the results."

Rick leaned forward to watch Leo's expression, chuckling. "She's telling the truth, you know. Her mother was the mayor's wife's best friend in high school. I can't tell you how many people in high standing throughout the state owe her father their lives. Hell, her brother coached the governor's son in pee-wee football. She has more clout than you'd think. I wouldn't push it if I were you."

Leo shook his head, not believing how out of his control the situation had become. "Your life is at stake, and you want to go it alone. It's suicide."

Alana shrugged. "Only if we can't come to some sort of agreement. You need me to draw the guy out. That's fine with me, if that's what it takes to catch him. I want to keep my life as normal as possible. I need that. So we'll have to come to a compromise."

"Compromise?" Leo asked. This was ridiculous. Didn't she understand the danger she was in?

A slow, smug smile spread across Alana's face. She sighed as she settled more comfortably into the bed, staring up at Leo, still looming above her. "I know. You're not the type to compromise. But this will be simple. As long as I can stay in my own home and go along with my life, you can do whatever is necessary to catch the guy."

"Define normal," Leo replied, thinking that the word didn't seem to apply well to her so far. If he had any sense at all, he'd slap some cuffs on her and take her in for her own good. But if what she'd told him was true, he didn't dare. The last thing he wanted was to be pulled from this case, not when he was so close.

Alana ignored the sarcasm lacing Leo's voice. "I want to be able to stay in my own home, work as usual, and maybe see my friends. That isn't too much to ask, with you using me to catch your killer, now is it?"

Leo shook his head in disbelief. That he was even considering this amazed him. Why did she have to be a stubborn little redhead? He was beginning to wish she'd been more of a vulnerable victim type. "If you're determined to go through with this 'life as normal' routine, I want someone on the inside. You won't be allowed to be alone, ever. Can you live with that?"

A cat-like smile slid across Alana's face, causing Leo's body to stiffen. "I guess I'll have to. That's what compromise is all about. I have to give a little, too."

Leo glared at her. How could she sound so reasonable while making these kinds of demands? "I don't like it, I'd rather have you in a more controlled environment."

"We can't always get what we want," Alana replied, her hand reaching up to touch the bandage covering her stitches, her expression haunted. "We can either work together, or you'll get no cooperation from me and I'll have every bureaucrat I know of breathing down your neck."

Leo's eyes narrowed, lips forming a narrow line. He hated the feeling of being backed into a corner, but he wanted to catch the killer. He'd do whatever he had to, and, by God, he'd make sure she wished she hadn't set this up. "Okay, it looks like you've got yourself a deal. But I'll be with you at all times. You do nothing without running it by me first."

Alana nodded, relieved and surprised that he was giving in. "I can live with that. Can you?"

"It doesn't sound like you're giving me a choice, does it?" The look Leo gave her had left many a crook trembling.

"No, I'm not," Alana answered, folding her arms across her chest and staring him straight in the eye.

Chapter Four

They drove through the neon dotted night for close to forty-five minutes. Leo was the first to hop out of the car. As much as he tried to hang on to his brooding silence, Leo couldn't help but gape at the massive, two-story house sprawling out in front of him. "How many rooms do you have?"

Alana had the grace to blush. She found the family homestead to be on the ostentatious side—but then, with the family rate, the rent was cheap. "Twenty-two, not counting the bathrooms. It actually belongs to my parents. They designed it and had it built about thirty years ago, when prices were lower. They retired and moved a couple of years ago, and I took it over."

Leo stood amazed. He hadn't realized how far from downtown Las Vegas she lived, and what that would mean property-wise. Alana's home was as far northwest of the Strip as you could get without ending up at Mount Charleston. He hadn't seen another vehicle and very few buildings since they'd turned off Ann Road. Knowing a little about her family now, and realizing that she was a performer, he expected some type of extravagance, but this blew him away.

"How much of this land is yours?" he asked, looking around but seeing no neighboring homes.

"About fifteen acres," she answered, but rushed to add,

"Like I said, it's not mine, it's my parents'. They rent it to me for a lot less than it's worth. They don't want to sell it, but they don't want it to stand empty. They like the idea of one of their children still living here, but not enough to just give it away to one of us. So, this was what we worked out when I moved back to Vegas."

Leo's lips quirked, thinking of his own modest, three-bedroom home. He'd been so proud when he saved enough for the down payment, going out and buying Max right away. But this was incredible. Real people didn't live this way, at least not normal ones. And that's what he was, normal.

On the bright side, he wouldn't be slumming it on this assignment.

Rick hopped out of the driver's seat and helped Alana out of the car while Leo continued to gawk. He hooked his arm around her shoulder, taking most of her weight.

"I can walk, Rick," Alana complained, uncomfortable with the extra attention added to the embarrassment caused by Leo's ogling of her home. "I've got stitches in my head, not a broken leg."

"Do you always have to be so stubborn?" Rick asked, keeping hold of her elbow when she would have jerked away from him.

Alana tilted her head and raised a single brow, stretching herself to her full five foot eleven inch height before poking him in the chest. "I'm a Devlin, we're bred that way. What's your excuse?"

A mischievous smile lit up Rick's face as he pushed her finger away. "It's the bad company that I keep, what else?"

Leo walked behind the two, carrying an overnight bag, and wondering what he'd gotten himself into. Alana wanted to hold on to her normal life, one of Leo's own greatest desires. If he was honest with himself, it was the real reason he agreed to her plan. But he had to admit, he hadn't seen anything as yet that he would consider *normal* about her life.

"I hope the two of you don't keep this up all the time. I'm here to protect Alana, not as a volunteer for experiments in the loss of sanity," he grumbled.

Rick smirked, glancing sideways at Alana. "I like him, Mom. Can we keep him? I promise to feed him everyday."

"Only if you promise to clean up after him, too." Alana laughed and ripped her arm from his grasp, palm swinging to slap him on the back of the head. "It's a good thing you're *not* staying. I think killing a man in front of a homicide investigator would go hard on me."

Rick stopped in his tracks, shock crossing his features. "What do you mean, I'm not staying?"

"Just what I said," Alana replied, crossing her arms and glaring at him. "You can stay tonight, since it's so late, but that's it. It's bad enough I'm acting as 'bait-girl'. I'd rather not see my best friend in the same boat. Anyway, I'll be seeing you most of tomorrow, to go over changes in the show, remember?"

Rick shook his head, his expression becoming obstinate. "I'm not leaving you alone."

Alana stopped in front of Rick. With her three-inch heels, they were eye to eye. Watching her staring down her *friend,* Leo wondered idly what it would be like to be able to stare a woman in the eye, without having her use stilts. But, then again, he didn't want to be looking into the expression gracing Alana's face. For a moment, he didn't envy Rick whatsoever.

"But I won't *be* alone," Alana replied. "I have my own personal, police bodyguard. I have to trust him to know what he's doing. And, as a good friend told me, I can't always depend on you being there for me. What's the point in trying to keep my life normal if I start acting different?"

Rick folded his arms across his chest. Alana knew that he didn't want to back down, but he didn't have a choice either. When it came down to it, she was the boss.

"I hate this, Alana," he said, disgust dripping from his voice. "I don't like the idea of you being dependent on a total stranger for your safety, but it's your call to make, not mine. Just remember I can be here in less than ten minutes if you need me. And I'm not leaving in the morning. I'm staying until you force me out, if only to work on the show. That is, if you consider work something *normal* to do."

Alana smiled as she patted Rick's arm. "That's fine."

Leo couldn't fight back his slight snicker. Rick sent him a piercing glare over Alana's shoulder. "You take care of her, hear me? If anything happens to her, I'll hold you personally responsible."

Leo's brows arched as he pulled himself up to his own full, imposing height, chest puffing. No way was he letting Alana's *friend* intimidate him. "Threatening an officer is a crime. I hope you realize that."

Though outweighed by a least thirty pounds of pure muscle, Rick refused to back down. After growing up with the Devlins and all that entailed, very little scared Rick. "It's not a threat. It's a promise."

Alana turned Rick's face back to her. "Down boy. I'll be fine."

Rick didn't look reassured, but marched into the house without another word.

Leo grimaced, watching Rick stalk away. "I didn't take him for the type to back down that easily."

"It's not a matter of backing down," Alana answered,

wincing as Rick slammed the door closed behind him. "It's doing the sensible thing. You're here to protect me, and you don't need the distraction of another person. Now let's get you settled in."

Alana opened the door and led him inside. Leo's first impression was that of walking into a rainbow, bright colors reflected from every corner. A huge amethyst geode sat by the entryway, sparkling with the fluorescent light from the open doorway. Stained glass windows turned the light gathered from security lamps outside into colored patterns gleaming on the translucent mother-of-pearl colored tile floor. The walls themselves were white, but bright paintings, done in both realistic and impressionistic styles, were displayed prominently. A jungle of plants sat in the corners of the room, vines climbing up to the vaulted ceiling.

Alana giggled at the stunned expression on Leo's stoic face. "I know. It's a little hard to take in all at once, but my mother loves color and living things. I take after her in that respect. She decorated this area. Don't worry, though, the whole house isn't like this. We each decorated different rooms, so no one style is dominant. A bit schizophrenic, I know, but interesting at least. Now let's get you upstairs before you suffer sensory overload."

They climbed a vine-covered spiral staircase to the second floor.

"I feel like I've stumbled into Middle Earth," Leo muttered under his breath, while gripping the intricately carved oak banister.

Again, Alana laughed at the image, her own hand gliding along the wooden railing. "Mother would be proud then. I've always thought that was the look she was striving for when she planned out the foyer." Alana lead him past several large doors before stopping. "I'll give you the full tour in the morning, but feel free to wander about as much as you want. The layout is simple, so you shouldn't get lost. I'm assuming you'll want a room close to mine, so I'm giving you my sister's. You'll have to excuse the décor in here as well. Her tastes run to the girly."

Alana opened the door to a large, spacious room done in muted pastels, a relief to the eyes after the color collage downstairs. A large, Victorian four-poster bed dominated the room, matching well with the cherry wood bureau and roll-top desk. Various glass bottles decorated the bureau while Monet prints graced the walls. The plush beige bedding with numerous pillows looked incredibly comfortable for such a formal setting, while the faint scent of hyacinth clung to the air.

"Well," Leo said, dropping his bag, "it's not a very man friendly room, I'll grant you that. Where will you be?"

"Right next door." Alana gestured to a door Leo assumed was a second closet. "The rooms are connected by a bathroom, so be sure to lock the door when you're in there, unless you want unexpected company. But that way, if I need you, you'll have easy access."

"Then no locking the doors. I'd hate to waste time dealing with locks when the whole purpose of me being here is to be able to help you quickly if needs be."

"Whatever you say, you're the expert here," Alana was quick to agree. "I think we can both live with that. Now, I'll go down and talk to Rick for a while. I don't know about you, but I'm too wound up to go to sleep yet, no matter how late it is. You can look around to your heart's content. We'll be in the den." Alana studied the walls, not meeting Leo's gaze as she dropped her first surprise into his lap. "I do have one houseguest here, Amber Wentworth. I didn't mention her before because I knew you'd want to get rid of her. But she's had a hard time of it lately and needs the support. She should only be here tonight."

Leo's eyes flashed. He was in charge of her safety. How dare she decide who is a threat and who isn't without discussing it with him first! "You have someone else in this house that I wasn't told about, that I haven't had time to run even the most basic background check on. You call this a compromise?" He kicked the bedroom door closed, then leaned back against it. "We need to get a few things straight here. You are not running this show."

Alana held her hands out towards him, palms forward. "Before we have this fight, I think you should meet Amber. You'll understand everything once you see her. She's fragile, Detective. Even you'll be able to see that kicking her out tonight would do her serious damage. She'll leave with Rick tomorrow, maybe even sooner, I promise you. Just meet her before you make any decisions."

"She isn't my concern. You are." Leo resisted the urge to scream at her. It wouldn't do any good anyway. There were only a few hours before dawn. At that point, he'd kick out everyone not involved in the case.

Leo nodded, mind going over the other massive security issues that this monstrosity of a house raised. The other people had to go. "We'll meet downstairs, and I expect you to introduce me to this woman. After that, we need the time to sit down and get a few things straight."

"Oh, I agree," replied Alana, slipping out of the room and closing the door with a smirk. Leo had a lot to learn if he thought to control this situation. This was Alana's turf, and he'd do well to remember that.

Twenty minutes later, Alana sat on a plush leather couch in front of a roaring fire, drinking a steaming cup of chamomile tea. Chills racked her body in the stuffy room, a delayed reaction to the attack. Knowing the cause didn't help ease the discomfort. If the home remedies didn't work, she'd call Fiona and ask what she would suggest. Alana hoped the tea and the warm fire worked. She didn't want to worry her sister.

She looked down at the woman sitting on the floor near her feet. Alana tried to get Amber to sit in one of the other chairs, but the woman refused, saying she felt safer on the floor. So there Amber sat, painfully thin arms wrapped around her knobby knees, rocking back and forth while humming an off-key tune.

Rick stood by the fireplace, staring down at the woman's shaggy blond head, pity filling his face.

The door swung opened to a harried Leo. Alana couldn't help but think of how cute he looked all rumpled, like a well-loved Teddy bear. If one ignored his grumpy expression, that is.

Amber had a different reaction.

With a shrill squeak, she scrambled to the other side of the room, huddling in a corner, arms raised over her head, whimpering. Rick went to her, kneeling down, rubbing his hand against her back and mumbling to her.

Leo froze in the doorway.

Alana walked over to him, pushing him back out of the room. "Give Rick a second to calm her down," she said, closing the door on the panicking woman.

Leo shook his head, anger lighting his eyes. "What's wrong with that woman? She's practically skeletal, and it looks like she took hedge-trimmers to her hair."

Alana looked back at the closed door, lips pursed. "She might have done just that. I'm not certain. She's had a rough time, let's leave it at that." Alana smiled at his mutinous expression. "Trust me, Detective, there's nothing you can do to help her. The demons she's wrestling with can't be controlled physically, can't be arrested and brought in for questioning. But you can see why I didn't want to kick her out tonight."

Leo crossed his arms and stared at the thick, oaken door, listening to the echoes of the woman's whimpers. "Personal demons have human origins. Those I can cuff and stuff for what they did. No woman, no person, should look like that, be that terrified."

"No, no one should. But first she needs to fight her way free of her fear. That's what Rick and I are doing, helping her. If there is any person responsible for her pain, I'll report it to you personally." Leo didn't look convinced, still looking at the door. Alana reached up to turn his gaze back to her. "That's all I know at this point to tell you."

Leo jerked away from her touch as though it burned. "If you don't know who caused that, I'll have to agree with you for now, but I will check back with you to find out more. Do you have someplace for her to go tomorrow?"

Alana nodded. "If she's not ready to go home, I'm sure that Rick can take her to his place. Don't worry. We'll see that she's taken care of. She's not your responsibility."

The door opened. Rick stepped out, his strong arms wrapped around the tiny, shivering woman. "See, Amber," he whispered, "Leo's a friend of Alana's, no one to be afraid of." He gave Alana a pointed look. "I'm going to take her to the conservatory. Will you be meeting us?"

Alana nodded, watching Amber tremble in Rick's arms. It was obvious that Amber didn't have much time left. Amber had been drained to the last limits of her endurance by the creature tormenting her. It would have to be dealt with tonight, or she might have no tomorrow. "Detective

Grady and I have some things to go over first. I'll join you after that."

"You should get some rest. Your body needs to recover." Leo's eyes were locked on the pathetic woman supported by Rick's embrace.

Alana place a single hand on Leo's shoulder. "I will, don't worry. I think Amber needs me more than I need rest. If I have to, I can sleep the day away."

Leo shrugged off her hand, then shouldered his way back into the den. "It's your decision."

Alana stared at his back before waving Rick away.

Leo stood pacing in front of the fireplace when Alana stepped in the room. He turned towards her. "Do you have any idea how many outside doors this place has, not to mention windows?" he asked, rubbing his temples.

Alana walked over to the couch she'd been lounging in, picked up the cup from the side table, and took another sip of tea. "I can't say I've ever taken the time to count them."

Leo rolled his neck, his hands kneading his shoulders, trying to relieve the ache from the stress-filled muscles. "After tonight, I'm taking you somewhere else. This place is a nightmare. There's absolutely no way I can keep you safe here."

Alana turned and walked to the bookcase standing to one side of the fireplace. She pushed against it, causing it to roll open. "I think this might help calm you a bit."

The wall behind the bookcase was covered with mini-televisions. Lights blinked, and a computer keyboard slid forward. "My father was a private investigator until he retired. He had a thing for security, too. This place has one of the best security systems around. Not perfect, mind you, but pretty darn good, if I do say so myself."

Leo whistled. "I'll need to go through all this, but in the

55

morning. No way will I be able to decipher it all in one night."

Alana pushed the bookcase back in place. "Now you know why I wasn't worried about staying at my home as opposed to one of your safe houses."

"I guess so." Leo lowered his towering form into the large couch. His lips curled into a gentle smile as the butter-colored leather embraced his sore body. He picked up a sandwich from the tray on the coffee table and looked askance at the two silver urns.

"Coffee or tea, your choice."

Leo grunted and poured some coffee. Silently, he settled back and watched the flames dance.

Alana sighed when it became apparent that Leo wasn't going to start up a conversation. She had to admit, she wanted more from him. She hadn't felt this secure with, or attracted to, a man since her one debacle in college. But how did you approach a man like Leo, so stoic, especially under circumstances like these? Not the best time to try and talk up a guy, that's for sure. "So, I guess since we're going to spend so much time together, we'll need to get to know each other better."

Leo shrugged, trying to block out her disturbing presence by concentrating on his steaming cup. "That depends on how we're going to go about this. The way I see it, you've decided to run the show. I'm here in a bodyguard capacity. That doesn't require a lot of getting to know you. And it would be better if we didn't. It could become a distraction."

"I don't know. If you knew me better, you might be better able to predict the tactic the killer will take." Alana sank down in the couch next to him, folding one leg beneath her to face him. She flicked one of her long, curly red locks behind her ear and stared into his steely eyes.

Leo felt his temperature rise. He had a sinking feeling that it wasn't caused by the fire in front of him, but by the heat Alana's closeness seemed to be stoking. He found himself wanting to babble, something that hadn't happened since high school. "Okay, you want to get to know each other. How about we stick to the important issues for now, things that could come to play in my investigation? What about your work? You said you wanted to keep working while we continue the investigation. What's your usual schedule?"

Leo paused for a breath, wincing at how stupid he sounded. *Way to impress her with your professionalism. Bet she feels secure in your hands now. Better yet, don't think about your hands in connection with her. Dear God, what am I thinking? She's pretty and sexy. So what? This is Las Vegas. You can see sexy at any casino. Get a grip. She's a job.*

Alana didn't seem to notice his preoccupation. "Well, Monday and Tuesday nights are dark. But Rick and I meet to talk business, plan new illusions, that sort of thing. Of course, being a magician, I'll expect most of those meetings to be private."

"I'm not going to run out screaming all the secrets to your tricks." Leo leaned back, glaring at her.

"Nevertheless, I'd feel better doing it that way. It shouldn't be a problem for you. We meet here anyway. We'll be in a different room from you, that's all."

Leo didn't look convinced, but let it slide. "What about the rest of the week?"

"Well, we perform twice nightly, one show starting at seven and one at ten. We rehearse starting around noon. That's if we don't have any special shows planned. Actually, we're not dark this Tuesday. We'll be doing a show at noon for some critically ill children from the Children's Hospital of Las Vegas."

Leo turned away from the fireplace to face her. "Really? I wouldn't have expected that. Do you do those kind of shows often?"

Alana hid her disappointment at his obvious shock. *Nice to know what he thinks of me. The idle rich thing again, that's just perfect.* "Yes, I do. My sister volunteered there through high school and college. She got me interested. I visit there twice a month, doing what I can to cheer up the kids and their families. Then, twice a year, I do a big show at the casino for the worst of the children and their families, at least those who can leave the hospital." Alana paused for a moment, her face falling into shadows. Her voice became strained as she continued. "About half of the kids who come to the first show don't make it to see the second one."

Leo reached out for her hand, only to pull back. He hated feeling her pain, knowing that he caused it. He cast around the room, trying to think of something to change the subject, to distract her. He spotted a familiar set of books on the bookcase.

He walked over and plucked one off its shelf. "Dev Kirby. He's my favorite mystery author. Are these books your father's?"

Alana shook off her maudlin thoughts and fought a grin. "In a way. That particular *copy* is mine."

Leo looked puzzled by her answer. "How can the copy be yours but also your father's?"

Alana answered with a question of her own. "That's the first one in the series you have, right?"

Leo nodded.

"Read the dedication."

Leo flipped through the first few pages. "Let's see. 'To

Alana, Adain, and Fiona, my greatest creations.' This was dedicated to you?" Leo's head jerked up. "Dev Kirby is your father?"

Alana shook her head. "Not exactly. Dev Kirby is my father and mother. Kirby is Mom's maiden name. She was a criminal psychologist before she retired. She creates the villain and the crime while Dad figures out how he'll be caught. It works well, don't you think? After they moved to Ireland to retire, they got bored. So they started writing."

Leo stared at her, like she'd grown an extra head.

"What? I thought he was your favorite author. You have something against being related to people who live off their creativity?"

Leo slapped the book shut, not liking the direction this conversation was going. "No, not exactly. My parents are artists."

Alana's eyes widened, not expecting that kind of background from such a self-contained man. "Really? That must have been great growing up. Do you get to see them often now? I haven't seen much of my parents since they moved."

"It depends on what commune they're living in at the moment. Right now it's in Maine, so no, I don't." Leo's eyes froze over, the muscle in his cheek twitching. He put the book back on the shelf. "But we've gotten off the subject. Is there anything else about your schedule that I should know?"

"No," Alana whispered, not certain what she'd said to make him close up or how to fix it. "Nothing else."

"Then I don't know about you, but I need some sleep. We'll work out the rest in the morning. Good night." With that, he spun around and all but stormed out.

"Good night," Alana replied to the empty room.

Chapter Five

Rick stood alone leaning on the door to the conservatory when the click of Alana's shoes against the hardwood floor brought him to attention. His hand rubbed at the tic twitching by his eye. "She's not going to make it, is she?" he asked without preamble.

Alana considered lying to him about his high school friend but couldn't. She shook her head. "No, not if we don't do something tonight."

"So what's the plan?" Rick asked, glancing back at the closed door. Worry deepened the chocolate brown of his eyes.

Alana took his arm and lead him away from the room, away from Amber's sensitive hearing. "First, I ought to tell you what we're up against. I suspected it from the first, but I hoped I was wrong."

Rick grabbed Alana's arm, jerking her to a stop. "Why do I get the feeling that I'm not going to like this?" he growled.

Alana looked down to where his hand gripped her and answered with a single word, *"Cearb."*

Rick backed away and let out a low whistle. He turned to stare at the door again. "The Killing One, that's what's draining her, tormenting her? But why?"

Alana ran her fingers through her red curls, fighting for calm. "Someone sent it to her. I can't think of any other way for this to have happened." She shook her head, clearing it. "But that's not important at the moment. We'll track the source down later. We have to break the connection between Amber and the cearb tonight."

Rick nodded, turning down the hallway to the back door. "Then we should go prepare the *nemeton* right away."

Alana placed a restraining hand on his arm, turning him back to her. "No, we won't be able to use Dad's sacred grove this time."

Rick stared down at her in disbelief. "You're kidding, right?"

Alana grimaced but still managed to meet his eyes. "I don't have the strength to cast a full protection circle as well as perform a ritual of separation." Alana clenched her hands at her side. "I've already done two shows, cast an emergency doppelganger glamour to escape the bastard who attacked me, and used a mesmer glamour on Detective Hunter. I'm running on empty."

Rick threw his hands up in the air in disgust. "Then what are we going to do? You can't risk a confrontation with a cearb without some protection. The nemeton is the best place for High Magicks. If you aren't strong enough to ward it, what other options do we have?"

"We'll use the basement room. It's soundproofed, so no problems with the detective upstairs, and it has built in wards. They may not be as strong as casting a full circle of protection, but I won't have to waste as much energy jump starting the protection already there." Alana watched Rick's face closely.

"We don't have a choice, do we?" he asked, shoulders sagging.

Alana didn't spare any time on false hopes. "Not if we want her to live. I'll start the preparations. You calm Amber down as much as you can before you two join me."

Alana completed her casting circle with a last sprinkle of salt as Rick and Amber entered the room. Black and white candles lining the walls provided nominal, flickering light to the room. Sticks of frankincense burned in each corner, the pungent aroma causing Alana's sinuses to close and her eyes to water. *Damn, forgot to take my allergy pills again.*

Rick hopped over the circle of salt, swinging Amber into his arms and lifting her over and setting her back on her feet. Alana stepped forward and took Amber's icy hands in her own, giving them a brisk rub. "Everything is going to be fine. It ends tonight. You only need to do as I ask."

Through hollow eyes, Amber stared at Alana. Her body shivered, bones threatening to rattle apart, but nodded in agreement.

Alana's lips pursed. She looked to Rick, whose face remained blank. She could see that he understood how much she was risking by putting this together without proper preparation.

Alana released Amber's hands and strode to the nearest wall. She took a breath, reaching deep within the core of her being. She laid both palms against the stone, pushing outward with the same energies she called to create her glamours. Her palms tingled and glowed against the cold stone, the light traveling outward along lines etched in the wall. An intricate design came to life, covering the entire room, wall to wall; ceiling to floor. When Alana lifted her palms, the energy clung between her and the wall for a brief moment, before snapping back into place around her hands.

She walked back to the center of the room, picking up a small dagger that lay on a piece of white silk at the exact center of the floor, where a circle surrounded by a triangle was etched deep into the stone. She raised the ritual athame above her head, her glow traveling up to the tip, sparking outward. "I call upon all those gods who have been invoked here before, upon all the magics cast in this space, guide me in my works this night."

She placed the athame back on the cloth, and then approached Amber. Reaching into her pocket, Alana withdrew a short gold chain with a simple onyx pendant hanging from it. She looped the chain around Amber's neck. "Wear this close to your heart, for protection against those who would wish you harm."

Amber's skeletal fingers clutched the pendant as Alana guided her to the center of the room being careful not to disturb the circle of salt. Alana pushed her down to kneel inside of the circle. Rick moved to stand outside behind Amber while Alana kneeled facing her, also inside the circle.

Alana placed her fingers against the stone-etched circle. The magics worked into the circle sucked at her energy, ripping it from her. Her hand trembled as the central circle of protection flared to life. She felt drained as an emptiness grew inside her. Ignoring the growing blankness at her core, she lifted her athame again, kissed its hilt, and began tracing another circle around Amber. "Now I cut the ties that bind, I free what feeds upon the mind. Creature sent, be revealed to me. As I will, so mote it be."

The warding circles flared a blinding white. The salt foundation Alana had poured crackled and charred a deep black. Alana heard Rick's swiftly indrawn breath as a pungent smell of rot permeated the room, overpowering the frankincense. The skin on her back prickled, the hair at her nape bristling. She fought the urge to look at the creature behind her, instead concentrating on pumping more energy into the roughly etched circle she had scratched around Amber, her power cutting through the links that chained Amber to the cearb.

Alana heard the cearb moving in the shadows behind her, seeking entrance, weakness in the circle. A deep growl rumbled and echoed off the walls.

Amber's back bowed, and she screamed as Alana's magic found the line of power holding her to the cearb. Alana's energy twisted around the link, seeking the best area to break it, following it back to the creature. The line tightened, resisting Alana's power.

As her power reached the cearb, Alana's awareness of the cearb grew. She could feel its anger, its hatred of all living things. She could taste its hunger, the black emptiness inside that craved a living soul to fill it.

Worse yet, Alana could sense the creature clawing its way towards her. It moved around the second circle, sniffling the ground. As it came within her line of sight, Alana tried not to look at it. But her eyes were drawn to its monstrous, dark form. The size of a small bear, it moved on all fours with the inborn grace of a cat, tail switching and claws digging into the stone floor. Its muzzle dripped yellow-green saliva that sizzled where it struck the floor. Row upon row of shark-like teeth gleamed and gnashed in its mouth. An angry, pulsing line of twisted red and purple energies shot out of its chest directly into Amber's.

Alana grasped the hilt of her athame, shoving at the line with all her strength, both physical and magical. The cearb launched itself at the circle, clawing and wailing. Alana flinched as it tore into her magic. The circle wrenched more power from her, twisting her stomach and forcing a gasp from her. Sparks flew as the warding bowed inward, but held.

Rick moved towards the cearb's back, slipping in behind the maddened beast. As the warding exploded outward under the onslaught, he snaked his arms under the neck of the cearb, jerking it back. "Hurry!" he cried as the cearb pitched and writhed in his grasp, its drool raising blisters where it hit his skin.

Reaching deep within herself, Alana pulled out all her reserves. The protective wards fell away as she drew back every drop of power she could. Her hair whipped around her face, and her entire body pulsed with white and blue light. The glow spiraled down into her hands as she raised the ceremonial blade over her head, slashing down at the line of power.

The beast howled and broke free of Rick as the line parted. It leapt forward, its paw slashing out even as it began fading from sight. Alana gasped as the spectral claws slammed through her, tearing not her flesh, but her very soul. She let out a single keening wail before collapsing into a heap, her last sight the rigid face of Detective Leo Grady standing in the doorway.

Alana awoke to a throbbing ache behind her eyes. Her hands slid over the smooth satin beneath her as she blinked to adjust to the bright light of day. She stared up at the silk-draped oaken beams of her enormous bed, taking stock of the various pains throughout her body.

"Think you'll live?" Rick asked from the far side of the room where he lounged in the overstuffed medieval throne sitting by her bathroom door.

Alana pushed herself up, sliding an extra pillow behind her back and pulling her burgundy, satin comforter under her arms. "I don't know. You tell me. What time is it?"

Rick sauntered to her bedside, handing her a steaming cup of tea. "Around four o'clock. You've got the detective downstairs worried. He almost took you back to the hospital until I convinced him that you'd been pushing yourself too hard for days now and just needed the sleep. If you hadn't woken up by this evening, I wouldn't have been able to hold him off." He gave her a worried look before collapsing beside her. "Hell, I might have brought you in myself."

Alana smiled and patted his hand. "I'm fine. You were right. I pushed myself too hard, but I'll be fine. More rest and a good meal, that's all I need."

"I called Fiona." Rick raised a hand to silence her as she struggled to sit straighter. "I know you hate involving family, but I didn't know what to do for you. She said to drink mint tea with as much honey as you can stomach until your head clears up. Then she suggests fruit first, maybe some pasta if your stomach can handle it. No meat until tomorrow. You need fuel you can convert quickly and easily until you have all your strength back."

A worried frown marred Alana's calm features. "The cearb got me. I remember the feel of his claws ripping into me."

Rick leapt to his feet and to stare out the window. "I know. I saw. That's why I called your sister. Because the cearb wasn't corporeal at the time, the damage is minimal and only on a spiritual level, a temporary drain. Your powers may be a bit sluggish for a while, but nothing permanent. She suggests you pay particular attention to rituals of the Barley Moon next week. She says the harvest rituals will help you replenish yourself."

"You didn't mention the other problem to her, did you?" Alana knew that Rick didn't like resorting to contacting

Fiona, but worried what he might have told her once he had.

Rick snorted, still looking out the window, fingers clutching the sill. "Of course not. I recommend that you do, though. You know she'll find out on her own. Fiona's always been the worrier. If you don't tell her about the mortal after you, she'll still know something's wrong and will believe the worst."

He was right. Her sister, more than her twin brother, kept close tabs on all the family. But Alana wasn't ready to call in the troops yet. "When the time comes," she assured Rick, before changing the subject. "How's Amber doing?"

For the first time since she'd woken, Alana watched the customary smile slide across Rick's face as he turned towards her. "Much better than she was, better than you are. She's eating and she's getting her color back. Give her a few days and a trip to the hairdresser, and she'll be her old self again. I'm taking her to her sister's house, now that you're up and around."

Alana sank back down into her cocoon of pillows. Amber would do better in familiar surroundings, with her family around her for support. They weren't finished yet, but the worst was over. "Good, I'm glad she's better. Later, we'll have to find out who did it and prevent anything else from being sent to her. But she should be okay for a while. Tell her to keep the onyx and to come back in two weeks. She and I should both be strong enough to finish by then."

Rick nodded and headed for the door at her dismissal. "I'll send the detective in before I leave. He'll want to see you himself, and I'll feel better knowing someone's with you while I'm gone."

Alana winced at the censure in her oldest and closest friend's voice. "It's better that you not be here. We'll let the detective do his job, and catch his criminal."

Rick leaned his head against the closed door for a moment before turning back to face her. "But I don't have to like it, leaving you like this. I'm going to put out some feelers, find out more about this Detective Grady. If he's going to be protecting my Protector, he'd damn well better be good at his job."

"I doubt you'll find anything else." Alana shrugged at Rick's expression of disbelief. "He feels right for the job. I know I'm not as good at reading people as Fiona, but even I can feel the dedication in Detective Grady. I'm willing to put my trust in him." Alana gave Rick one of her mischievous grins. "But that doesn't mean I won't be looking into things myself, once I'm up and swinging again."

Rick grinned back as he opened the door and stepped out of her room. "You do that. And let me know if you need anything."

"Don't worry. That's your job, Helper, and I'm not about to let you out of it that easily." Alana jerked forward as pieces of memories from the night before came rushing back. "Shit, tell me I didn't see Grady last night."

Rick grimaced, clasping his hands behind his back. "I was working my way up to telling you."

Alana groaned. "The whole night was a comedy of errors. How much did he see?"

"I'm not certain," Rick answered, rocking back on his heels. "He won't say anything to me. He also won't stay in the same room with me for long either. So I think it's safe to say he saw the cearb."

Alana slapped her forehead with her palm and collapsed back into the bed. She muttered unintelligibly for a moment, before looking back up at Rick. "Great, that's just great. And I'm not even strong enough to cast a mind wipe spell on him. By the time I am, the memories will be permanent."

Despite the seriousness of the situation, Rick smirked. "Looks like you're going to have to trust the good detective with more than your safety."

Alana grabbed a pillow and flung it across the room at him. Rick blocked it with one arm and a soft chuckle. He left without another word, leaving Alana to settle in with her overly sweetened tea and wait for her next interrogation.

Leo didn't leave her waiting for long.

The door flew open, Leo's shape leaning against the frame, arms akimbo. He stood, staring at her, expression unreadable, for what seemed an eternity. "So, you're conscious. How do you feel?" he asked, voice gruff, as he stepped forward, feet sinking into the russet shag carpeting. His eyes never left her face, watching her every movement.

Alana sat her cup on the bedside table, sloshing a bit of the liquid as she misjudged the distance. "Like somebody hit me in the back of the head with a crowbar."

Leo's expression darkened, not appreciating her grim humor. "I think that's the least of what happened to you last night. Do you want to explain what the hell was going on downstairs?"

Alana shrugged. "That depends on what you saw."

Leo reached her bedside, grabbing the pole of the four-poster closest to her head, the wood groaning under the pressure as he wrung it in his grasp. "Don't screw with me, Devlin. I saw some freaky shit go down, and then spent most of my day trying to think of how to explain it to my chief if you didn't regain consciousness. I'm not up to games right now."

Alana's face went blank, eyes haunted. Dark memories

seized her mind, separating her from emotion. "It won't matter if I tell you. You'll never believe me."

"Try me."

Alana released a pent up sigh, blinking as exhausted tears threatened to spill. She could feel the limits of her endurance like a tightened string running through her body, from head to toe. It was about to snap. "I guess you could say you and I are in similar occupations. It's your duty to protect and serve. I do the same. The only difference is that I go after things that aren't human, more along the line of 'things that go bump in the night'."

Leo stared down at her, face blank. At the sound the wood in his grip was making, Alana feared that a two hundred year old antique would shatter in his hand. "That's ridiculous, something a TV exec comes up with when ratings are low."

Alana cocked her head to the side. "Then how do you explain what happened last night?" she asked, a snide little sneer in her voice.

"I don't," replied Leo, fingers of his free hand raking through his hair. "I'm trying not to think about it. I've seen murder scenes that are less likely to give a person nightmares than whatever that creature was."

"I'm a witch, does that make things easier for you?" Alana waved her arms over her head. Had her powers been with her, sparks would have flown from her fingertips. Instead, the faintest whiff of wildflowers floated off her body. "I'm a descendant of the fey. The blood of the Sidhe Queen Aine runs through my veins. To stay in the mortal world, my ancestor swore that he and all his offspring would act as guardians of the mortal realms, protecting its inhabitants while hiding the existence of the Otherworld from them. And so it has been for over two thousand years."

Leo remained silent, but dropped his hand from its grip on the bed and took a step back.

An instant of pain reflected in Alana's eyes. "Let me help you. This is where you curse at me, call me vile names, accuse me of being insane, and leave."

"If it weren't for what I saw, I would, at least the calling you insane part. But I saw what I saw. You may be a magician, but nothing would explain that thing." Leo looked down at Alana's sunken eyes, drawn face, and pallor. "It was to help that woman, Amber. That's why you said I couldn't help her."

"Yes."

"Why didn't you do something like that to the killer last night?"

A whimper threatened to shred its way out of her chest. "I wish I could have. Casting a spell takes time and preparation, unless you're gifted. I can throw an illusion without preparation, that's my talent. Anything else, I have to work for. As it is right now, I'm so drained I couldn't change my eye color."

Leo's face shut down, denial written in every frozen muscle. "I won't pretend to understand all this, or even believe it. But you look horrible, and I'd feel better if we let a doctor take a look at you."

It was obvious from his looming stance that Leo had prepared himself for a fight. Instead, Alana shrugged and swung her feet over to the steps at the side of her bed. It was a little enough thing to give in on. She had a feeling that there would be more than enough to fight about later. "If you insist. I can tell you, the diagnosis will be acute exhaustion. It's not the first time this has happened, and it won't be the last."

Leo's face softened. He rushed to her side, offering an

arm for support. "Humor me. I need you for the case. To keep you in top form, I'll do whatever I have to. The quicker you understand that, the better off you'll be."

Chapter Six

Darkness and silence filled the house, an hour before dawn. Both Leo and Alana had long since fallen into deep, exhausted sleep. Neither heard the slight tinkling sound of broken glass or the quiet snick of a lock being undone. Neither stirred at the hushed steps climbing the stairway and sliding down the hall. Neither heard the pause of those steps before each bedroom door as an unknown assailant stopped to listen to the occupants.

While the silent alarm *was* triggered, almost no noise echoed through the vast hallways of the Devlin house. No warning given.

Alana would never be certain what awoke her, if she heard the squeak of her door opening or sensed that she was no longer alone. But she woke moments before strong hands clamped around her throat, cutting off her air.

Her eyes widened as panic sent surges of adrenaline through her body. The mask worn by her attacker gave him the anonymous aspect of death himself, come to claim her. The bitter taste of bile collected in the back of her mouth, along with the metallic tang of blood from biting her tongue. The bruising force of her attacker's grip on her throat stopped any shriek, reducing all utterance to a wheeze. Frantically, she gasped for air, her throat beginning to swell from the intense pressure. She clawed at the hands squeezing about her neck, thrashing her body and fighting for a single breath. She lashed out with her fists and feet, punching and kicking at the man's body.

In complete silence, her attacker grunted as she made contact, but squeezed tighter.

Stars began flashing before Alana's eyes while her room began to dim. Her struggles became weaker as her body tried to keep what reserves it had concentrated on keeping her vital organs functioning, holding on to life.

Despair spread through Alana, seeping her will. She thought of all she had left undone and unsaid. She groped at her bedside table, trying to grab anything that might stop him, force him to let go long enough for her to breathe. But in her weakened state, her fingers fumbled over objects. She couldn't clamp down, no matter how hard she tried. But she did manage to send the objects on the table crashing to the floor.

That was enough.

The door leading to the other bedroom crashed against the wall, a half-dressed Leo hurdling forward, gun in hand. Even in the darkness, he could see the struggling forms tossing on the bed. Bitter rage heated his blood at the sight of Alana fighting for her life, every primitive protective instinct rising within him. With no clear shot, his muscles tightened as he jumped into the fray.

The attacker cursed, rolling off Alana. Leo's finger's grazed the man's sleeve as he lunged for the door.

Leo paused, seeing Alana coughing and gagging, but alive. His desire to check on her battled against his need to catch the one who had harmed her. Alana waved him away as she wheezed. Leo stood frozen for another precious second staring down at her, then dashed into the darkened house after her attacker.

Massaging her throbbing throat and waiting for the

pounding beat of her heart to slow, Alana could hear the sounds of the two men stumbling down the stairs and running across the tile floor.

Then there was silence.

Fear for Leo's safety began to swell within her. Without him, she would be dead. His quick response was all that had saved her life. The thought of him being harmed now, in her defense, terrified her. Still unsteady, she dragged herself off the bed to lean in the doorway, waiting for Leo's return. She was the first to hear the faint shriek of police sirens.

Once more, Leo found himself sitting next to Alana on the couch in the den. But this time, neither felt like talking. One of the officers had been kind enough to get a blanket to wrap around Alana's shoulders, helping to fight the tremors that racked her body. Reaction ripped through her, causing violent, uncontrollable shakes. Tears glistened in her eyes as she listened to the officers discuss the break-in and attack.

She didn't care that the man had placed a large layer of packing tape across a window before breaking the glass, pulling the shards away. She didn't care that it took him longer than anticipated to open the window because of the metal rods her father had placed in the sill. She certainly didn't like hearing that he must be an electronic genius, bypassing most of her father's security system. She owed her life to Leo and a single redundancy in the silent alarm system. Alana didn't want to know how easy it was for him to gain entry to her home.

All Alana wanted was for the officers to leave, for her life to go back to normal, for none of this to ever have happened.

Leo's eyes turned to glacial slits as he watched each fearful and angry expression slip across Alana's face. He pulled her to his side, rubbing her arms, trying to give what comfort he could, knowing there was little he could offer. Looking at her now, he wondered why he'd felt any fear of her or her powers. She was a normal woman, scared for her safety. Her home had been invaded, her sense of security stripped away. He wanted to tuck her away somewhere secure, where no harm could come to her. He wanted to give her security. But nothing he could do, short of catching the maniac who attacked her, would give her back that peace.

"I don't know why I'm acting this way," Alana said between the chattering of her teeth as she burrowed her head into Leo's shoulder, soaking up his warmth. "I wasn't this frightened when he attacked me the first time, and he hurt me a lot worse then."

Leo fought the impulse to place a gentle kiss on her tousled head. Right now, she didn't need to be accosted by the feelings growing inside of him, inappropriate as they were. She needed comfort, and as uncomfortable as he was with the role, he was all she had.

"This is your home," he whispered. "You're bound to be more frightened after being attacked here. It's normal, nothing to be ashamed of." Leo pulled her closer to tuck her head under his chin, letting her shivering body absorb his warmth.

Alana sighed and snuggled in his arms. "I don't know what I would have done if you hadn't shown up when you did. I'm not this weak. I hate being this weak. I feel silly saying it, but I owe you my life."

Leo tried to ignore the blooming sense of pride that her comment caused. "It's my job to protect people, provide them with a sense of security." Leo grinned, squeezing

Alana's shoulders and rubbing circular patterns on her back. "Not to mention, from what I've seen, you would've figured something out yourself. You're a fighter. You wouldn't have given up. I don't think your assailant would have kept the upper hand much longer."

Alana swallowed, wincing at the stab of pain the movement caused her swollen throat. She had come so close to losing everything tonight. She couldn't let herself be vulnerable again. Something had to be done. "Then you have more confidence in me than I do. My entire family, including Rick, told me that a girl in today's world needed to know self-defense, if only to ward off muggers. I never listened to them. Too stubborn and sure of myself, I guess. Yesterday, in the hospital, Rick promised to teach me some. God, that feels like ages ago."

Leo was glad to hear her begin planning ahead instead of brooding on what might have been, like most of the survivors he'd dealt with over the years. She was the type who wouldn't let this destroy her. She would have a life after this was over; she'd make certain of it. "I think it's a bit late for that. It takes time to become proficient in any form of martial arts, if that's what you mean by self-defense. But it wouldn't hurt to start. I'll be sticking close to you for the next few days, maybe even weeks. I could teach you a few tricks that might help, at least to stall and draw attention."

"It would pass the time." Alana looked over at the officers, still discussing the crime. "What are we going to do now? And when are these guys going to let us go?"

"What we do now depends on what I can clear with my superiors. They weren't crazy about having you come back here to begin with, not that you left us any other option. But as soon as I know something definite, I'll tell you."

Leo watched as the forensic team tramped past the

den, heavy packs in hand. "As for when they'll let us go, that depends. I figure I'll have you tucked into bed somewhere safe within the next hour."

Alana started shivering again and clutched the blanket around her shoulders, nails sinking deep into the cloth. "I hope so. I don't know about you, but I'm dead on my feet." Hearing herself, Alana flinched. "Boy, that was a bad choice of words."

Leo gave in to one of his lesser desires and hugged her, giving Alana what solace he could while keeping an emotional distance. "I don't know about that. I think it's good that you can joke about it, no matter how morbidly."

Alana stiffened, before sagging against his chest. "Yeah, well pardon me if I don't think my death is good comedic material right now."

Leo's mouth flattened to a grim line. With Alana curled on his lap like a kitten, he loathed the thought of what could have happened to her. He'd seen her face down a monster with just a glowing dagger, and then watched a single man nearly choke the life out of her with his bare hands. Rage seethed within Leo. The bastard better pray that when Leo caught up with him they weren't alone. Otherwise, Leo feared what he would do to the man for causing such a strong woman to hit her breaking point.

Realizing the inappropriateness of his thoughts, Leo pulled back from Alana, watching her expression. His hands tightened to fists at the sight of the bruises forming a chain around her neck. "Listen. I need to call Gabe and let him know what's happening. Will you be alright alone for a while?"

At Alana's unflinching nod, Leo stood and walked to a small room connected to the den. The room was sparsely furnished, with only a massive leather chair and a telephone table. Leo dropped into the chair and dialed Gabe's cell phone number. *The man is never in his own home. How he talks so many different women into sleeping with him, I'll never know.*

"Hello," a deep, sleep-filled voice answered.

"Get your lazy butt out of whatever bed it's in. I need you," Leo replied with little sympathy. Why should his partner get all the sleep?

Gabe groaned before asking, "Why? What's going on?"

"He struck again," Leo snapped, temper simmering close to the surface. "Alana's alive, but it's not safe for her to stay here."

"Damn," Gabe cursed. Leo could here his partner scrambling. "Are you taking her to a safe house? Do you want me to meet you there?"

"No. I don't think laying low is going to work. This is the second time he's known where a victim was being kept. He's either keeping a much closer eye on his targets than we thought or there's a leak."

"Damn," Gabe muttered again, not sounding surprised.

Leo clutched the receiver. "Right. So enough keeping out of sight, I'm taking her to my house. I want you to call the precinct. I want a heavy presence around my place, at least two cars within sight at any given time."

Gabe snorted. "They're not going to want to spare that much man power, and you know it."

"Remind them that this is a priority case," Leo replied. "The big wigs at city hall want this case broken as soon as possible, before the press catches on. I think that will convince anyone to give me what I need."

"You've got it. Anything else?"

Leo glanced down at his watch and flinched at the early morning hour. "Come by my place around ten. I want you to stay inside with Alana for a couple of hours. I think it's time I question Burke again."

"Like I said, you've got it. Sure you don't want me earlier?"

This time Leo snorted. "Are you kidding? I've got to get *some* sleep tonight, or this morning, or whenever the hell it is. I'll see you at ten."

Alana smirked as they drove up to Leo's home. Tired as she was, she could still see the humor in their relative choice of homes. "I don't know how you stopped yourself from running, screaming, when you saw my place. Your home could be straight out of a Norman Rockwell painting." At Leo's expression, she rushed to add, "But it's very nice. Homey even."

Leo looked with pride at his one story, red brick home, surrounded by a white picket fence he'd put up himself. It took a long time to find the place he pictured in his mind throughout childhood, a home where he could put down roots. He could keep all the things that made a house a home, and never feel deprived.

Hearing his master pull in, Max came bounding through his doggy door, panting and slinging drool as he went. He scooped up a well-loved chew toy and flung it in the direction of Leo's car.

Alana shook her head watching Max's playful antics. "Even the requisite dog, everything you could want from an old-fashioned, family home. You know, I didn't think they built houses like this in Vegas, not anymore. Isn't there a city ordinance or something about every home being made of stucco and no Tom Sawyer fencing within city limits?"

Leo flashed Alana a dark look. "Very funny. I don't remember giving you a hard time about your home. And believe me, yours is much more impossible to believe than mine. My home may be Norman Rockwell, but at least I didn't take design tips from the Winchester House and the Addams Family."

Alana guffawed at the image, rocking back and forth, tears of laughter pooling in the corners of her eyes and her arms clutching her stomach. "True, but I didn't picture you as the suburban dream home type," she retorted once she managed to catch her breath.

Leo shrugged as he hopped out of the car to struggle with the bags in the trunk. "You've just met me. I don't think you're qualified to make any judgement calls about what suits me."

A thoughtful smile curved her mouth as she watched Leo's tight backside. She had to admit, for such a big man, he was mostly muscle. "I've always prided myself on being an astute judge of . . ." she paused for a moment to watch his thigh muscles ripple beneath his jeans, *"character."*

"Well, you missed on this one," he replied, not catching her innuendo. "Now let's get you settled in."

Leo dragged his overnight bag out of the car along with the one that Alana had thrown together before leaving her house. He guided her down the sidewalk going to his front door, between the two large pine trees shading his yard. Max scampered around them, spraying drool and tripping Alana. Leo reached down and scratched his ears, eliciting a groan of pure doggy pleasure.

"Quite a guard dog you got there," Alana commented as she watched Max roll over in the grass, begging for a belly rub. "Very dignified."

Leo ignored the criticism. He juggled the bags to fit the key in the door. "Max knows when to guard and when to greet. He's been well trained. He knows friend from foe.

Anyone I bring here with me is a friend. Plus, I bought him for company, not security. Few people are stupid enough to break into a cop's house."

"Yeah, well hopefully it'll stay that way." Alana peered around his shoulder for her first look at his living room. His home reflected a canvas of neutral colors, from the light tan of his carpeting to the deeper browns and forest greens in his furniture coverings. Each window had heavy wooden shutters instead of the vertical blinds Alana was used to seeing in most homes. All the furniture was also made of sturdy wood, except for the delicately carved piano sitting in the corner. Alana swept her fingers along the keys. "Do you play?"

"Not really," Leo answered as he dropped the bags on his couch. "But I feel that a house isn't a home without one."

Alana glanced at his back in puzzlement, before sitting down and pecking out a haunting melody.

Leo stared at her, placing a casual hand on her shoulder. "That's beautiful. What is it?"

Alana smiled, images of happy family time dancing through her head, and continued playing. "Oh, just something my dad would play for my mom. I think one of my ancestors wrote it, but I'm not sure. My mom loved it though. Dad would play it anytime he thought she was a little put out with him. He called it his dog house insurance."

"I didn't notice a piano in your home," Leo commented, sitting down beside her on the bench.

"Oh, Dad built a cottage in the back of the main house. He said that way he could play as loud as he wanted to without disturbing anyone. It has a music room, a small solarium, and an area where I practice my dancing."

"Dancing?"

Alana chuckled, changing to a rowdy Irish pub tune Rick's father had taught her. "Yeah, it was my mom's idea. It was her way of curing my slouch."

Leo looked at the tall, straight form sitting beside him and frowned. "I don't get it."

"Well, being over six feet tall, you may not have noticed that I'm just shy of six foot myself."

Leo shrugged. "I noticed that I didn't have to bend over so far to look you in the eyes. When you're six four, everyone seems short to you."

Alana giggled in delight. "Once upon a time, I would have sold my soul for someone to call me short. I got my biggest growth spurt in junior high. I'm sure you know how cruel kids that age can be, so I tried making myself look shorter. I even prayed that God would make me shrink. Needless to say, that didn't pan out. When Mom noticed how I was slouching, she sent me to dance class. I guess she thought the posture and poise would carry over."

Leo let his eyes glide up and down her straight and slender body. "Seems to have worked."

Alana blushed at the approval in his eyes, but chose to ignore it. "Well, it took a while, but in the meantime, I fell in love with performing. I continued dancing through college. I only quit dance after I quit college to come back here and give my magic show a real try."

"Sounds risky, quitting school like that," Leo replied, leaning one hip against the piano as he let the music she played flow over him.

"It was," she answered, her fingers flying across the keys. "But college wasn't working out for me. It was my parents' idea in the first place. I wanted to perform, and I loved magic more than dance."

"So, you didn't have your heart in your classes and

flunked out?" Leo asked.

She shrugged matter-of-factly. "No, I was doing pretty well in my business courses, but other . . . social problems came up and I decided to leave."

He tilted his brow, looking at her uncertainly. "Social problems?"

Alana's face went blank. She snapped the cover over the keys and rose from the bench. "I'd rather not discuss those. So which room is mine?"

Leo let her change the subject, sensing the pain beneath her words. He grabbed her bag off the couch and led her back into the house. "I'm giving you the middle bedroom. It's closest to mine and, as it sits against the garage, it has no windows. It'll be dark, but safe."

"Safer than my place?" Alana replied with a snort.

Leo's eyes darkened with concern. "We'll have police cars keeping my neighborhood under constant surveillance. My doors have bolt locks and the shutters on my windows are reinforced with steel. It's not perfect, but enough to slow the guy down. We almost had him tonight. If he keeps this up, you shouldn't be locked up in here for long."

Alana shrugged with forced indifference. "I'll call Rick in the morning and have him meet me here to go over the show. I still want to perform, especially Tuesday. It means a lot to the kids. That will be all right, won't it?"

Knowing how important it was to her and thinking it would be the perfect place to set a trap, he gave her a brief nod. "We'll put extra security on you, and I want to be close every minute. That might mean having me backstage. I hope you don't mind my being in on your trade secrets."

Laughter floated up from her still aching throat. Alana shook her head, tossing him a mischievous grin. "Oh, that won't be a problem. Remember, my magic is real. I doubt anyone would believe you if you told them."

A sour look crossed Leo's face. "I'm trying not to think about that."

Alana reached out, placing her fingers against his arm, needing to touch him. "Believe me, not thinking about it doesn't work. It sneaks up and bites you in the ass when you ignore it."

Chapter Seven

Leo eased the door open, not wanting to wake Alana yet. He knew that she would want to be awake before Gabe got there, certain she wouldn't be up to any surprises after the night she had lived through. But he also wanted to see her lying in innocent sleep, to see her vibrant, red hair spilling like silken fire against her white pillow. It was a bit perverse to torture himself this way, but he had to know if she was as beautiful asleep as she was awake.

He slid into the room, eyes locked with the peaceful figure lying bundled on his guest bed—so pure, she almost glowed. Watching her gentle breath, it was hard to believe that she was a popular, local magician with a psycho after her, even harder to believe she was a witch, part fairy.

Leo wished that he had met her under different circumstances, wished that he didn't know as much as he did about her.

Looking down into her oval face, pale, and rather delicate, he could only pray that after this was over she'd give a hulking, brooding giant of a detective the time of day. Then he wondered if that was what he really wanted.

She mumbled something and snuggled deeper into her pillow, one hand beneath her cheek, the other folded against her chest. Her pert, little nose scrunched while her full, red lips pursed. How a woman could seem so lush and yet so adorable at the same time was beyond him.

Gently, he reached out and shook her shoulder. Voice soothing and calm, he whispered, "Alana, you need to wake up. Detective Hunter will be here any minute."

Alana muttered more unintelligible grumbles and burrowed farther beneath the blankets, curving her knees against her chest. An infectious grin curled Leo's lips, warming his cold expression. Had Alana seen it, her heart would have fluttered. As it was, her eyes screwed closed, fighting to keep hold of her dream world.

Sitting beside her, Leo leaned over to whisper in her ear. As his lips neared her cheek, Alana turned. Leo found his mouth brushing hers.

Leo tried to jerk back, the reaction shooting through his body from so minor a contact shocking him. But the sleep-drugged Alana would have nothing of it. Her arms wrapped around his strong shoulders, pulling him down into the bed beside her.

Her mouth nibbled on his own, driving all thought of what he should or shouldn't do from his mind. All he could think of were her warm lips brushing his own, radiating pure delight through his bloodstream while melting all his resolve. He groaned and buried his hands in her fiery red hair, yanking her into his chest, claiming the kiss for his own.

Alana regained consciousness to the rich heat of Leo's mouth and the sharp, spicy scent of his cologne. The semi-erotic dreams she had been having, with him as guest star, melded with reality. Her hands ran over his cloth-covered shoulders, the thin cotton of his T-shirt doing little to keep the heat of his body from scorching hers. Her nails dug into his shoulder blades, craving closer contact.

She didn't know how this had started, but she wholeheartedly gave herself over to the tantalizing sensations.

Leo groaned with approval at Alana's passionate surrender, rewarding her with a kiss that was both slow and
drugging, a kiss her whole being could melt into, luxuriate
in. His lips moved across hers in a gentle, but firm caress.
The light massage sending currents of pleasure to all
reaches of her body.

Feeling her response, he increased the pressure, coaxing
her mouth open for a more intimate caress.

Alana whimpered and pulled him closer, trying to nestle
deep into his chest, where no one could pull her from her
indulgence. At that moment, she would have given anything
to him, so enwrapped was she in the pure desire coursing
through her.

Only the shrill, persistent buzz of the doorbell broke the
two apart.

Leo stared down at Alana in shock, panting, her floral
scent encompassing him. What on earth could he have been
thinking? This was just another case. And she was not the
type of woman that a man who wanted a normal life should
even consider getting involved with.

Not able to meet her eyes, Leo jumped up and muttered,
"That'll be Gabe." He turned and raced to the door.

Alana placed her fingertips against her throbbing mouth
and closed her eyes. She could feel the heat and pressure of
his lips on hers. It had been so long since any man had
kissed her, so long since she had felt the strength and temptation of a man's mouth against her own. Too bad it didn't
seem to mean as much to him. But then, what else did she
expect? He knew what she was, end of story.

With a sigh, she pulled herself up and stumbled to the
shower.

"So, for a man who didn't have watchdog duty last

night, you look like death. Did we have a rough night, bed hopping?" Leo taunted his partner, while fighting the image of Alana draped, moaning, across his guest bed. He knew that image would be etched in his mind.

"Jealousy is such an ugly emotion," Gabe replied, running a hand through his rumpled, golden hair. His blue eyes, framed with dark circles as they were, still had the twinkle of a consummate tease.

Alana froze in the doorway, the picture made by the two detectives too intense for *any* woman to break without a little gawking time first. Gabe had the boyishly handsome face of a local high school sports hero. He looked innocent enough to make a woman want to be the one to corrupt him, and worldly enough to make a woman wonder if he would corrupt her.

Yet Alana found herself drawn to the strong welcoming presence that was Leo. He wasn't the most handsome, but his strength drew her. With his height and stature, he felt like a comfortable Teddy bear, someone you could trust and feel safe near. Coupled with his amazing eyes, looking at him sent warm shivers through Alana's body, especially since it had yet to cool down from his kiss.

Gabe cast Alana a suspicious look, with her hovering at the door like a shadow waiting for dawn. A worried darkness passed over his features. "Is there a reason why you're lurking in the corners?"

Alana shook her head, walking into the kitchen to take a seat at the breakfast nook. "No, just enjoying the view. It's not every day a woman gets to wake up to coffee with two gorgeous hunks."

Seeing his partner had no intention of answering the flirtatious comment, Gabe elbowed Leo. "I don't know about Grady here, but you can look at me any time, babe."

Alana winced at the cloying endearment. Since her breakup with Jack, she'd developed a definite dislike for easy endearments. Still, Gabe seemed harmless enough, not meaning to insult. "I wanted to let you know that I called Rick. He'll be over in about a half-hour."

Leo nodded without thinking, taking another deep sip from his mug. He could not make himself meet her eyes. "That's fine. I'm going out. Gabe is going to stay here with you. A couple of uniforms are outside watching the place. You should be safe while I'm gone. Do whatever you need to. I'll tell you what we're going to do when I get back."

Alana was surprised by Leo's abrupt manner. She was trying to play down the whole kiss thing, as it was obvious that he wanted to forget it. But he didn't have to be cold about it. It's not as if she threw herself at him. He was the one to come into her room, after all.

"Fine. Rick and I will keep busy hammering out some snags in our show. That is, as long as Gabe doesn't mind being left to his own devices." She glanced over at the detective to find him staring at her.

"With a view as gorgeous as you, that shouldn't be any hardship," he replied with a brash smile and a wink.

A queasy feeling filled her stomach. Alana was glad that Rick would be there soon. Gabe's ogling was beginning to get on her nerves.

Leo's mouth thinned as he glared at his partner. "Remember, you're working here, not trawling for your next bedmate."

With that, he slammed down his mug and stalked out of the room.

"Boy, somebody got up on the wrong side of the bed this morning. Or maybe *in* the wrong bed." Gabe gave Alana a questioning look once his partner was well out of sight.

Alana wrinkled her nose and shook her head. "Don't look at me. I have no idea what's eating him. I barely know the man, remember?"

Gabe considered that for a moment before agreeing. "Yeah, Leo's never been one for socializing."

Alana cast an interested glance at Gabe as an evil little idea occurred to her. Here was her chance to find out what made Leo tick, not to mention her chance to see if her powers were recovering. Here was a man who worked with Leo day after day. Who could know Leo better? It wasn't *right,* using her powers for such a mundane and selfish cause. But considering all she had given up because of her duty and powers, she figured being a little self-serving for once wouldn't hurt. And Gabe had made such an easy subject before.

In her mind, she recited the simple chant, fingers twisting behind her back. She felt the answering surge of power, not as strong as usual but enough for a simple spell.

Gabe's brow wrinkled as he sniffed the air. "Are you wearing perfume? I didn't notice it before, but I smell flowers. Not Leo's normal home scent, too dainty."

Alana leaned forward with a reassuring smile. "It's a special blend. I make it myself. Now why don't you tell me more about Detective Grady? I'd like to have a better understanding of the man I'm trusting my life to."

Looking into her trustworthy eyes, Gabe found himself compelled to answer before he could even think of why he shouldn't. "Well, I've worked with him the last two years, since we both made detective. He's a bit of a loner, hard to get to know. Kinda gruff, if you ask me."

Alana nodded in understanding before urging him on. "Is Leo involved with anyone? I'd hate to find myself facing some jealous girlfriend over my staying here."

91

"No, no girlfriends," Gabe was quick to reassure her. "He hasn't been in a relationship for about four years from what I can figure, not since his injury."

"Injury?" Alana coaxed.

Again, Gabe answered without hesitation. "Shot and stabbed in the line of duty. I don't know much more than that. He doesn't talk about it. But I heard he was engaged until then. Chick dumped him in the hospital, least that's the way the rumor mill tells it. Women never stick with a guy when the going gets tough."

Alana let that comment slide, intent on pumping him for more information while she could. It was difficult to hold this kind of spell over a person, at least if you didn't want the person to suspect something, and she hadn't recovered enough to hold any spell for long. She had a few more minutes at most before she needed to release him. "So, even though you're his partner, you haven't gotten to know him?"

Gabe gave a weak laugh. "Hell, I don't even know his real name. Heard he had it legally changed to Leo a few years before I met him. No one knows what it was before he changed it. He always called himself Leo."

"Really?" Alana asked, beginning to ease out of the spell, as not to alarm him. "So there's nothing else you can tell me."

"Other than he likes to give me a hard time over my love life, no," Gabe shook his head, looking dazed. "I'm divorced. My ex is dead, killed in a car crash last year. I can do what I want with whoever I want as long as we're both consenting adults."

Hearing the pain lacing his angry words, Alana regretted pushing him this far. She dropped the spell as quickly as she could. "I'm sorry to hear about your wife. You must have loved her a great deal."

Gabe ran his fingers through his hair. "Yeah, you think you know someone. She and my daughter were run off the road in a hit and run about a month after the divorce was final. We'd been separated a year by then." Gabe struggled to continue. "They never found out who killed them. My ex-wife and I weren't even on speaking terms, but my little girl had so much life left. It's hard to believe she's gone."

Alana's face filled with sympathy. She hated hearing of anyone dying through violence, especially when a child was involved. "About a year ago, huh? That would be the crash on the North 15 that was on the news for several weeks."

"Yeah."

Alana's voice roughened with shared sorrow. "I'm sorry about your loss. How old was your daughter?"

Gabe sighed, one elbow on the table and his head leaning in his hand. He felt exhausted. "Eight. All I ever wanted to do was protect her, but I wasn't there when she needed me most."

Alana placed her hand on his, giving what comfort she could while letting go of the last vestiges of her spell. After what he told her while under compulsion, she felt horrible about using him that way.

You always end up paying for using your powers for your own gain, if only in guilt.

Again, Alana found herself jumping at the buzz of the doorbell. Gabe jumped up, hand going to his shoulder holster. "It's probably your friend, but stay here until I give the all clear."

Alana nodded, guilt mounting as she watched him rubbing at his temple. Using a glamour coupled with a spell like that, in such close quarters and at such intensity, gave the recipient one hell of a headache.

Gabe escorted Rick into the kitchen. Rick shrugged his backpack over one shoulder while sniffing the air and watching Gabe rub his head. Rick cocked his head at her. Alana looked back at him, eyes wide and full of innocence.

"So, where are we going to talk about the show?" Rick asked, looking at Gabe.

Gabe smirked at the dislike in the other man's voice. "Don't worry about me. I'll crash up front here, with one of Leo's books. You two can go into the back bedroom and talk secrets all you want."

Rick gave Gabe a barely civil nod, before taking Alana's arm and leading her in the direction Gabe had pointed.

"What do you think you're doing? Detective Grady knows about you. If he finds out you're pushing his partner, all hell is going to break loose." Rick dropped the backpack as soon as the bedroom door closed behind them.

Alana didn't even ask what he meant. "I was getting more information. You don't expect me to go into this situation blind?"

Rick dropped on the bed, bouncing. "No, but I don't trust that guy. Detective Grady seems like a straight shooter. He's helped you once, so I can't say anything against him. But there's something about that guy I don't like. He doesn't feel right."

Alana plopped down next to him before giving him an impish glance. "It couldn't have anything to do with the fact that he could give you a run in the player department, now could it?"

The look Rick gave Alana was filled with hurt. "You know me better than that. I have *never* seen women as a type of competition. I haven't found the right one to settle down with yet. So no, I'm not jealous of his ability to make conquests, thank you very much. I don't like him. There's something wrong with him."

Alana reached out with a single finger to tap him on the temple. "Hello, I'm the one who's supposed to have the whole psychic thing going for her, not you. He's susceptible, not a very strong personality. That's what you're picking up."

Rick looked doubtful, but let it drop. "You're probably right. But keep your eye on him, for my sake. Now, I brought you a few things." He reached into the bag beside him and pulled out a small cylinder. He held it up in front of her before putting it in her hand. "It's mace. I'd feel better if you were armed, but since you haven't used a gun before, you'll be safer with this. It won't stop anyone dead, but it should slow them down."

Alana slipped it into her pocket, amazed at how small it was. "Thanks for the thought. Leo said he'd show me a few things too, if I wanted. But for now, I'd like to talk about the show. I need to get my mind off this, or I'm going to go insane."

Understanding her feelings, Rick gave her a quick hug, before pulling out a pad of paper to take notes on. Neither noticed the silence descend in the next room.

Chapter Eight

Leo eased his car into an empty parking space outside of the Hands of Brotherhood Mission, one of the few even on a Monday morning. Business must be booming in the soul saving industry.

White-knuckled, he gripped the steering wheel and gazed up at the structure built on greed and duplicity. The two-story building consisted almost entirely of white marble, not an easy commodity to find in the Nevada desert. The golden gilding on the windowsills and its stained glass were the only things that broke the purity of color. The Hands of Brotherhood Mission, created from the fear and gullibility of its parishioners. What shocked Leo the most was the fact that a couple of squad cars were parked in parishioner parking, the officers being members come to worship.

Leo couldn't believe that one of his own could be taken in by a shyster like Charles Burke, a man more concerned with his bottom line than the condition of his followers' souls. This monstrosity of white, gold, and stained glass infuriated him. Burke's average followers lived below the poverty line, yet gave all they had to keep his message alive. He preyed on the elderly, living on fixed incomes, or the poor and despairing. He had some middle-class followers, but no one with enough money to spare to build a place like this. They gave what they couldn't spare.

And his message, one of intolerance and hatred, should be buried under a pile of shit as far as Leo was concerned.

Forcing his muscles to relax, Leo left his car and entered the eye-piercing greeting hall. He stood for a moment in the doorway, blinking. The sounds of hell-fire and brimstone preaching echoed from the main chapel, along with pre-recorded organ music.

All the trappings of a well thought out con.

A large, heavy hand fell on Leo's shoulder as he stepped towards the sounds of the service.

"Something I can help you with, Detective?" a harsh, grating voice inquired. Leo lost feeling in one arm as the hand clenched.

Leo looked up at the man addressing him. Randolph Grear, Burke's personal assistant, glared down. Leo grimaced. He had hoped to avoid another run-in with this ape, a man who made Leo feel like a midget Adonis in comparison. Standing over six and a half feet tall, his face pox marked and with a scar running down his jaw, the older man looked more like a mob enforcer than a secretary. To make matters worse, he was tenacious as a bulldog. The last time they had met, it took Gabe and him over four hours to get past the man.

Randolph continued scowling down at Leo.

"I need to speak with Mr. Burke again," Leo said, jerking his shoulder out of Randolph's meaty grip, dusting off his jacket, and straightening his tie.

"Is this an official visit?" the larger man asked, towering over Leo and eyeing him with suspicion.

Leo pulled himself up to full stature, voice dropping several octaves. "I can make it one, pull him off the pulpit and take him down to the precinct. If that's what you want, I'll be sure to let Burke know it was your idea. I thought he'd prefer doing it here, voluntarily."

Randolph's eyes glittered as he considered Leo's words. His face contorted as he backed down. "You'll have to wait. We're taping this morning's service. Mr. Burke should be ready to talk in about an hour. You can come back then."

Leo's head cocked, eyes steady. No way was he letting Randolph put him off. "Or I can wait here."

Randolph looked ready to argue, but must have thought better of it. With a shrug, he led Leo down a side hallway. "Right this way. You can wait in one of the vestibules until Mr. Burke is ready for you."

After seeing Leo settled in one of the long benches, Randolph scowled at him one last time, then trudged back to the receiving area.

Leo glanced up as a man in a stark white suit and mustard yellow tie sauntered towards him. With a broad grin, and not a single salt and pepper hair out of place, Charles Burke reached down to shake his hand.

"I'm sorry for your lengthy wait, Detective Grady. Several of my parishioners wished to speak with me. I couldn't leave them waiting, of course. It's one of the duties of a spiritual guide to be there when needed." Burke pumped Leo's hand, grin never dimming even as it turned apologetic.

Leo smiled back, cheek muscles aching with the effort. "Of course."

Burke gestured to one of the rooms behind him as though speaking to the police for the second time caused him not a hint of worry. "If you'll follow me, we can speak in my office. It's much more comfortable there."

I'm sure it is, Leo thought, trying not to wince as he pulled himself up from the hard wooden bench he'd been sitting on for close to two hours. His knees creaked and his back cracked, but he was able to keep from stumbling.

He followed Burke into a sparsely furnished office, with only a desk and one large chair behind it, and two facing it. The walls were stark white while his desk and chairs were made of white wood and leather with metallic gold accents. There were no plants, or any other sign of life. The only two decorations hanging on the wall were a golden cross, in Celtic design, and a claddagh, golden hands clasping a golden heart, the logo of the Hands of Brotherhood Mission.

Leo had to admit, he was developing a certain respect for Burke and his people. It took a person with a strong constitution to withstand such monochromatic surroundings for any length of time.

Burke sat down behind his desk, gesturing for Leo to join him. Leo was not unaware of the fact that the seats facing the desk were several inches shorter than the one Burke occupied. *Likes to keep people in their place,* Leo thought as he felt the momentary panic of falling before hitting the seat.

Burke placed his folded hands on his desk and leaned forward, the perfect picture of honesty and concern. "Detective Grady, Randolph told me that you had more questions for me. Don't tell me you still think I had anything to do with those poor, unfortunate souls' demise. As I've told you, I work for God. Murder is the work of Satan."

"Then can you tell me why three of those poor, unfortunate souls had been threatened by you before they were attacked by someone doing Satan's work?" Leo asked, voice calm and smooth, reaching out to set his recorder on the desk.

Burke raised an eyebrow at the device, but kept his smile

in place. "Detective Grady, I told you before, I do not threaten people. I warn my parishioners to stay away from certain unsavory elements in our society, for the good of their immortal souls, of course. It is the duty of any good shepherd to protect his flock, after all. But I don't threaten people. If those who are sinners do not change their ways, it is their own choice. They have free will, and God will judge them accordingly in the end."

"Then can you explain the letters received by Savannah Price, Manuel Rodriguez, and Alana Devlin?"

Burke leaned back, his smile now reflecting confusion and concern. "I never sent them any letters. I recall speaking to my parishioners about them, though. The woman, Price, took money from people to divine their futures. She did the Devil's work, and my people were warned about her. Rodriguez lured children into his shop to convince them that magic is fun, leaving them open to the practice of witchcraft and the worship of Satan. And that Devlin person, not only does she flaunt herself on stage, inciting lust, she lures people into believing in witchcraft. She teaches children about magic. So, of course, I spoke to my parishioners about them and others like them, warning them away from sin."

Leo wondered how Alana would react to Burke's description of her, the wild temptress. Instead, she was a self-proclaimed witch or fairy. Burke would have a field day if he knew half of what Leo was struggling to understand.

Burke paused for a moment, tapping one finger against his lips. "Perhaps a parishioner took my message further and tried to save the sinners themselves, in my name. I didn't encourage them. I wouldn't want my flock near those people. And I can't say I'm sorry or shocked by what happened to them. When you play with forces you do not understand, it is only a matter of time until you are burned in your own fire."

Leo resisted the temptation to roll his eyes heavenward, wondering what God thought of what this man did in his name. Leo knew for a fact the man preached intolerance of any person believing in a different religion, or different version of his own religion. His little tirade on the three victims was nothing compared to what he said about Catholics, Jews, Protestants, Baptists and all others who didn't think much of the Burke way of finding God. His T.V. shows preached more hate than love. "Thank you very much for the sermon, Minister. Now, did you happen to warn your people about anyone else that I should know of? Any other future victims in the making?"

"I don't appreciate your insinuation. The only one I've warned them about recently is that gypsy woman who works in the Silver Coin Casino's theme park, Elise McMann. I don't believe I've heard of anything happening to her."

"Not yet, anyway," Leo couldn't resist taunting. "Can you tell me where you were the last two nights, at between midnight and four o'clock?"

Burke almost scowled, but caught himself. Instead, he tilted his head in simulated thought. "Last night I have to confess to being home alone, asleep. No alibi there. But the night before, from the hours of eleven to one, I was taping a special service. One of my oldest parishioners passed away and wanted his funeral to be broadcast live. That was the only time slot available at the station. Heaven knows how many viewers I had that evening, besides those attending the actual service, but I am certain there will be enough to testify as to my whereabouts. Now if that's all the questions you have for now, I need to be going."

"What about your man, Grear? Where was he?"

Finally, Burke began looking flustered. Smile fading, he kept his voice even and civil. "You'd have to ask him. I'm his employer, not his keeper. He's left for the day, but I can supply you with his address."

"I have it." Leo reached forward and snapped off his recorder, slipping it back into his jacket pocket.

Burke rose, opening the door. "Then I'm sure you don't need my help."

Leo smiled at Burke's blatant desire to get rid of him. It looked like he'd worn out his welcome with the good man of God. "You do know if you have anything to do with this, I'll catch you. You need to watch your step."

Burke's eyes fell to slits, but his mouth regained his trademark smile as he escorted Leo to the door. "And you, son, need to be more careful with your soul. I understand the need for earthly justice, but be careful of whom you seek to defend. It wouldn't do for you to be pulled into their world of depravity. Who knows what could happen to you?"

Leo struggled to keep the sneer from his face as he walked out the door. But he couldn't resist one last jibe. "I'll keep that in mind. Along with a tenet that my mother stressed to me as being one of the most important in the eyes of God."

"Oh, what is that?" Burke inquired, false interest coating his words.

Leo turned to look straight into Burke's eyes. "Judge not lest ye be judged. Something *you* should keep in mind."

Chapter Nine

Stepping out of the Hands of Brotherhood Mission, Leo's eyes relaxed at the normal brightness of sunlight. He took a deep breath to clear all the negative feelings Burke and his whole set up brought out in him. As he walked to his car, he pulled his cell phone out of his jacket pocket and called Gabe. Maybe this new person Burke mentioned would be able to shake things loose. Something had to give.

Not waiting for a greeting, Leo barked, "Gabe, see what you can get me on an Elise McMann. She works as some sort of fortune-teller at the Silver Coin. I'm headed there now, but I need to know if we have anything on her, anything at all."

"Elise McMann, right. What do you want . . ."

Leo tensed as Gabe broke off. Panic set in, setting his heart racing. He stood motionless, hand frozen in the act of reaching for his car door, as the sound of a struggle, one he could be no help in, increased. He relaxed when Alana's voice screeched out at him from the receiver. "What about Elise? Has that monster done something to Elise? If he has, I swear, I'll turn the little jerk into a toad, if it takes me a hundred years to figure out how to do it."

Leo blanched at her choice of threats. She said that she had to work at anything more than an illusion, but who knew the truth? "Nothing's happened to her as far as I know. I found out that Burke has mentioned her by name in one of his sermons, as he did you and two other victims. I want to contact her, see if she's been threatened. She could be the next target. How do you know Ms. McMann? Is she like you?"

Hearing her sigh of relief, Leo could almost see Alana melting into a chair. "No, not like me, she's a gypsy fortune-teller, the real deal. She's a friend of my parents, the closest thing I have to a godmother. She's in her early eighties, for crying out loud. She doesn't deserve anything like what happened to me to happen to her. She's a sweet old lady. I don't think she's ever hurt anyone in her life."

Leo tried not to laugh out loud. "You have a gypsy godmother. Somehow, I'm not surprised. But I thought it was supposed to be a *fairy* godmother. Get your wires crossed somewhere along the way?"

"It would be redundant in my case. Now what's going on?"

"Listen, everything's fine. I just want to talk to her, get some information. And give her a warning. That way she can protect herself."

"I'm coming with you."

"No way," Leo responded while slipping into the driver's seat, clutching the phone with his shoulder and struggling with the seatbelt. "You're staying right where you are, where you're safe. No way am I letting you put yourself at risk. Ms. McMann may be the next target, but you're the prime target—the one in danger, in case you've forgotten."

That steel he was beginning to hate slipped back into Alana's voice. "Just try to stop me. I'll have Rick and Gabe escort me, if it'll make you feel better. Between the two of them, I'll be safe. We'll meet you there. She should be at work. Meet me in front of the amusement park area, and I'll walk in with you."

Leo banged his head against his steering wheel before replying. "Okay, I'll agree, because I know you'll find a way to come anyway. At least this way you'll have some protection. But you have to promise to stay close to Gabe and Rick until then. And if I tell you to leave, you go right away, no questions and no arguments."

"Whatever you say."

She paused for a moment before adding, "Thanks."

Leo snorted. "I don't know what you're thanking me for. It's not like you ever give me an option anyway."

Hanging up, he closed his eyes and sighed before pulling into traffic. *I don't know how she does it, but that woman could give lessons in tying people in knots.*

Leo waited outside the casino, a steady stream of tourists and hopeful locals passing him at the doors for several minutes before Gabe's car pulled up. With the car still rolling, Alana jumped out and dashed toward him, her worn jeans snuggling against her long legs and her soft, untucked cotton shirt flapping in the breeze. "Are you certain she's alright?" she panted.

Leo put a steadying hand on her shoulder, pulling his eyes from how her shirt outlined her breasts. Seeing the rosy hue of her flush, Leo started to slide his hand up to feel the heat. Only the sight of his partner stopped him. He pulled away, shoving both hands in his pockets, rocking back. "According to the management, she's working as we speak. Are you sure there's no way I can talk you out of tagging along?"

Leo smiled as Alana put her hands on her hips and tapped her foot. "No way. The guys can stay outside and guard the perimeter. I'm coming with you." Seeing Leo wanted to argue more, Alana added, "She won't believe you're serious otherwise. I want to be certain that she understands the danger she's in. She tends to blind herself to negative energies. But she'll listen to me, believe what I tell her."

Leo wasn't happy with the situation, but gestured for Alana to lead the way. He noticed many male heads turning to watch her as she walked through the park, towards the fake gypsy encampment. A fierce, territorial instinct rose within him. He walked as close by her side as possible, glaring at every man they passed.

Alana gave him a puzzled look as they drew to a stop in front of a magenta and gold silk tent. Leo looked back in all innocence, pulled back the cloth covered entrance, and swept his hand before her. "Ladies first."

Alana shook her head at his strange behavior, but ducked inside without comment.

A small, birdlike woman sat behind a scarf-covered table, the soft glow of candlelight flickering around her. A few curled and silvery locks escaped from the bright red scarf held on her head by gold mesh, framing her delicate face. Gold and silver dripped from her neck, ears, and arms. Little gold bells laced the edges of her shimmering purple shawl, tinkling with her slightest movement. Even with all the wrinkles, Leo could tell that at one time, she had been a striking beauty. It still shined from her dark brown eyes.

Her bright smile lit the darkened tent, not at all the spooky old crone that Leo had expected. "Alana, my darling child, how are you? Please sit, you and your young gentleman. I didn't know you were coming."

Some fortune-teller, Leo thought. He eased down in the over-stuffed, brightly colored chair next to the one Alana took, trying not to look too uncomfortable with his bizarre surroundings. So this was what Alana's life was like. For the first time, the thought bothered him. He kept his welcoming smile plastered on his face. Fake smiles were becoming an occupational hazard. He hoped his face didn't freeze that way, as his mother had always threatened.

The elderly woman cast him an impish gaze, recognizing the look of discomfort on his face. "And who's this handsome young skeptic?" she asked. "Anyone I should warn your parents about?"

Alana tried not to blush, or even make eye contact, twisting her hands in her lap. Auntie Elise had more power than she let on. Alana knew Elise had expected them. No one surprised Elise. Worse, Alana recognized the incense filling the air, patchouli for love. Alana was afraid she knew what lay out in the open for the old woman to see. "Not quite. This is Detective Grady. Auntie Elise, he has some things to talk to you about. I want you to listen without making any judgements."

Worry added more creases to the woman's wrinkled brow. A single delicate hand fluttered at Elise's throat. "A policeman? Is everything alright, dear?"

"For now," Leo answered, reaching forward to take the woman's other frail hand in a comforting embrace. "And I'm trying to keep it that way. But I need to ask you a few questions, if you don't mind my taking up your time."

Alana watched as Elise patted Leo's hand, getting a feel for his character, deciding whether or not he was worthy of Alana. She recognized the vague expression sliding across Elise's face, the separation from the physical world. "Of course not, dear boy. But you'll have to return the favor. If I answer your questions, you'll have to let me do a reading for you." Her crafty eyes slid to Alana, who shook her head. "If just to get a good feel for you."

Alana rolled her eyes. Auntie Elise was as overprotective as her father. He insisted on holding something of her dates' before she left the house. People in the older generations could be so nosey.

Leo nodded in agreement, though his stomach clenched. He didn't like the idea of letting the old witch look into him but sensed her need to look out for the daughter of her friends. "If that's what you want, I think I could spare a few extra minutes."

Elise giggled, nothing like the cackle Leo expected from a woman who made her living telling fortunes. Then she patted his cheek, reminding him of his grandmother. "I think I may end up liking you, young man."

Leo pulled away and reached into his jacket pocket. "I hope you don't mind my recording this. I take horrible notes, can't read my own handwriting."

Elise waved her hand towards him, setting the bells stitched into her clothes chiming a cheerful tune. "Oh, I don't mind. I'd prefer you didn't during my time, though. Mechanical devices tend to disturb the flow of energy necessary for a good reading."

Leo pictured the dim room he caught Alana casting in, with its flickering candles. He'd tried his best to block that from his mind, especially the image of the disgusting creature ready to pounce on Alana and the split second of mindless panic that froze him in the doorway. Leo's body tightened while he looked for a good place to put his recorder. "However you feel most comfortable," he managed to say after loosening his throat with a soft cough. "I appreciate any help you can give me. Now, have you received any threatening mail?"

Elise seemed taken aback by the question. "Yes, I have. From that nasty Burke man, or one of his people. Quite an intolerable little bigot if you ask me, using the Christian tenets to preach hatred. But to each his own." With a frown, Elise turned to Alana. "Now before you start scolding, I didn't see any reason to involve you. The man who wrote it is a coward, hiding behind his paper and pen. He wouldn't do anything to me. Trust me enough to know that I would look into his heart."

Leo looked at Alana, surprised that she didn't have something to say to this. Alana touted herself as a Protector, but she didn't try to protect a woman who meant this much to her.

Instead, Alana remained silent, not even attempting to contradict Elise.

Leo looked back at the old woman, trying to size her up, to see what it was that Alana placed her trust in. "Do you still have the letter?"

"Yes, I think I put it in my chest in back." Elise blushed and gave a sheepish grin. "I'm a bit of a pack rat, never throw away mail. You can't tell when something may be important later on. I'll be happy to find it for you before you leave. May I ask what this is about?"

"It concerns an ongoing murder investigation. Some of the victims received threats before the attacks."

"Oh dear, not anyone I know I hope?" she asked, eyes flying to Alana, searching her. Alana kept her mind blank, letting Leo do his job.

Leo answered instead. "I'm afraid I can't mention any names to you. That information is on a need-to-know basis."

"He attacked me twice, Auntie," Alana whispered, knowing the woman would pick up the aura of physical violence surrounding her.

Elise nodded, coming out of her seat and around the

table to take Alana in her embrace, placing a soft kiss on her forehead. "I hope you've called your father or your sister to ask about this. I'm certain that they could help. I know your talents don't run in that direction. Maybe I should do your reading before you leave as well."

Alana shook her head. "You know I don't like to do that. The future will come in its own time. Without foreknowledge, I can appreciate the good and not be preoccupied with the bad."

A musical laugh bubbled up from Elise, nostalgia reflected in her eyes. "Stubborn, just like your father and your brother. But you know best, it *is* your life. But do be careful. You need to remember to protect *yourself* as well as others."

"I will," Alana answered, struggling to keep her deepening doubt from reflecting in her voice.

Elise turned to Leo as she glided back to her seat. "I'm sorry, but I don't think there is anything else I can tell you. I received the letter two days ago, and nothing has happened."

Leo tried not to let his disappointment show on his face. They needed a break in this case. "That's alright, ma'am. Having a copy would be helpful. The other victims didn't keep their letters. We only have the word of their relatives that the letters even existed. But you should be careful. You could be on his list of victims."

Elise smiled, a wistful look creeping into her eyes. "I'm eighty-three years old, young man. I'm not afraid of dying. I've lived a good life and have made my peace with it. If something happens to me, it happens." At the horrified expression on Alana's face, she added, "Not that I'm looking forward to leaving this world anytime soon. No, I think I have quite a few years left in me. I'll survive to see three more Devlin weddings, if nothing else. But I'll be careful. Now, if you'll turn off your recorder, I believe it's my turn."

Leo pocketed his recorder again and shifted in his seat. Alana smiled at his obvious discomfort, reminding her of a six-year-old waiting in a dentist's office.

"What do I need to do?" he asked, voice filled with suspicion.

Elise gave him a comforting look. "First, you need to take a deep breath, dear boy. I'm not going to eviscerate you and look through your entrails. That's not my cup of tea. I've gone beyond that sort of nonsense."

Elise reached for a delicately carved, wooden box sitting below the single white candle. Alana's face lit up with recognition. "Adain made that, didn't he?" she asked.

"Yes, your dear brother gave it to me before he left last month, called it payment for all the advice I tried to give him." She shook her head sadly while running her fingers along the carvings. "I wish the boy would listen to me, but he's off to find his destiny for himself. I think he'll be pleasantly surprised, if he lets himself be."

She opened the box and tapped the deck of cards it contained in front of her. "I need you to shuffle these until you feel comfortable with them. Then hand them back to me. I do the rest."

Leo looked at the deck, one eyebrow quirked, before taking it from her. He shuffled the cards awkwardly, more cards in the deck than normal playing cards had. It made it difficult to hold them all in one hand, even one as large as his. After a few minutes of struggling with them, he handed the cards back.

Elise slid her hand across the deck before dealing out the first six cards in a diamond pattern, with the second card dealt lying across the first. "This is the most common pattern used in tarot, the one most people are familiar with. It's not the way I like to use the cards, but for you it feels right. Let's begin."

Looking down at the first card, a smile lit Elise's face while Alana looked uncomfortable. Even Leo could see what that particular card must mean, and refused to look in Alana's direction.

"First we have those things that are influencing you in the present." Elise ran her fingertip across the picture of a couple locked in a passionate embrace. "The Lovers. A romance is blossoming for you."

She then lifted the second card, which had crossed the first. "That fits well with this card, representing your immediate influence, the Empress. Here is a card representing female power. A strong woman, comfortable in her own strength and influence." Looking at the woman's picture, Elise glanced up at Alana with a wicked grin and a wink. "Interesting that she's portrayed with red hair, don't you think?"

Alana stared at the ceiling.

Elise continued, ignoring the blush mounting both Alana and Leo's cheeks. "Now this is something I like to see. This third card stands for the best possible outcome you can have under present circumstances." She held up the brightly colored card, depicting a gleaming gold chalice surrounded by clear running water. "The Ace of Cups. You have the opportunity for great joy, abundance, and happiness, if you follow your present path."

Looking down at the next two cards, a frown marred her face. So much pain here. "I'm glad to see you with such a possible future. This next card represents your distant past, those things that still guide you today."

"What's the problem?" Leo asked, interested in spite of

himself. He glanced down at the happy family painted in a perpetual embrace, all staring at a chalice-covered rainbow. "It looks good to me."

"And normally it would be. This is the Ten of Cups, which represents security, home, and family. But it is in the reverse position. You didn't have a very secure home life when you were younger. You didn't feel like you belonged or that you had any roots. Were you adopted, or uprooted somehow?"

Leo thought of the countless moves his parents made, the number of different schools he went to and shook his head. "Not exactly, but I can see the relation."

Still frowning, she pointed at the next card, with its happy couple, each holding a beautiful chalice. "This is your *recent* past that still holds influence over you. Again, it's in the reverse position. The Two of Cups reversed. I see a painful separation, a broken romance in your past."

Leo didn't agree or disagree this time, but his mind locked on the image of Tina the last time he saw her, standing over his hospital bed, tears running down her cheeks as she ripped his heart out and stomped on it. He saw the diamond ring that he'd saved several months' pay to buy being thrown to the floor.

Even Alana could feel Leo's pain as he stared down at the card. Without thinking, she reached out and took his hand. He clung to her, never looking up.

Elise continued. "I think the thing you need to learn is though you may have had pain in the past, you need to learn to let it go. These influences can become obstacles to the happiness destined to be yours."

"What about this last card?" he asked, shifting in his seat, uncomfortable with the direction she was going, needing to change the subject.

"Oh, this isn't the last card, you still have four more to be dealt, the most important four. But this card represents something or someone who will influence your future. It too is in the reverse position. You need to be careful of who you trust."

Leo looked down at the picture, a knight on horseback, carrying a single cup. "Why?"

Elise tapped the card as she spoke. "In reverse, like this, the Knight of Cups represents lies. It is a man full of deceit and treachery. But, in your line of work, you must see these types of people often."

Leo grimaced while he watched Elise deal the last four cards in a row beside the others, holding Alana's hand even tighter. The old gypsy's face became more pensive as she looked down at the final pattern.

"Well?" he asked, drawn in.

She pointed down at an austere man wearing a crown and holding a sword. "This card represents *you*. We have the King of Swords. You're a controlled man, determined and efficient. It's a good card for you, as it also represents someone concerned with justice."

Elise then tapped her finger on the next card, another knight, carrying a sword this time, instead of a cup. "This, on the other hand, shows how others *see* you, appropriate for your occupation. The Knight of Swords is a defender, one who protects others." Elise grinned at Alana. "It's a card I used to draw often, when Alana was younger and would let me read for her."

But then Elise looked down again. She frowned at the last two cards, expression both puzzled and disturbed. She pointed to the first, depicting an innocent young boy. "Here are your emotions, your deepest desires or fears. It is the Fool. He represents folly and extravagance. Foolishness. I have to assume that this is a fear, not a desire. But I don't understand it."

Leo's face paled, thinking again of his parents. "Then let's go to the last card."

"The tower," Alana whispered. Leo could hear fear in her voice. Glancing at the picture, he saw a tall tower with a man's figure being blown from the top, crown flying from his head and fire spewing after him.

Elise shook her head. "You must be very careful, Detective. This card represents the final result, what will happen. While I told you earlier that joy and happiness were the best results you could hope for considering all that influenced you, this card says otherwise. It is a card predicting a severing of old beliefs, deception, loss of the stability that you hold dear. It is a card thought by many to be the most hopeless in the deck, the worse possible draw, worse even than drawing Death. Watch yourself."

With that, she swept all the cards back into the deck and put them back in the box, clicking it shut. "Now, I've done what I can to help you. I'll find that letter, and then I think you should leave. Alana?"

Alana started out of the fear-induced trance the reading had placed her in. "Yes, Auntie Elise?"

The old woman's face was grim as she looked at this young woman who meant so much to her. "For once, don't follow your twin's example. Listen to me and listen well. Protect *yourself* for a change, and watch out for your young man. He will need all the aid you can give."

Chapter Ten

Later that evening, as Leo stepped out of the shower, a spicy aroma wafted in the air, along with the raucous sound of rock music. His mouth watering, he took a deep breath and absorbed a sense of completeness that he'd never experienced in his own home before, not quite certain how he felt about finding it now. Reaching down, he pulled on a pair of gray cut-off sweats and a white T-shirt, then padded barefoot to his kitchen.

Alana stood writhing in front of a sizzling pan, stirring and singing along with the loud, nearly unintelligible lyrics blasting from the radio. Watching the show, Leo had the sudden urge to wrap his arms around her and kiss her neck, but settled for leaning against the counter next to her.

"Do you always sing to yourself while you cook?" he asked, a playful grin splitting his normal somber face.

Alana melted at the warmth shining from his glacial colored eyes. Her fingers curled around the spatula, resisting the desire to run them through his damp hair. Being in such close quarters with Leo had a strange effect on her. She hadn't decided what she wanted to do about it. "It's the only way to make certain that everything turns out the way it should. Every meal needs a little music to coax it along, to help give it spice. Let me guess. You just shove everything in the microwave and watch T.V. until it beeps at you?"

Leo reached around her waist to lift the lid off one of the pots. The smell of tomato and chili drifted up from the rice filled pan, causing his mouth to water even more and his stomach to growl. "If that were true, you wouldn't have found all the ingredients for what smells like an excellent Mexican dinner."

Alana slapped his hand with a wooden spoon. Leo grinned, but backed away from her territory, palms raised. Alana muttered under her breath, wagging her spoon at him, before answering. "Well, it's pretty simple, just tacos, rice, and beans. The only thing that took any skill was the *sopaipillas*. One of my mom's old friends taught me how to cook them. I hope you have honey. Nothing tastes better with sopaipillas than honey."

Leo reached into a cabinet, flourishing the jar with a smile. "Don't worry, I'm fully stocked." He placed the jar on the counter, leaning closer to her. "But you're not giving yourself enough credit. This smells way better than what I order at a Mexican restaurant, but you didn't have to go to all this trouble." He reached over to sneak a peak in another pot, only to retreat at Alana's warning glare. "Not that I don't plan on taking full advantage of it. But that means tomorrow night is on me. I make a mean eggplant Parmesan."

Alana wiped her hands on the plain, canvas apron she'd found hanging from a hook near the refrigerator. "You've got yourself a deal, but for now, how about setting the table. I'm about done here."

"You've got it," he replied, turning to the cabinets to her right.

Alana peeked as Leo stretched up to reach the plates, his T-shirt hiking up enough to offer her a glimpse of his well-defined abs. She loved watching his muscles ripple, like steel coated in velvet. There was nothing like good eye

117

candy to get the appetite going. Too bad nothing was stored in the bottom drawer. Those sweats looked like they would hug his butt. Alana had a thing for a well-shaped butt.

"You know," Leo commented, not noticing Alana's preoccupation with his physique. "I didn't take you for the type of woman to cook dinner every night. You seem more the take-out type to me."

Alana forced her eyes back to her pots and pans, stirring the meat. "Well, I'll admit to doing more than my fair share of restaurant hopping. But that's for convenience. It's a waste to cook a big meal for one person. But I do like to cook. My mom made sure we all could, even my brother. Everyone needs the skills to make a home and take care of themselves, don't you think?"

Leo carried the dishes to a small breakfast table set into an alcove on the far side of the kitchen. Mechanically, he set the table, lost in memory. "I agree. I was the cook in my family. My parents forgot about meals unless there was someone around to remind them. I got tired of hot dogs and T.V. dinners by the time I was ten. So, I started collecting cookbooks and experimenting. The one good thing was, with people as distracted as my folks, I never got complaints." Nostalgia glowed in his face as Leo laughed. "Not even when I used the wrong kind of crust for a quiche I made. I used a sweet dessert crust instead of a plain butter one. It was disgusting, but I got no complaints."

Alana laughed along with him, switching off the burners and putting the sopaipillas on a large plate. "I think everyone has one of those stories. I remember making my mother a chocolate cake from scratch for Mother's Day one year. It would have been great, but I used the wrong kind of flour, the kind that isn't self-rising. You could have used that cake for a discus, but Mom never complained.

I'm surprised she didn't chip a tooth."

"Yeah, I guess parents are like that."

Alana picked up the plates from the table and heaped food on them both, while Leo poured some Chianti he had stuck away for a special occasion. Alana sat across from him and let the dry red wine soothe her worn nerves.

Watching him, Alana brought up the subject foremost on her mind since the visit to Elise. Here was a way to test out his attitudes towards magic. "By the way, did Gabe give you a hard time about the fortune-telling thing? I had a feeling that he didn't approve of your approach, wasting time with tarot cards."

Leo thought about the shocked expression on Gabe's face when they told him what had taken them so much time. You'd have thought they'd been in the amusement park sacrificing small children to a demonic horde from the look Gabe had given them. Gabe wouldn't even look in Alana's direction after that.

Not that that's a bad thing, Leo thought, remembering his partner's reputation with women, before answering Alana's question. "No, he doesn't believe in wasting time humoring people. So he did rib me some about it, offering to stop and pick up a crystal ball while he was off-duty. But it made your aunt feel more comfortable with me, so it was worth it. I never put a lot of credit into the whole fortune-telling thing before. Now, I don't know what to think. Meeting you has changed my view on the issue. I'm not comfortable with it, though. What about you? I noticed you didn't let her read you."

Alana shrugged, taking a bite of her taco while dodging his gaze. "I don't mess with things I'm not comfortable with. I'm superstitious that way. I wasn't given the power of divination, so I feel I shouldn't know about my own future.

Even in castings, I only seek information about the past and present."

Leo tore off a piece of a sopaipilla and doused it with honey. He tried not to moan as it almost melted in his mouth. "Do you believe Elise is safe, as she says?"

Alana wondered what Elise would say if she could hear the protectiveness in Leo's voice. It would raise him higher up on the list of possible matches for her favorite honorary niece. "Yes, she's safe. I've never known her to be wrong, especially when she is so certain. Do you want to tell me she was off target with what she said about you, that nothing struck a chord?"

Thinking of the card with the two lovers entwined, Leo grimaced. "I'd rather not get into that subject right now, but what about her little warning to *you*? What did she mean with all that stuff about protecting yourself for a change? Are you in the habit of ending up like you did yesterday, so exhausted you pass out?"

Alana grimaced, putting down her fork and pushing back her empty plate. "I've been told I have a savior complex. My family and friends worry about me, because I tend to go overboard helping others. Giving too much sometimes, wearing myself thin, like the benefit tomorrow. Here I am, worrying about other people when I'm in so much trouble myself. Not that the show is going overboard, with you planning a trap and everything, but it's an example of what Elise meant. It isn't only the magic."

Leo nodded, seeing how her soft heart could get her hurt and understanding how people who cared about her would worry about it. But this was an opening to discuss some important issues that needed to be settled. "Speaking of the show, we need to set up some ground rules, if we expect to flush out our criminal friend. What's your usual approach when you put on something like this? What do you do?"

Alana paused for a moment, trying to break her routine up into steps. "Well, Rick and I get to the showroom about two hours before show time, to make certain all the gear is ready and to get ourselves together for the performance. It takes a good half-hour to get dressed and put on the stage makeup. The show itself lasts an hour, unlike our usual performances, which run about two hours. Not being in good health in the first place, we don't want to wear the kids out. There'll be about thirty kids, plus their families and a few of the doctors and nurses at the performance, less than a hundred people total. After the show's over, we get cleaned up and go out for lunch before we have to come back and get things ready for our evening performances."

Leo nodded while mentally ticking off the security issues he would have to address. At least it was a small, enclosed environment as opposed to the huge auditoriums some Las Vegas performers used. That made his job easier. "Okay, we'll try to stay as close to your normal pattern as possible, but I want to have a few of my men, including Gabe, scattered in the audience, as well as myself backstage at all times. That way, I can keep my eye on you. And we'll set up a signal that you can use should anything unusual come to your attention."

"Fine by me." Alana glanced down at the empty plates, amazed that they had finished. But it was nice to cook for someone else for a change, especially someone who liked her food as much as Leo did. "Why don't you grab the rest of the wine and we can check out the fireplace you have in the living room? I could use the quiet time and the company."

Seeing the stress she held under control just below the surface, Leo patted her hand and grabbed the bottle and glasses without protest, following her out of the room. Alana snuggled into his overstuffed couch, while he lit the fire. Max padded in and curled at her feet.

Alana reached down to scratch Max behind the ears as Leo lowered himself down beside her. "This is one thing that my dad did right when he designed our house."

"What?" Leo asked as he topped off her glass.

Alana took a sip and sighed, slipping off her shoes and wiggling her toes in front of the warm flames. "It has a fireplace in all the main rooms. There is nothing as good as cuddling up in front of a toasty fire to help you relax after a long, stressful day. By the way, I wanted to tell you that I love your home."

Leo raised a single eyebrow, wondering if she was serious or not. "Oh, really? I wasn't too sure you would. It's quite a bit different from the one you live in."

Alana grinned at the comparison, definitely Rockwell versus Winchester. "True, but it's comfortable. It has a warm and welcoming aura. I've seen a lot of houses in this town that I wouldn't be able to call a home, but that doesn't apply to this one."

Leo couldn't help the swell of pride her comment caused. His home meant a lot to him, being the first one he'd ever had. "I'm glad you like it. That's the feel I was looking for when I bought the place. With the job I'm in, you need a place you can retreat to."

Alana stretched out further, taking most of the couch space. Not that Leo minded. The more space she took, the closer it brought her to him. He couldn't complain about having her practically sitting in his lap. He may not have been part of the dating scene in a while, but he wasn't that stupid.

"You accomplished that. This is the first time I've felt

relaxed since the attack." Alana yawned, her eyes drooping. "A good night's sleep tonight, and I should be back up to full strength in time for the show tomorrow."

Seeing the little sleep from last night catching up with her, Leo reached over and pulled her to him, giving her his shoulder to use as a pillow. "Don't worry about anything. I know the last few days have been hard for you. And tomorrow won't be any better. But everything will be over after tomorrow night. Until then, let me do all the worrying for both of us. I'll make certain that nothing happens to you. I give you my word."

Alana closed her eyes and gave into the comfort he offered, sinking further into his warm embrace. "My Knight of Swords," she whispered into his chest, a smile lifting her lips as she allowed herself to fall into a deep, peaceful sleep.

Chapter Eleven

Dressed in a Victorian style nightgown and carrying an old and worn Teddy bear, Alana glided onto the darkened stage. Her attention focused on the well-loved toy in her arms, with its missing button eye and its silver coat of chain mail.

Leo looked around, but Rick was nowhere to be seen. He must be preparing for some type of grand entrance. Leo shifted his stance, leaning against a wall while surveying his surroundings. Nothing out of the ordinary yet, and the show was nearly over. It was beginning to look like this afternoon was a bust. At least there was the chance of the bastard showing at one of the regular evening shows, and the wait had been entertaining. After watching her perform, Leo had new respect for Alana. Even knowing she used real magic, she impressed him with her showmanship, the work that went into setting up each illusion.

The spotlight narrowed on Alana as she sat down on a brass, four-poster bed positioned center stage and cuddled the toy bear. A soft, classical tune played in the background, loud enough to be heard, but not loud enough to identify. Alana tucked her feet beneath her and looked out into the audience of young, enwrapped faces.

"When I was a child," she began, "I saw magic everywhere around me, in every story my mother told, in every dream that I had."

She placed a soft kiss on the Teddy bear's nose before holding him up to view. "I remember the stories my mother told me, the ones I believed with all my heart. That belief brought me back to this old friend, tucked away in my attic."

Must have taken her years to find it again, Leo thought, picturing what an attic in her house had to be like. Still, he found his attention riveted to the stage, captured by the sound of Alana's voice as she told her tale.

She danced the bear in the air, gliding across the floor before turning and cuddling him into her chest again. "His name is Sir Ted-Ted. Not very creative, I know, but it felt right at the time. You see, when I was little, I had nightmares almost every night. I knew that monsters lived under my bed and in my closet, just waiting for their chance to get at me. But no matter how often I told them about it, my parents couldn't see the monsters. So every night, I would hide under my blankets and cry myself to sleep."

Alana paused for a moment, letting the children absorb what she had said, compare it with their own nighttime terrors. Then she continued.

"One night my mother caught me cowering in my blankets and asked me what was wrong. When I told her, she smiled, patted my hand, and sat with me until I fell asleep. The next night, she brought me Sir Ted-Ted, and she told me a secret."

Again Alana paused, watching as the children leaned forward in their seats.

" 'Every monster,' she told me, 'has one thing that it fears. One creature that all monsters know is stronger than they are. When they see this creature, they are the ones who run and hide in terror. This is why parents give their children Teddy bears. Teddy bears, who love children more

125

than anything in the world, are the only things that monsters fear. This was the best monster-fighting Teddy bear I could find, and now he will protect you.' "

Alana smiled, her expression soft, and looked down at her bear.

"With that, Mother gave me Sir Ted-Ted and tucked me in. I never had a problem with nightmares or monsters again."

Her story told, Alana lay down on the bed. The bear sat at her feet, looking out for danger. Mist rose around the bed, giving it an Otherworldly glow in the stage lights. The smell of flowers floated through the air as the music changed from comforting classical to a more primal tune. Snickering and cackling ran over the speakers as several people, dressed as monsters, crawled and scurried on stage to surround the bed.

Suddenly, blue light flashed and someone leapt off the bed. Leo blinked for a moment, trying to clear his vision, surprised to see Alana lying in the exact same position. Sir Ted-Ted, now life-size, stood over her, chain mail, sword, and all. His well-worn face and missing eye seemed noble and protective, fierce in this larger size.

The children in the audience gasped as he turned to confront the monsters.

Sir Ted-Ted struggled against his foes, waving his sword and intimidating some, while throwing others off-stage. Like a well-choreographed dance, the fight ran for several minutes, gluing the children's eyes to the stage.

When the stage cleared, he turned back to the bed, kneeling before it.

Alana sat up, looking shocked. She walked over to Sir Ted-Ted, bent down, and placed a tender kiss on his furry nose. Again, lights flashed, sparks flying up from where the two stood. Wind machines kicked in, whirling glitter around the couple. Suddenly, in Sir Ted-Ted's place, Rick stood, wearing the same chain mail and carrying the same sword.

Alana turned to the applauding audience and winked. "Did I mention, I also love the story of Beauty and the Beast?"

The children burst out in laughter and cheers. Alana walked forward as Rick headed backstage, still panting from the fight. Leo reached out to help Rick pull off the mail. He was amazed by the weight. "I'm impressed. This feels heavy enough to be real."

Rick reached for a towel and glass of water. After wiping his brow and taking a long drink, he replied, "It is real, belonged to one of Alana's ancestors. You'd be amazed at what she has tucked away in that attic of hers."

Leo snorted, the comment echoing his earlier thought, and turned back to the stage. Alana sat at the edge, speaking to the children.

"There is something that each and every one of you knows better than any adult. Life *is* magic. You are surrounded by daily miracles, the sun shining down from the sky, a quick glimpse of a humming bird, a sudden rainstorm. All these things have a magic of their own. When you are young, you can see it in every moment of your lives. Never forget that, no matter how hard things may seem. Life is a daily miracle."

She smiled down at a little girl in the front row wearing a ball cap that did little to hide her lack of hair. "Now, for my last trick. I want each of you to reach under your seats. I think you'll be surprised."

Each child scrambled to reach under his or her seat, each finding a package about the size of a shoebox that they hadn't noticed before. Wrapping paper flew throughout the room, followed by squeals of delight. Each child found a Teddy bear, a different color, with different expressions, wearing different costumes.

Alana reached behind her back, pulling out Sir Ted-Ted again, plopping him down on her lap. "I hope you like your gifts, and I hope they bring you as much happiness as Sir Ted-Ted did me. They were designed and made with love and care especially for each of you. I hope you've enjoyed your time here with me as much as I've enjoyed mine with you. For now, I must say farewell."

With a whooshing sound, followed by a flickering of lights, Alana vanished from the stage.

"Well, what do you think?" Alana asked Rick as she and Leo came out of her dressing room. The smell of wildflowers clung to her, but she had managed to scrape all the makeup off, a struggle that served to entertain Leo, who wore a smirk.

"About what, your obvious lack of privacy?" Rick asked in return, puffing up and glaring at Leo.

Guessing at the overprotective, big brother turn of Rick's mind, Alana crossed her eyes at him. Foot tapping, she stopped dead in front of him, forcing his attention to her. "No, I mean about the new disappearance. Do you think it's an improvement over the old ending or not?"

Rick shrugged and moved around her to continue walking towards the employee exit. "It's more dramatic than before, I'll give you that. But I think it needs something. Maybe some pyrotechnics, sparklers, flares, or maybe even a little fire. Give me a few days to rig something up, and we'll try it again."

"Sounds dangerous," Leo replied, an unfamiliar panic

rising in him at the image of Alana surrounded by flames. He didn't like the way that thought made his palms sweat.

Rick put his arm around Alana's shoulders, pulling her into his side. "I wouldn't do anything to put my honorary little sister in danger. Unlike some people."

Alana punched Rick in the ribs, jerking out of his grasp. "Cut it out. I know you didn't like the plan to begin with, but nothing happened to me. No one showed up to threaten me or attack me. And if they had, I told you Leo would watch out for me. You refuse to listen to anything I say."

Rick glowered at Leo again, not pleased with her automatic defense of the man. "I don't like the idea that he wants to use you as bait, that's all. He's supposed to be keeping you out of danger, not putting you into the line of fire."

Leo's temper flashed, his eyes turning cold, his voice frigid. "I don't want to put Alana at risk. But since she was determined to go through her normal routine, I saw no harm in taking advantage of the situation. The protection had to be put into place anyway, why not use it to put the bastard away? Alana would be much safer with him behind bars."

Rick bristled, but he had no time to respond.

A man lunged forward, out of the shadows, as they walked through the exit door. Leo thrust Alana behind him, reaching for his gun.

Rick took a more direct approach, grabbing the man by the throat and slamming him against the wall.

"What the hell!" the man managed to choke out, before Rick picked him up off his feet by his neck.

"Who are you and what did you think you were going to do?" Rick roared, shaking the much lighter man whose toes grazed the ground.

"My name's Dylan Russell. My family and I were at the show. I wanted an autograph for my daughter, Janice. She's got leukemia, and this was the first time I've seen her smile in over a year. I wanted to thank Miss Devlin and get her to sign the tag on my daughter's bear. That's all, I swear," the man babbled, still dangling several inches in the air.

Alana pushed Leo out of her way and took the stuffed animal from the man. As if it was nothing unusual, she spoke to the man in a calm voice, reaching out with a little of her power to soothe him. "You'll have to excuse my friends. I've received some threats, and it's made them jumpy."

She ran her fingers over the bear, its pure white body dressed in full armor. "I remember your daughter. I've been by her room several times on my visits to the hospital. I'm glad she liked the show today, and I'd be happy to sign her bear. Do you have a pen, Rick?"

Rick let the man slide down the wall. "You mean to tell me, there isn't a pen in that monstrosity you call a purse?"

Alana forced a giggle. "Silly me, I forgot about that. Has Janice thought of a name for her bear yet?" she asked as she dug for a moment before finding a felt tip pen.

The man straightened his jacket, still keeping a fearful eye on Rick. His voice shook a little as he answered. "Sir Abracadabra. She wanted to name him after something that would remind her of you. She's a big fan, and the show meant a great deal to her. She wasn't expecting you to give her anything. The bears were a great idea."

"I have a friend who owns one of those make your own bear stores. I persuaded her to donate the materials. I helped design the bears from what the children told me on my visits and got several friends together and had a huge stuffing party a few weeks ago. I thought the kids would appreciate the results, if not the effort." Alana grinned and signed the tag to Janice and Sir Abracadabra.

She then handed the toy back with an apologetic smile. "Again, I'm sorry for the misunderstanding. I hope you're not hurt."

The man shrugged in the face of her sincere words, finding it hard to hold a grudge against someone who had done so much for his daughter. "It's okay. I can't believe that anyone would want to hurt you. Not after all the effort you've gone to for my daughter and the other kids. But I guess there're crazy people everywhere."

Looking at the two grim guards standing over Alana, the man turned and scurried away.

Alana glared at Rick.

"What?" he asked, expression anything but apologetic. "I didn't know who he was. What did you expect me to do, wait until you were bleeding on the ground before I did anything to defend you?"

Alana poked him in the chest with a single finger. "I didn't expect you to leap into action, like some dim-witted superhero. If he had been the killer, he would have been armed. Have you become bulletproof when I wasn't looking? This is why I've tried to keep you out of this mess. At least I know that Detective Grady will respond in a professional manner. He protected me, without assaulting the first stranger we met."

Rick crossed his arms and scowled down his nose at her. "Oh yeah, I'm sure Detective Grady is all professional. No unprofessional thoughts running through *his* mind."

Alana's eyes narrowed. "I suggest you think about your next words. I'd hate to have to hurt you. It takes a long time to learn all those tricks, and I'd hate to have to find a replacement."

Rick looked into Alana's face, really looked, and then

cursed. "Okay, I'm sorry. But I do want to talk to you about things later, privately."

Warn me, you mean. But Alana realized that he meant well, he just didn't want to see her hurting again. He feared her growing feelings for Leo, how vulnerable they made her. Watching out for her was part of being her Helper, something that had been drummed into him since birth. "That's fine. Now, Leo and I will meet you at the pub. You go ahead. We'll call if anything comes up."

With one more menacing glare at Leo, Rick stalked down the aisle to his car.

"You want to explain what that was about?" Leo asked, watching the other man's retreat with suspicion.

"Not really."

Leo raised his eyebrows, but let the subject drop. Contrary to what they both had told him, Rick seemed to be acting more like a jealous lover than a brother figure. He needed to get some answers from the two of them, both for his investigation and for himself. He had no desire to be the guest star in a love triangle.

Preoccupied as he was with images of Alana and Rick intertwined, he didn't see the golden sticker on his windshield right away. When he did, picking out the image of golden hands clasping a golden crowned heart, he jerked Alana to him, forcing them both a few steps back.

Rick heard Alana's small shriek two cars away. He ran to them as Leo pulled out his cell phone to call it in.

"What's going on?" he asked, not liking the pallor overpowering Alana's cheeks.

"He was here," she whispered.

Rick ran his hands up and down her arms, trying to warm her while Leo spoke over the phone in clipped, staccato sentences.

Leo snapped closed his cell and stared at the two for a moment before speaking. "I've got people coming. They'll check the car out and make sure it's safe. We'll stay until they get here. Then I suggest we do lunch as planned. It will give us time to talk."

Chapter Twelve

The darkened but lively pub stunned Leo as he walked out of the quiet afternoon sun. Knickknacks, posters, and other odds-and-ends brought to America from Ireland by the owner covered the walls and ceiling. A band blasted from the side of the room in front of an area cleared of tables. As they played a spirited tune, a young woman pulled people from their seats to show them how to do a jig. A few patrons even beat their tables with their glasses and sang along with the band.

While he and his parents didn't see eye to eye on many things, Leo held a great deal of pride in his Irish heritage. Under any other circumstances, he would have delighted in the surroundings. But he found it hard to concentrate on the joy around him with all the negative emotions waging war within him.

The moment of stark fear he had felt as the man approached Alana in the parking lot stunned him. He never feared for his own safety, but the thought of her being harmed caused his mouth to dry up. He hadn't even thought, reacting on instinct as he shoved her behind him, shielding her with his body. And she put herself in danger from countless supernatural creatures regularly, if her story about Protectors was to be believed. He could not guard her from those threats.

Then there was the jealousy simmering below the surface, as he watched Rick put a hand behind Alana's back and to guide her to a table. *Friends, my ass.*

"Busy for a weekday at lunch isn't it?" Leo asked, trying to ease his own tension, but appalled by the coldness that crept into his voice.

Alana leaned close to yell in his ear, brushing against his arm. "I've never seen the place any other way."

Leo struggled with the rising temperature caused by her slight contact as Rick whistled at a buxom brunette waitress, whose warm smile brightened the room. With hands on hips and foot tapping, she scolded, "Carrick Murphy, I missed you last night. You left before my shift even started. What's a girl to think about that, I ask you?"

Rick reached up and patted her hand. "A girl like you need never worry about a thing like that, Deirdre me love. I keep telling you that you should drop that no good husband of yours. I'd be more than willing to take his place."

Deirdre spun away with a snort. "And for how long, I'd be asking? How long before you went flitting away to the next pretty young thing to give you the eye? I'll be staying with a man I can depend on, if it's all the same to you." She turned and gave Alana a commiserating glance. "I don't know how you put up with the rogue. I'd have given him up for a lost cause ages ago."

"Putting up with him is easy. I never, ever date him. That's the key. I stand back and watch the female carnage." Alana met Rick's insulted glare with an innocent smile.

Leo couldn't help but watch Deirdre bounce as she laughed. Here was the type of woman he expected Rick to attract, gorgeous, like Alana, but in a different way. With ease, Deirdre pulled out a pad and started writing. "Now let's see, that'll be one turkey and rasher sandwich and a Guinness for the flirt, one Irish stew and an ice tea for the lovely and ever patient magician, but what will this brawny, handsome man be having?"

"An Irish breakfast and an ice tea," he answered, ignoring her coy comment, and handed her the menu.

"Ice tea?" she responded with a flirtatious glance from under heavy lids. "Sure you don't want me to build you a Guinness? We even pour it cold for you tasteless American types."

Leo shook his head and returned her playful manner with a faked glare. "I like my Guinness warm as it's supposed to be. Only a barbarian would drink it cold. Not to mention, my granddad would have my head if I drank it any other way. But I'm on duty right now, lass, so no liquor for me."

"A policeman, eh. And a right striking one at that." Deirdre gave Alana an impish grin followed by a bawdy wink. "If you don't want to keep him, I might be tempted to throw out Bill and try my hand with him."

"Hey now, if you give up your husband, I have first dibs," Rick called out, folding his arms across his chest and looking crestfallen.

Deirdre swatted the back of Rick's head. "You'd be too high maintenance for the likes of me. I'd spend most of my days shooing the other women off of ya. Now behave, or you'll be wearing your Guinness, not drinking it."

Rick leaned back and laughed. "Ah Deirdre, I do love you. You're a fine woman, a veritable Venus. And you know how to keep a man in his place. Why can't I find another woman like you?"

Alana answered as Deirdre walked off with their orders, dodging dancing customers. "Too handsome for your own good, that's the problem. You scare the good ones off and are left with all the harpies."

Rick rubbed his cheek, pondering the problem. "Maybe if I scarred up my face a bit, I could attract better attention."

"Maybe if you let the swelling in your head go down, you'd notice the others," Leo said, watching as a sweet young brunette glanced at Rick, before quickly looking back at the floor.

Rick puffed his chest out and leaned forward. "Are you accusing me of being stuck on myself?"

Leo pulled back, shaking his head. He didn't know why he had said it, but he might as well tell Rick the truth, now that he'd put his foot in it. "No, not stuck on yourself. Just blind. If you want a good woman, they're out there. Looking like you do, you shouldn't have a problem catching one's eye. The harpies with looks equaling your own distract you. You need to notice the ones that may not look like they walked out of Fredrick's catalogue."

"You're saying the only good women are ugly?" Alana asked, warning etched on her lovely face. The grip she had on her fork made Leo nervous.

"No, just that Rick here's only noticing the playboy packaging, like that lovely little thing sitting over in the corner." Leo nodded in the direction of the brunette he'd seen looking at Rick earlier. "She's not drop dead gorgeous, like Rick, but she's nice looking. Attractive even. She has the look of a woman with a kind heart, if that's what Rick's looking for. But you can tell that she's shy. And *he* hasn't looked twice in her direction."

Rick gazed over at the woman, seeing her avoid making any type of eye contact with him. "As if she'd give me the time of day. I know the type. They assume that I'm a player, a lot like you do."

Leo shook his head at Rick's misinterpretation of the

woman's actions, sighing. "I bet if you went over and asked her to dance, she wouldn't say no."

Defensiveness laced Rick's voice. "And what makes you the expert? I don't recall you mentioning having a good woman waiting for you at home. If I remember correctly, all you have at home is a dog."

"I said it would be easy for *you*." Leo answered, trying not to wince as the insult touched a nerve. "Not many good women want to risk hitching up their fates with a stubborn old police detective."

Rick's face closed down in denial. "I still don't buy it."

Leo shrugged, indifferent to the other man's belief. "Then prove me wrong. Go ask her to dance. I assume you know how to jig. Tell her you'll show her how. If she refuses, then I was wrong and you win. If she says yes, then you get a dance with her and you win. It's a win/win situation, seems to be little risk involved."

Rick clenched his jaw, and pushed away from the table. "I still say she'll shoot me down, but no risk, no gain."

As she watched Rick stalk towards the other woman's table, Alana squeezed Leo's hand.

"What was that for?" he asked, puzzled.

"For getting him to listen to what I've been trying to tell him for the past two years." Alana watched as Rick started talking to the woman, watched as her face lit up with laughter at something Rick said. "He's the type who needs to have someone, a woman with a kind heart, some strength to her, but who needs him as well. Deep down, I don't think he feels he deserves it, so he avoids the type of woman that would be best for him. He tells himself that she'd never be interested in the first place. I'm glad he listened to you. Now maybe he'll be able to find someone."

Leo stared at her in amazement. "You're really not interested in him are you?"

It was Alana's turn to look puzzled at his question. "Of course not. I thought I told you that."

Leo shrugged, staring at the opposite wall, where the band was set up. "Yeah, but looking like he does and seeing how close you two are, it's hard to credit."

"Well, it's the truth. He's too much like a brother to me, and I'm not the right type of woman for him, too set in my ways. He needs someone who needs him. I like having Rick around, but I don't need him." Alana watched Leo, to see how he was taking what she said. Maybe this was the reason for the distance he held between them.

"Under normal circumstances, I don't think you'd need anyone," he replied, still focusing on the band.

"Maybe not need, but everyone wants someone they can be close to, and I don't mean physically. But today we're working out Rick's problems, not mine. And we seem to be doing a good job at it."

She gestured to where Rick took the young woman's hand and led her, grinning, onto the floor.

Leo showed no surprise. "I knew she'd say yes, she'd been watching him since we walked in the door."

Looking around at the throng of bodies packed into the little pub Alana had to ask, "Do you always notice things like that even with so many people milling around?"

Leo watched as Rick spun the woman, demonstrating one of the intricate steps to her. "I like to people watch, but I'm especially sensitive to it when I'm on duty."

Alana tried to hide the disappointment his answer caused her. "So you consider yourself on duty right now, Detective?"

Leo leaned further back in his chair, crossing his arms against his chest. He kept his expression blank. "I'm here to protect you, Ms. Devlin. I don't know what else to call it."

"How about calling it down time?" Alana grabbed his hand and dragged him from his seat. "With your Irish heritage, you should be able to dance a wee bit. So take a girl for a turn on the floor."

Before he could say anything, Leo found himself on the small dance floor, spinning a laughing Alana in his arms. People around them cheered, pounding their cups on their tables. The music played, bubbling up through his blood, causing his feet to move faster and faster. Looking down into Alana's shining face, Leo had never felt so right about anything before in his life.

It was as if she belonged in his arms.

As soon as that thought crossed his mind, he pulled her to a stop and retreated back to the now food covered table.

Alana, panting, fell into her seat. She pushed her hair back from her face and took a long drink from her tea before asking, "What's wrong? For a moment there, I thought you were having fun."

Grim faced, Leo replied, "I'm not paid to have fun. The two of us need to get something straight. I have a job to do. Any feelings between the two of us could jeopardize that job, jeopardize you."

"And who said anything about feelings?" Alana glared at him over her tea glass. "I wanted to have a little fun. You don't think I know my life is in danger? Hell, every day, our lives are in danger. Even without a killer on the loose, we don't know how long we'll be here. There are no guarantees. As such, I plan on enjoying every moment that I'm given on this earth. If that means I want to dance the jig during my lunch with a sexy police detective, then by God, I'll do just that."

Leo pulled her out of her seat and across his lap, causing

her to gasp. "You can't tell me that's all this is about. I know better."

With that, he crushed her mouth under his.

At first, his kiss was ferocious. He ate her, all of his frustration focused on her mouth. His fingers speared into her hair, twisting her head this way and that to achieve a better angle, a closer connection. Alana went rigid in his arms, shocked by the intensity of what was happening. But ever since their first kiss, she had craved this, craved the taste of his mouth on her own. She sank into him.

Leo's mouth crushed against her lush lips until they parted. With that little bit of surrender, Leo gentled the kiss, licking and nibbling at her lips instead of bruising and biting. His fingers ran through her hair, caressing and gentling her. Alana's sweet moan entered his mouth, setting his entire body trembling. The tip of her tongue reached out to trace his lips.

Pure heat shot through his body, shocking him out of the trance her mouth had put him under.

Leo tore away, thrusting Alana back into her chair. Her hair tumbled loose from the barrette anchoring it, falling in fiery waves around her shoulders.

In a strained voice, he continued. "This is what I'm talking about. I'm attracted to you and, considering your response, I don't think I'm alone in that. But while the killer is on the loose and after you, I have a job to do. And that has to come first, for both our sakes. Things like that little dance out there can't happen again, not until this is over. Things like that kiss must *never* happen again until then."

Alana pressed a shaky hand to her lips, disturbed by the strength of the feelings he'd shown. She'd had no idea of the depths of emotion he hid from the world. And, somehow, they called out to something deep inside her.

The two sat in silence, not certain what to say and wondering what the other was thinking. Then Leo's cell phone rang.

Not wanting to leave her alone, even for the amount of time it would take to answer the call, Leo gestured for Rick before walking out the door to hear better.

Rick plopped down beside Alana, his face split with a wide, excited grin. "Her name's Joan. She works at the library a block from here, and she gave me her number. I hate to say it, but maybe Leo's right. I should have been paying more attention way before this. That was a lot easier than I thought it would be."

Silence was Alana's only response. Rick peered at her. Seeing the stunned expression on her face, he asked, voice soothing, "Hey, what's the matter, Curls?"

Panic laced Alana's voice as she answered, "Oh my God, I think I'm falling for him."

Rick scooted his chair closer and pulled her hand away from her mouth, letting her fingers dig into his palm. "I know. I've been wondering how long it'd take you to realize that. It may not be as bad as you think, though. He seems straight-laced and closed-minded at first, but he does have some redeeming qualities. He cares about people. That's a plus, right? I mean, most guys don't notice all that relationship stuff. I'm a perfect example of that. But he did. And he was willing to stick his neck out and give me some good advice. I don't think he'll go weird on you, like Jack did. He already knows the worst. Maybe you should give him a chance."

Alana shook her head, fighting the sickening panic beginning to turn her stomach. "I couldn't stand to see that look in another man's face. Not a man I loved. You have no idea how it feels to see utter repulsion on the face of someone who means that much to you. To know that you caused it and there's nothing you can do about it. No, I can't risk feeling like that again. It hurts too much, Rick—too damn much."

Leo's chilly voice sounded behind them. "Get the waitress to pack this up. We're leaving right now."

Holding herself together with crossed arms, Alana turned to face him. Leo's craggy features were frozen in an emotionless mask. Her heart skipped as she stared into his icy expression. "What's wrong? What was that call about?"

"There was a primitive explosive device fixed to the bottom of my car, along with a nice little note." For a man who looked so cold, pure angry heat radiated in his words. "We're canceling your next show. He made explicit threats against both you and the audience if you perform again tonight."

Rick stood, waving Deirdre down. With a decided lack of playful banter, he settled the bill and began piling food into the Styrofoam boxes she quickly provided. "I'll give you a lift home. I'm assuming your car is out of commission for the time being."

Leo reached to take the boxes from Rick, letting the other man help Alana from her seat. He didn't trust himself to touch her after what happened earlier. "An officer is dropping a new one at my house for us to use for the time being. But we need to take some time and regroup."

Rick nodded, pulling a silent Alana through the crowd. "I'll swing by later tonight to see what's going on. Call me if you need anything."

Leo was shocked by the other man's offer, with its utter lack of hostility. The corners of his mouth curved up into a smirk. "So, she gave you her number, did she? I knew I should have put some money on that wager. Live and learn, I guess."

Rick didn't reply, just grinning in return.

Her thoughts and feelings still in turmoil, Alana followed the two men without comment.

Chapter Thirteen

Silence echoed through Leo's home, the two occupants going their separate ways the moment they entered the house, avoiding any contact with each other. Anger, doubt, and hurt simmered below the surface. The oppressive atmosphere drove Max outside with his tail between his legs. Anything was better than watching the two humans brood.

Alana sat in her room, staring at a blank wall. Doubt gnawed at her chest, chipping through the defenses she'd built around her emotions. She didn't know what to do, what to think. She couldn't love the man. He'd made his feelings clear. There was no future in it, and Alana needed a future. She was wrong about her emotions. She had to be. But, God forbid, if she wasn't wrong, what was she going to do about it? Should she try her best to repress it, or should she try to convince Leo to give a relationship a shot? Should she risk opening herself up to the pain again?

While Alana wrapped herself in her uncertainties, Leo puttered about in the kitchen, making his promised eggplant Parmesan, distracting himself from the guilt that pounded him. Alana was perfect, a kind and beautiful woman. The type of woman a man meets maybe once in a lifetime, if he's even that lucky. But she was trapped in a horrible situation, one he couldn't in good conscience take advantage of. Emotions developing under these kinds of circumstances were suspect. Even if he could risk letting his own feelings show now, when the danger still threatened her, it was very possible that after the danger passed, she would have no more use for him. He couldn't set himself up for that kind of pain. Not again.

Viciously, he stirred the sauce, splattering his pristine stovetop. Worse yet, she wasn't close to being normal. Leo craved normal. What would happen if he let himself be dragged into the bizarre life that she led? Monsters, spells, and fortune-telling, that's what he'd be forced to live with, never knowing what was waiting around the corner to pounce on her. Faced with creatures like the one he saw her fight, Leo was of no use to her. How could any relationship survive that pressure?

Lost in morbid thought, Leo jumped as the phone rang.

In her room, Alana didn't even blink at the sound of the phone, trapped as she was in her own dark thoughts and emotions. She didn't have the energy to move. Her emotions twisted inside, leaving her physically worn.

Leo came into her room with slow, heavy strides. He stood inside the doorway with his shoulders slouched, as if expecting a blow. Pity filled his eyes.

Alana's stomach clenched at the sight. "What is it? What's happened now?"

Leo didn't know of any way to soften the blow. "It's Rick. He was attacked an hour ago, on his way home," he answered in a dull and troubled voice.

Every muscle in Alana's body clenched, heart stopping. "Is he okay?" she asked, unshed tears gleaming in her eyes.

Leo swallowed, trying to ease the tightness clenching his throat. "He's pretty messed up, but the doctors say he's fine. He's conscious, but they have him on painkillers, so there's no telling how long he'll stay awake. They plan on keeping him there at least one night for observation. We can go see him, if you want."

Alana had already leapt off the bed in search of her shoes. Watching her flit about the room cut at Leo. He hated being so powerless, powerless to stop that maniac from hurting her, even emotionally. Nothing he did seemed to help.

Instead, he did the only thing he could. He turned his back on her pain, leaving the room to start the air-conditioning in the car.

Leo stayed outside, talking to the guard at the door and waiting for Gabe. Alana tried to hold a smile on her face as she approached the hospital bed. The battered figure lying on the bed held little resemblance to the handsome young man Alana had watched dancing only hours before. A mass of cuts and bruises covered his face, his right eye swollen shut. His right arm was in a cast. The doctors told her that he had two broken ribs and a concussion, but no internal injuries. It was as if, as soon as the killer was certain that Rick had been rendered helpless, he just walked away. The one thing connecting Rick's attack with the claddagh killer was a button found pinned to his back.

"Rick?" she whispered, more afraid now than when she had been the one lying in the bed.

"Curls, is that you?" his hoarse voice whispered in reply.

Alana sobbed as she reached down to run a hand along his injured cheek, careful not to cause him any more harm. "And who else would drag themselves out to see about a sorry sot like you on such a beautiful afternoon?" she asked with forced cheer.

Rick's swollen lips curled and a little sparkle shown in his left eye. "I don't know. There's a cute little nurse hanging around. She said she'd be back to talk to me later.

If I play my cards right, there might be a sponge bath in it for me."

Alana chuckled though her throat still ached with unshed tears. "That's my best bud. Always looking on the bright side."

Rick shifted in his bed, wincing with the movement. "Yeah, if I'm going to be stuck here for a while, I might as well keep myself occupied."

He paused for a moment, a bit of his impish side shining through. "You do know that I was joking at the pub when I said that maybe I should scar up my face a bit to catch a better girl. I think one of the Fates must have heard me and thought I was serious. Remind me to hold my tongue next time."

Seeing the pain his earlier movement caused, Alana lowered herself to sit beside him on the bed, careful to avoid jostling his IV. Leaning forward, she kissed him on the chin. But her eyes clouded as she pulled back. "It's nothing to joke about, Rick. This is my fault. If I'd done what I was supposed to, done my job as a Protector instead of depending on human law to solve this, you wouldn't be in this position. I failed you, Rick."

Rick reached out for her hand, giving it a weak squeeze. "This was not your fault. None of this is. It's the fault of some maniac who's become a self-proclaimed vigilante against the magically inclined."

Alana crossed her legs and hugged herself, ignoring Rick. "He didn't want us to do another show. That's what he said in the note he left on Leo's car. He couldn't get to me, so he went after you. I promise you, I'll do everything within my power to stop him. He won't hurt anyone else. I'll do what I should have done in the first place. I *will* stop him."

At the pity in Rick's expression, Alana leapt to her feet and began pacing in front of the window.

Rick nodded his head. "Just be careful. Don't jump in half-cocked. You've never done anything like this before. You've never even gone against a supernatural threat by yourself before, only with your father or me. I want you to take every precaution. I won't be around to help you."

Alana walked over to the window and leaned her forehead against the cool glass, closing her eyes. She couldn't look at Rick. Guilt ripped at her with the sight of his battered face. "I will, starting now. I can't see the future or the past, but I'm going to contact those who can, get what information there is. I'm taking your cell phone, in case I run into any trouble of the earthly variety."

Wishing he could do something more to help her, Rick answered. "Take whatever you need. They left my personal belongings in the dresser over there. But you'll stop at the house before you do anything crazy, won't you? You'll need more than that can of mace I gave you. And I don't just mean for physical protection. If you're going to call on the Others for help, you'll need all the protection you can get. They don't take kindly to being pulled into this plane of existence and tend to be a little nasty about it."

Alana straightened and braced herself before turning back to her friend. "Yes, I know. I'm not a complete novice. I haven't worked without a net before is all. But I'll need to pick everything up without Detective Grady knowing about it."

"So, I take it you don't plan on letting him come along?"

Alana ran her hands up and down her arms, fighting the chill that shivered through her at the thought of Leo getting that good a look at her world. "No. No way am I pulling him in on this. This is my business for now."

Understanding shone in Rick's eyes. "Just promise me you'll be careful."

"I will." Alana sat down beside him once more, trying not to flinch when she looked down at him. "What are you going to tell Leo when he comes in and finds me gone?"

Rick grinned. "Don't worry. I can't wait to see the look on his face. How should I know how you got out without being seen? I have a concussion and am on more drugs than I can count. You could have flown out the window for all I know. I assume you just walked out the door. How am I to know why he didn't see you leave?"

"How indeed?" she replied while calling on the magic necessary to change her appearance. Leo and the guard posted didn't look twice at the young blond nurse who left the room moments later.

In a cab reeking of sweat and stale cigarettes, Alana began laying informational groundwork. She dialed a long distance number known by heart and waited for an answer.

"Book, Bell, and Candle, how may I help you?" a calming voice began, causing Alana to smile in spite of herself. She hadn't realized how much she missed her family since they'd all gone their separate ways, even just hearing their voices.

"Fiona, this is Alana. I need you to do something for me."

A sigh echoed across the country. "I move all the way to New Orleans, and I still get hassled by relatives. What can I do for you, big Sis?"

Alana darted a quick look at the cab driver, making certain his attention was elsewhere. He was enamored with the hard rock station blaring from his radio. Tapping on the steering wheel, he was deaf to the world.

"I need some of your special magic," Alana answered in a hushed voice.

Panic laced Fiona's reply. "Have you been hurt? I knew something was wrong. I meant to call last night. I had a feeling that something was happening out there, something bad, but I wasn't certain if it involved you or Adain. So I shoved it to the back burner, convincing myself you'd call if you needed me. I've been so busy here. I should have called."

"I'm fine," Alana rushed to calm her sister. She didn't have time to deal with panic. She needed to have this call done with before she got to the house. Too many things waited for her to do there. "No need to worry about me. Rick's a little beat up, but nothing that won't heal on its own. You don't need to come dashing down here for a rescue. No, I need you to try and *see* something for me."

Alana could picture her sister shaking her head in unwavering denial. Fiona had never been very comfortable with using her Second Sight. "It doesn't work that easily, Alana. You know that. It's only a secondary power, and one I don't have much control over. I can't call it up like I do a healing, and it's more draining."

"I'm asking you to try for me." Alana paused for a moment before continuing, knowing what Fiona's reaction would be to what she planned on trying next. "You're not my only hope. I'm exploring other avenues as well."

Fiona gasped at the realization of what Alana meant to do. "You're not thinking of doing a calling by yourself, are you? You've never done that before, not without Mom or Dad being there to help. Rick told me how your last casting drained you. If you rested, you should have the strength to work, but you can't be at your top energy level. You need to be very careful dealing with the kinds of powers you'll be contacting. One misstep and you could be spending eternity in one of the Otherworlds."

Alana's voice took on a desperate tone. "I know that, and I will be careful. I'm not a complete amateur after all. But this is important. I'm dealing with a serial killer, Fiona, and not a supernatural one at that. He's killed five people. I need all the help I can get. I'm out of my league here."

Ever the voice of reason, Fiona tried to coax her sister from her present course of action. "Then why not leave it to the police? It's what they're there for. We're held to the promise to protect mortals from *Otherworldly* threats; things normal people can't protect themselves from. This doesn't fall under that directive."

Hating to worry her, Alana hadn't wanted to tell Fiona the truth. She didn't want Fiona to know the danger she was in. Her sister lived too far away to be of any physical help. On the other hand, it was only a matter of time until Fiona ferreted out what was happening, and she'd never forgive Alana for not telling her.

"The killer's coming after me. I've been attacked twice, but I wasn't hurt. I've been under police protection ever since. Because of that, the bastard went after Rick. That's how he was hurt." Alana paused for a moment, her voice growing shaky with built-up emotions. "Fiona, I can't sit around waiting for things to happen, not when he's hurting my friends. I have to stop him, before anyone else gets hurt."

Realizing there was nothing she could say to change Alana's mind, and not certain if she wanted to, Fiona could only offer what support she could give from such a distance. "I'll see what I can see. But I've been working hard on a case here, and I haven't had a chance to recharge, so I'm not sure how much good it will do. I fried myself trying to force a vision last night, but I'll try for you. I just can't guarantee that it will work. It's all I can offer."

Alana smiled and held the phone a little tighter, wishing she could give her little sister a hug. "Don't force anything and hurt yourself, but I would appreciate the attempt. I'll owe you big time for this, I know. Call me on Rick's cell if you get anything, anything at all."

"I will." Fiona stopped for a moment before adding, "And Sis . . ."

"Yes?"

"Be careful."

Chapter Fourteen

With solemn strides, Alana approached the circular grove of oak trees hidden behind her house. A single humming bird brushed past her face, following the lush scent of cape honeysuckle. A wisp of nostalgia filled her with longing. It felt strange going to the grove without her father, unsettling even. Her father always handled this side of things, contact with the other races, worried that his children would be too much of a temptation for some of the creatures that answered the call. It was only in the last few years before his retirement that he began showing his children how to perform a calling. Without his comforting presence, or that of Adain or Fiona, everything felt wrong, wrong to stand within the circle alone, without her family.

Alana stumbled as she reached the trees, tripping over the robe she wore and the lengthy cord that tied it. The long, brown wool of her robe danced around her feet, making it hard to walk while carrying her bag of tools. It also made things even more sweltering in the heat of the Las Vegas afternoon. Alana blew at a stray curl sticking to the sweat on her forehead as she pulled the robe up with one hand. Under other circumstances, she would put off the ritual until nighttime, when the magics were stronger, and the air cooler. But there was no time for delay.

No time, that's the story of my life.

Entering the grove of trees, she stepped over the circular

154

ditch dug around the altar and lined with river rocks. At each of the cardinal directions, a square, marble slab lay embedded in the ditch, two white and two black. On each of these stones, Alana knelt and placed a different colored candle before turning to prepare the altar.

Her mind went to Leo as she faced the altar, wondering what he would think of her if he saw her now. A forthright, honorable cop like him would be shocked out of his socks at the sight of her heavily cloaked figure, carrying occult instruments. What he'd seen with the cearb was nothing compared to a true ritual, having been a slapped together affair. Even her ex-boyfriend had never seen her as she worked; she'd only made the mistake of telling him about it. Considering his reaction, she didn't want to imagine what Leo would think of her in her present outfit or worse, if the casting called for her to go skyclad.

Leo was probably right not to get involved with her. Then again, maybe her dancing nude in the moonlight would intrigue him.

The ritual she was to perform was a mixture of the two traditions practiced by her parents. Her father had practiced Druidic rituals, passed down from his ancestor who had lain with a member of the Tuatha De Danann and was the first placed under the geis of protection. Her father hadn't called on that particular side of the family for help often, but he was very careful to follow their rules when he did. While he refused to worship them, he always said you should pay them their proper respect when requesting their aid. They tended to have a nasty, creative temper if not treated by the standards they devised.

Her mother, on the other hand, had been an eclectic Wiccan, using a mixture of symbols, myths, and ceremonies when practicing what for her was a religion. Alana found it useful to borrow workings from her mother, as many of the rituals helped her focus her powers better than those taught by her father.

The mixture of the two traditions tended to be heavy on the visual symbolism, and therefore intimidating to the uninitiated. It brought to mind shades of Macbeth.

On a small pedestal situated in front of the stone altar, she placed four objects to show respect for the Druid traditions: a small iron cauldron, a miniature sword, a miniature spear, and a piece of granite chosen and polished by her own hand, each representing one of the four sacred objects of the Tuatha De Danann. She then took the crane bag from around her neck and set it in front of the other objects, bowing as her father had taught her.

Turning to the altar itself, she took her bag and pulled out a white cloth, trimmed in black with a golden pentagram embroidered in the center. She smoothed it over the surface of the altar. On each of the two back corners, she put a single bee's wax candle, one white and one black, sticking to the two colors associated with protection. On top of the pentagram, she placed another candle, a swirling mixture of black and white.

In front of the center candle, she laid two bowls, filling one with salt and one with water. To the left of the candle, she placed a plain brass chalice, polished to resemble gold, and filled it with wine. To the right, she set her athame, the sharpened, dual-edged blade made of silver, etched with an apple leaf design. She ran a single finger over the blade, thinking of the work her brother had put into it for her. The handle was made of an oak dragon, a piece of oak naturally twisted from a honeysuckle vine wrapping around it. She found the piece while visiting her parents in Ireland and asked her brother to fit it to her athame. Staining it a dark black and fitting one end with a piece of silver, etched with an apple blossom, he attached it to a blade made for Alana by a friend who was a jewelry designer.

Taking a deep breath to calm herself, she began preparations for a ward of protection. First, she walked to the ditch and filled it with a small line of salt. Then she lit all the candles and walked back to the altar to take up her athame.

Okay, show time.

Pointing her athame towards the yellow candle placed on the eastern square, she began. "Hear me, oh Paralda, Overseer of the Sylphs and Zephyrs, Governor of Air, Guardian of the East. I do summon thee to bear witness and protect this gateway to the Otherworlds."

A yellow glow surrounded the first candle as she turned to the red candle positioned to the south. Focusing her power and pointing her athame, she called out, "Hear me, oh Djin, Overseer of Salamanders and Firedrakes, Governor of Fire, Guardian of the South. I do summon thee to bear witness and protect this gateway to the Otherworlds."

A red glow flickered around the southern candle as she turned to the blue candle set to the west. "Hear me, oh Niksa, Overseer of Undines and the Mer-folk, Governor of Water, Guardian of the West. I do summon thee to bear witness and protect this gateway to the Otherworlds."

As the blue glow formed around the third candle, Alana turned to face the last, dark green candle. "Hear me, oh Ghob, Overseer of Gnomes and Dwarves, Governor of Earth, Guardian of the North. I do summon thee to bear witness and protect this gateway to the Otherworlds."

With those final words spoken, the line of salt within the ditch began to sparkle as the glow surrounding each candle began pulsing in a regular beat.

Alana raised the athame towards the sky to finish the

circle. "Let only good will and peace enter this working, touch this scene. As I will it, so mote it be."

The circular sparkle grew until a wavering dome enclosed the entire area, wrapping it in a peaceful aura. Alana turned back toward the altar, placing her athame down for a moment and raising the bowls of salt and water over her head. Setting them down again she placed a pinch of the salt into the water bowl. She then swirled the liquid, concentrating her energies on casting out all impurities. Finally, she sprinkled a bit of the combination over the center candle. "With the mixing of the elements, earth, air, water, and fire, I call upon my ancestors for guidance. Come to me, oh creatures of the elements. Come to me, oh ancient peoples. Heed my call and answer my plea. As I will it, so mote it be."

An eerie wind tugged the hood of Alana's cloak off her head and whipped her hair about her face. She flinched at the violent strength of the gale, but reached for her athame and gripped it. Raising it once more above her head, focusing all her energy on its point, she called out once more, strong and sure, "As I will it, so mote it be!"

As quickly as it arose, the wind stopped. Where nothing was before, the figure of a beautiful young woman stood swaying and humming in front of the alter. A gauzy dress of orange and gold danced around her legs, along with the ankle long length of shimmering silver-blond hair. The sweet scent of exotic flowers filled the air, and Alana could almost swear she could hear the sound of a lute or harp playing a lilting tune in the background.

Alana picked up the chalice of wine from the altar and approached the spectral figure before her. She bowed, arms outstretched, offering the cup to her visitor. "It is my honor to greet you, venerable spirit."

The woman smiled, flicking her silvery blond hair back from her delicate face. Not pausing from the haunting tune she hummed, the woman reached for the chalice and took a small sip.

"You are new to me, never having answered my call before. By what name may I call you?" Alana inquired, unsettled by her guest's lack of speech. She seemed a gentle creature, but one could never be too careful when dealing with the fey. *Never* judge one by its appearance. Her father pounded the quote about fair being foul and foul fair into each of his children's minds.

The woman stopped humming, looking up at Alana with eyes a soul-piercing shade of violet rimmed with gold. Still, she smiled, at peace. "You may call me by the name of my kind. I am Leanan Sidhe."

Alana swallowed. There was nothing like dealing with a creature you weren't familiar with. "I fear I do not recognize the name of your kind. What type of spirit are you?"

The woman's melodious laughter rang through the circle, sending a pleasant set of goose bumps dancing over Alana's skin. "Do not be concerned with your ignorance. I will not hold it against you. Most have not heard of me, knowing only of my sisters, the Bean Sidhe, or banshee. I am a spirit of life, a muse to music. Artists have pined for my divine aid, but you have nothing to fear of me, little cousin. As it is, the higher Court Faeries are busy, too busy to answer you themselves. They had only myself, or one of the Ganconer, to send. It was felt that you would have an easier time with me than with one of those hopeless flirts. And with you not being a milkmaid or shepherdess, the Ganconer wasn't to eager fight me for the honor of meeting you."

Alana allowed herself to relax, muscles easing, but still

kept up her guard. You could never completely trust one of the Sidhe. They didn't lie, but they also never told you the full truth. "I called you here to ask you for information not accessible to myself on this plane. From what you have said, is what is happening in my city known in the Otherworlds?"

Again, the Leanan Sidhe's lilting laughter echoed within the circle. "We know why you have called. It is what the various Courts of Faerie are meeting about, what they couldn't pull themselves away from to answer your call. The others sent me as messenger, to let you know the seriousness of what you now deal with. All the peoples of Faerie know of the one you face. He has killed seven humans of various fey ancestries. The Tuatha De Danann, Seelie and Unseelie Courts, as well as the Kingdoms of the Faerie are concerned with the well-being of their half-breed children."

Alana paused for a moment, letting what she was being told sink in. Something wasn't right with the information. "Seven killed? I thought there were only five dead, with Rick and myself the only other two victims?"

The Leanan Sidhe stared at the ground, hands clasped, shaking her head. Her voice held a sorrowful tone as she replied. "No. Seven has he killed to date. Seven with our blood are gone. Your mortal law has not found the first two, not connected them with his crimes. Though the attack on you and your Helper, who is also of our blood, does concern us as well. But it is the first two dead who will be your key."

"My key?"

Again the Leanan Sidhe shook her head, her hypnotic eyes meeting Alana's own, a deep well of sadness reflected there. "It is not my place to tell you outright who it is you seek. That is your duty, to find and protect. With that, I cannot help you."

Alana stared back at the spirit, shoulders thrown back, willing her to give more information, something she could use. "I thought my duty was to protect humans from powers they could not hope to face alone. Now you are telling me that I must find a way to defend the fey against human attacks as well."

Anger lit the faerie's eyes, quickly banked behind a placid veil. "No. I am telling you that if you do not find and deal with this threat, we of the Otherworlds will be forced to take matters into our own hands. You will not like the consequences. In our doing so, many of your humans will die."

A cold chill raced through Alana's blood as the possibilities tore through her mind. "What do you mean? What kind of consequences?"

The Leanan Sidhe's voice was hard and steady as she replied, "Those whose descendants have been killed call out for revenge, for the blood of their murderer. Even the more even-tempered of our kind are outraged by the deaths. You are to be given three times three days to bring this human to mortal justice before we send our own powers out against him. Those under discussion for the job of vengeance are the Sluagh, the Wild Hunt, or the Morrigna."

The color fled from Alana's face. Las Vegas would be in ruins if any one of those creatures were set loose upon them. "You would consider sending the Triple Goddess of War out of the Otherworlds and onto my city, much less those other vicious creatures?!"

Her face a careful sculpture of pity, the faerie answered, "You asked what may happen. I have told you. You have nine days to find the one and deal with this man by mortal means, before we are forced to send our own form of justice."

The Leanan Sidhe paused for a moment, considering the tone of her message and the irony of its carrier. "On second thought, perhaps my sister would have been a better choice to deliver this ultimatum. Warnings like this aren't what I would want to do for all eternity. But remember, the first two dead are the key to finding the killer."

The faerie shrugged and sighed before vanishing, leaving only the sound of her music in her wake.

Alana stood shocked and ill as she considered the monumental task before her. Nine days to find a killer. Nine days until havoc would be set loose on her city. Nine days.

How in God's name am I going to explain this to Leo?

Chapter Fifteen

Alana smoothed the pale blue cotton of her sundress across her ample hips and tossed a mousy brown lock behind her ear. Nondescript features and large, thick glasses covering plain brown eyes completed her illusion. She made her new appearance as unlike herself as possible, walking into the lion's den as she was. But she did nothing to hide her slight trembling as she approached the gleaming white desk of the secretary for the Hands of Brotherhood Mission, keeping her head bowed. She hoped it would be mistaken as shyness, not the stark fear that pumped muscle-tightening adrenaline throughout her body. She couldn't stop thinking that the man she was about to see had murdered seven people.

The petite blond behind the desk smiled at Alana. The confidence seeping out of the woman was nauseating. What was it about plain looking people that made some women feel better about themselves? "Mr. Burke will see you in a moment. He loves having a chance to speak with new people interested in joining our congregation. He feels that a true minister of God needs to keep in touch with his flock and their needs."

Alana smiled back as she twisted her hands. The woman gave her a pity-filled look, before turning back to her typing. Alana wasn't worth much more notice or consideration. She'd thought she would at least rate a cup of coffee, in a place so *not* lacking in financial support. But on the bright side, she *had* worked hard creating the illusion of a woman easily ignored and forgotten. It looked like the glamour was a complete success.

After what felt like an eternity with only the monotonous clicking of the secretary's keyboard for distraction, the office door next to the secretary's desk opened and the immaculate Charles Burke walked towards Alana, hand held forward to embrace hers. "Gloria, it's a pleasure to meet you. I understand you have some questions you'd like to ask me, as you're considering joining our church."

Alana rose to take his hand, fighting the urge to wipe her fingers on her dress afterward. The man oozed charm, reminding her of a well-dressed used car salesman or perhaps one of those time-warped gigolos that still haunted certain nightclubs. "Yes, while I find your church to be quite attractive, I'm not convinced of what it has to offer me that other churches don't. There are a couple of issues I want to get straight in my mind before I make any commitments. Not that I feel there is anything wrong with your church. I just want to know if it's right for me. I hope you understand."

Hearing the rambling in Alana's well-rehearsed speech, Burke broke out his patented smile, slid an arm around her shoulders, and guided her into his office. His touch alone sent bile racing up Alana's throat. "Of course my dear, I understand. When deciding the fate of your immortal soul, one cannot be too careful. Have a seat, Gloria, and I'll explain all that you wish to know."

Alana sat in the same seat Leo had occupied the day before, facing Burke's desk. She pulled what little power she had in reading and controlling people to her. It was a long shot, but perhaps she could get Burke to say something incriminating, give her something that she could take to the police and end this madness with. But she couldn't rush things. Pushing people was a delicate matter. "How long has your Mission been in existence?"

Burke leaned back in his white leather chair, hands crossed behind his head and a look of pure nostalgia crossing his even features. "Two years. I received my calling four years ago, but two years ago I found a few interested parties willing to donate enough money to begin the television outreach program. Moneys donated over the first year through that program were funneled into the creation of this building, our physical church."

Alana nodded, keeping the man comfortable as she pushed forward with a small amount of power, making herself seem harmless and trustworthy, the kind of person you could tell anything to. "You received your calling four years ago. What did you do before that, and what training did you go through during those two years before starting your parish here?"

Burke chuckled, a picture of perfect calm. It was a well-practiced speech, one he'd given hundreds of times before, on and off camera. "Actually, Gloria, I ran a small import and export business, a lucrative endeavor, if not satisfying. I decided that I wanted more in my life, that I wanted to help people, not sell them things. After I decided to make the change, I studied with various ministries throughout the Las Vegas valley, as well as doing missionary work in South America."

"And then you came back here." Alana met his eyes, willing him to give her more.

Mistaking her concentration for personal interest, Burke straightened, puffing out his chest. The smile crossing his face took on a flirtatious, even lascivious cast. "Yes, Gloria,

I came back here. There's no need in saving people from other countries if you are not willing to do what you can for those in your own back yard."

Alana tried not to show repulsion from the signals he was sending her way. And she hated the way he kept repeating her name, as if he were forming a connection between them by the number of times he said it. "I'm confused. From what I've heard on your broadcasts, you've given warnings about certain people in the Las Vegas community, people you say do the work of the devil. Yet I haven't seen you make any attempts to save them. I thought one of the tenets in the Bible dealt with not judging others, leaving that to God. Instead, one should try to convert those who don't understand His power. Why do you single out particular people and hold them up to your parishioners as evil, without attempting to save them?"

Burke's smile never wavered. He came out from behind his desk to stand closer to Alana, leaning against the desk, his knees brushing hers. With an air of supreme conviction, he answered. "Of course, Gloria, we should try not to pass judgement on the sins of others, focusing instead on our own weakness. I make my parishioners aware of the danger certain people pose to their own souls, how they hold out temptation. I wouldn't presume to say what fate those people in question have awaiting them in the afterlife. I don't want their corruption to spread to those I have taken up to protect."

Alana stared at him again, willing him to say something specific about what he had planned. She couldn't understand how a man who had to be a complete fanatic about magic could seem to care so little about the people he condemned. He was too calm about the whole thing. It didn't mesh. "I see. So, unlike some of the accusations I've heard against you, you are not preaching hatred."

Burke chuckled. Shaking his head in dismay, he answered. "Quite the contrary. I want people to understand God's eternal love and forgiveness. I've dedicated my life to leading others to salvation. If the people I've mentioned in past sermons came forward to embrace the Lord, they too would be forgiven. It would be an honor to think that I had any small part in such a conversion."

For a moment, Alana relished the irony of his statement. Here she was, in his presence, ready to embrace the Lord. Seeing as nothing was shaking loose in this line of questioning, she decided to switch tactics. "I'm glad to hear that. There is one last thing that confuses me, though. I hope you can clarify it."

Burke held his hands out before him, showing his openness to her questions. "Anything you want to know, Gloria, anything that would make you more comfortable accepting my message. I'm at your complete disposal."

Alana tried to keep her answering smile friendly, no easy task when confronting a person she believed to be filled with deceit. "Your parish is called Hands of Brotherhood Mission, but I've never heard of any missionary work being done here, with the exception of the work you tell me you did before founding the Mission. As an English teacher, the use of the word mission, when you don't do missionary work, seems misleading. I hope you don't mind my asking, but this does appear to be an affluent parish, with plenty of funds to spare in helping the less fortunate within our community. And yet, I don't know of any work your Mission has done for the community at large."

Burke's smiled tightened and his eyes narrowed for a moment before he answered. "Most of the moneys we raise goes to our television outreach program, though I am trying to organize some more direct community service programs such as soup kitchens and homeless shelters, that sort of thing. Gloria, perhaps you would like to help direct those projects?"

Alana knew he was hiding something here, she could see it in the way he held himself. But she couldn't see any connection. How could his finances have anything to do with the murders of people of fey descent?

Alana was afraid to push much harder, causing suspicions. Burke's mind was stronger than Gabe's had been, and pushing people to be truthful beyond their normal habits wasn't her strength, only a secondary power. She'd have to see if she could get information from his minions before she left. This visit was a bust. She'd have to think of another approach if she wanted to protect the city from supernatural reprisal. The clock was running. "It would be a challenge, helping others like that. Not something I normally do. I'll have to give it some thought. I want to thank you again for taking the time to alleviate my concerns. I think you have an excellent church."

Burke took her hand in a warm clasp between both of his as she rose from the chair. "Thank you for your interest. I hope I'll be seeing more of you in the days to come."

"Oh, I'm certain you'll see me again."

The door opened behind her, allowing a huge monster of a man to enter. "Ah, Randolph. Would you mind escorting this young woman to the door?" Burke took one of Alana's hands in both of his. "We lock the door an hour after our last service. This isn't the best of neighborhoods. Randolph will let you out. I hope to see you again soon. Be certain to pick up a schedule of our services before you leave. Whenever you're prepared to join with us officially, see my secretary for the paperwork."

"Thank you for taking the time to speak with me. I appreciate it. I'm certain you had a lot that you could have been doing during that time. I respect a person who puts the welfare of others above his own." *Unlike you.*

Burke smoothed his hair back, his smile spreading wider at the compliment. "Why, thank you, Gloria. But, as they say, it's all part of the job."

Alana plastered a fake smile across her own face in response, before turning to the hulking mass of a man lurking in the doorway. Randolph took Alana by the elbow and guided her out of the office.

As the door clicked shut behind them, Alana looked up at her large guide. Turning her influence on him, she inquired, "Can I ask you something? Is he for real?"

Randolph grunted, his long strides forcing Alana to pick up her pace towards the main doors or be dragged along behind him.

Alana struggled to keep up the concentration necessary to push for truthful answers. It was becoming more difficult to hold together all her magics and run the forty-yard dash behind Randolph. "Is that a grunt yes or a grunt no?"

The wrinkles in Randolph's granite face deepened. His voice grated on her nerves as he replied, "Of course he's for real. With all those people believing in him, and all the time he puts in, how can you doubt it?"

Alana winced as Randolph's grip on her arm increased, nearly cutting off the circulation to her hand. "No, I don't doubt it. I like to know what I'm getting into when it involves the welfare of my soul. It is the only thing we have in this world that we get to take with us. Working in a spiritual place such as this, you can understand the strength of my concerns."

"If you say so," Randolph replied, releasing Alana's arm

to undo the lock on the front door. Alana used the brief reprieve to rub her tingling fingers. "I've been working with Mr. Burke for two years now, known him even longer. He's got my respect. He's a man who knows what he's doing and where he's going."

"And where is that?" Alana asked, using her last bit of power to push at Randolph full force.

Randolph turned and gave her a penetrating look. "You sure you're here to join up? Seems to me like you have a lot of questions for someone interested in church membership. Most people aren't so . . . conscientious."

His mind felt like a rock wall standing against her powers. Alana's mouth twisted in disgust at her weakness, forced to focus all her energies back into keeping her disguise up. "Oh really? I thought everyone would check into things like this."

Randolph leaned back with arms crossed, blocking the door. His voice dripped dire threat as he spoke. "No, few people do. You wouldn't be trying to make trouble for Mr. Burke, would you?"

Alana let her eyes widen in shock. Taking a step back, she replied, "I'm not certain I know what you mean."

Randolph's eyes narrowed, not fooled by her innocent expression. "We get reporters around here sometimes, trying to make a name for themselves by smearing a good man like Mr. Burke. They think they can get a Pulitzer if they can prove he's just another religious opportunist using the television to get people's money. Mr. Burke's not hurting anybody. You'd think they'd mind their own business, wouldn't you?"

Alana nodded in agreement, tension tightening her muscles in preparation for battle. "I can assure you that I'm no reporter. I have no interest in Mr. Burke's financial dealings, beyond how they could help the community he serves."

Randolph stepped forward, until he stood mere inches from Alana. Looking down at her with hard eyes, he said, "Maybe you aren't a reporter, but that leaves me wondering who you are then. If I were you, I'd keep out of things here at Hands of Brotherhood Mission. We don't need trouble makers and non-believers." He leaned down close enough for Alana to smell the garlic he had for dinner on his hot breath. "Don't mess with things you can't understand, little girl."

Alana felt her powers flare protectively around her, before he stepped back to let her out the door. *I could give you the same warning,* she thought, staring up at him.

Alana stepped around his threatening bulk and pushed through the door into the fading daylight. The strain of keeping her glamour going for so long after working a casting on the same day began wearing on Alana. Waiting until Randolph walked back into the building, she released her illusion and headed for her car. She had nine days to catch a killer, and no idea what to do next.

So preoccupied with her dark thoughts, Alana almost missed the figure lurking beside her car. She came to an abrupt halt a few feet from him. Her heart hammered as the man leaning against her driver side door approached her, radiating pure anger.

"Don't say a word, I don't want to hear it. Give me your keys and get in," a chilly voice commanded.

Without argument, Alana tossed her keys to Leo and slid into the passenger's seat.

Chapter Sixteen

The sweltering summer heat in the car surrounded her, oppressive. Drips of sweat gathered at her hairline. Alana stared at Leo, not attempting to turn on the air-conditioning. She sat motionless, as though beside a large quantity of nitroglycerine ready to explode at the slightest movement. She watched with a building sense of unease as the tiny muscle in Leo's jaw ticked while his hands gripped and released the steering wheel over and over again.

"I should expl . . ." she began, her voice shattering the silence.

Leo held one hand in front of her face, never taking his eyes from the road.

Alana sat back, legs crossed and hands in her lap. Memories of sitting outside the principal's office came to mind.

"But . . ." she tried again.

He turned to face her. Alana recoiled at the cold, flat, cop's eyes that stared out at her. The temperature in the car plummeted. A lump formed in her throat, closing off any explanation.

"I suggest you *not* talk to me at the moment," Leo replied, his voice frigid and controlled.

Alana nodded in quick agreement, then turned to stare out the window at the darkness surrounding them. This recently opened part of the beltway lacked the lights that would eventually line it, leaving the road in a near pitch-blackness broken by the occasional headlights of approaching cars on the other side of the large, gravel median.

The gloom matched the feelings growing inside Alana.

Leo sped up to zip around one of the few cars traveling this bit of highway. Alana heard him take a deep breath as he eased his foot off the accelerator.

"I don't know what you thought you were doing or what you hoped to accomplish by the stunt you pulled today," Leo said, voice hollow.

Alana watched his hardened profile, trying to judge his emotions. "I only . . ."

Leo cut her off with a callous wave of his hand. "Don't say anything, don't try to explain." He rubbed the back of his neck, grimacing. "Do you have any idea what kind of havoc your little disappearance caused? You not only put yourself into God knows how much danger, but you wasted precious time Gabe and I could have used on the case. Instead, we spent an entire day combing the city for your sorry ass. If you don't care what my reaction might be, the fear you caused me, what about your friend Rick? Did you even consider what you put him through? There he is, in the hospital unable to help you, and you go and pull your vanishing act. What about his feelings?"

Alana waited for him to finish, her own temper growing by the second. "Can I respond now, or do you have more to say?" she asked, her calm voice covering the storm building inside her.

The corner of Leo's mouth edged up into a cruel half-smile at the sarcasm. "Oh, believe me, I have more to say to you, but you can *try* to explain your actions now."

Alana's eyes narrowed, temper flaring. She tugged at her seatbelt, turning in her seat to face him with a sneer. "Let's get one thing straight. I don't *have* to explain anything to you. I'm helping you with your case on a *voluntary* basis, letting you use me as bait for your killer. I'm not required to do anything, explain anything. One of my oldest friends is lying in a hospital bed because of me. You can't expect me to stand idly by. I needed to do something constructive. This guy's got to be put away if I hope to feel safe again. I knew Rick would understand, and I didn't think it would worry you all that much, considering I'm just a job."

Leo's grip on the wheel tightened, his knuckles whitening. Alana expected to hear the plastic pop at any moment. Worse, she suspected that he imagined the wheel being her neck. "Didn't think is right," he growled. "That's the only thing you've said that makes sense. You didn't think. You're lucky that Burke and his goon didn't figure out what you were up to. You could be dead right now. And you didn't even find out anything useful for your troubles, did you?"

Alana's body sagged into the seat, her eyes swinging back to look at the glow of city lights in the distance. "No."

Leo grunted, slapping the wheel. "I didn't think so. Burke's too smart for that. And how the hell did you get out of Rick's room in the first place? I was standing right in front of the door."

"I was the blond nurse that had been cleaning Rick's bathroom, the one Gabe hit on," she mumbled, refusing to look his way.

The muscle in Leo's jaw started ticking again, his fingers tapping the wheel in time with each tick. "That's damn creepy. I didn't realize it was you. How am I supposed to protect you when I can't even recognize you? I can't keep you safe when you put yourself in dangerous positions. You could have been killed."

"But I wasn't." Alana's voice sounded weak and defensive, even to herself.

Leo's eyes radiated disdain as he glanced at her again. "The way I'm feeling right now, I might finish the job. You little *idiot!* I'm working my ass off to keep you alive and you go off and risk your neck on a whim. I can't take any more explanations from you right now. I won't be held responsible for my actions. I don't want to hear another word from you until we get home."

"Yes, Daddy Dearest," she mumbled under her breath.

Leo chose to ignore her small rebellious comment. He couldn't be angrier with her than he already was. He'd spent the entire day with various images of her broken, lifeless body flitting through his mind. He was horrified to realize how much her life had come to mean to him. All day, the thought of Alana in danger sickened him. Finding her coming out of the lion's den sent his temper surging.

A heavy thump pushed the front of the car.

Leo's hands jerked at the wheel, fighting not to swerve from the impact. With no time to react, Leo looked out in horrified fascination. A harsh shriek pierced the air as a dark figure clawed its way up the hood, nails ripping through the metal. The familiar, hairy monstrosity glared up, snarling.

"Shit!" Leo managed to curse a split second before the creature reached the windshield. Its sickly green eyes glowed with voracious intent before the vaguely canine head reared back. Its bloodcurdling howl cut through the night, sending chills racing through Leo's body. A growl rumbled from between the creature's shark-like teeth seconds before its head smashed through the windshield.

Alana shrieked and grabbed for something on the floor in front of her as chunks of breakaway glass rained down on them. Leo squinted in the sudden rush of air slamming against his face. He jerked the wheel right and left, swerving the car across both lanes. The creature's claws, lodged deep in the hood, held it motionless throughout the violent maneuvers. Its head swung back and forth, nose quivering in search of its prey.

The creature's face turned away from Leo. It lunged through the window, focused on Alana. The gun strapped in his shoulder holster occurred to Leo too late for him to reach it. With one hand gripping the wheel, Leo sunk his fingers into the scruff of the thing's furry neck. He yanked back with every ounce of strength he had, holding its snapping jaws away from Alana's pale face.

The creature ignored Leo, digging its claws deeper into the dashboard. It pushed forward, snapping and shaking its head, slinging burning saliva. Blue and white sparks skipped and danced across the dash as it managed to tear into the wiring beneath.

Leo cursed, jerking the wheel toward the gravel median, his one arm straining under the pressure of keeping the car straight as it tipped and bounced on the uneven surface.

Leo's grip on the creature weakened as it twisted and writhed. Its oily fur slipped through his fingers. Leo watched as it rocked back on its haunches, cat tail twitching as it prepared to launch itself at Alana. There was only one thing to do.

The moment the creature loosened its grip on the dash to leap forward, Leo slammed on the breaks.

The creature flew out of the car, smashing into the ground and rolling several yards. Leo shoved the car back into gear, ready to peel onto the road.

Alana jerked her seatbelt off and jumped out, dragging her purse behind her.

"What the hell?" Leo gasped, fumbling with his own belt

and scrambling out after her.

Alana upended her purse, spilling the contents across the gravel. Falling to her knees, she pawed through the pile until she came up with a sheathed dagger. She pulled off the protective leather and kissed the blade. Leo stood in amazement as she held the blade to her forehead and mumbled while the monster shook itself off.

Leo jumped between the creature and Alana, pulling out his weapon and pumping shot after shot into it. With each impact, the creature twitched but kept coming. Running out of ammo, Leo dropped the gun. He stood with legs parted, knees bent, and arms out, preparing for the onslaught.

Leo felt a moment of panic as the thing snarled at him, displaying row after row of serrated teeth. But it stopped a few feet away, glaring and spitting. Leo felt the wind rise behind him, whipping at his hair, as a glowing red light encompassed the area, growing brighter and brighter before changing to a pure white. All sound ceased except for Alana's husky voice chanting.

"Hungry and seeking, true prey you lack. To your master, return your attack. Evil deeds rebound, three times three. As I will, so mote it be."

The white light exploded in brilliance, blinding Leo. He could hear the shrieks of the creature echoing around him. The wind tore at his body, forcing him to his knees.

Silence and stillness fell in an instant.

Leo staggered to his feet, turning to Alana. She sat in the gravel, shoulders heaving as she panted. Her hair tumbled in front of her face, blocking the beginnings of a massive bruise covering one cheek. Scrapes and scratches decorated both of her arms.

Leo knelt down, taking her cold hands into his. He pried

the fingers of her right hand loose of the dagger, his own fingertips tingling as they grazed the blade. Feeling the power in it, if not understanding, he placed it reverently on top of her fallen purse.

"Are you hurt?" he whispered, lifting Alana's hair from her face.

"I'm sorry," she replied, voice trembling. "This was my fault. I misjudged. I didn't think he would retaliate so soon."

Leo cupped her face, tilting it towards him, his fingers grazing her swollen cheek. "What do you mean?"

"Whoever hurt Amber, I expected more time to prepare," was all she managed to say before she started to topple.

Leo scooped her up and carried her back to the car. His heart dropped back to its normal place in his chest when he saw her curl on her side in the backseat. She was alive. She was safe.

No thanks to him.

Chapter Seventeen

Alana regained consciousness lying on the fluffy brown couch in Leo's living room. She eased up with one hand on her head trying to keep her brain from sloshing too hard against the inside of her skull. Her head throbbed all the way to the tip of her nose. Even her teeth ached. She thanked every god she could remember that Leo left the lights dimmed.

"I have some tea if you'd like," Leo said from the doorway. Alana started, wincing as pain exploded behind her eyes. "I remember Rick bringing you some the last time," he continued, voice expressionless.

Alana groaned, sliding the hand from her head to her churning, queasy stomach. "You have mint or chamomile?" she asked through chattering teeth.

"Mint."

"Sounds perfect. Drown it in honey. I could use the sugar burst."

Leo turned without replying. Alana forced her feet to the floor and started taking stock of herself. Other than various cuts, bruises, minor burns, and aching muscles, physically she was fine. Remembering the sight of those gnashing teeth so close to her face, the smell of its fetid breath, Alana shuddered. Thanks to Leo, the cearb didn't get close enough to do much damage.

She held out one hand, palm up, and concentrated on

light. A faint floral scent rose around her, barely noticeable. A tiny, pale glowing ball appeared, hovering inches above her palm. Its light, cool to the touch, flickered but held. Not much, but at least she hadn't completely drained herself.

Hearing Leo in the hallway, she closed her hand on the orb and leaned back. "How long was I out?" she asked as Leo leaned over the coffee table to put her cup on a coaster.

"About two hours. It's just past midnight. I put your purse in your room after I tucked you in here, where I could keep a better eye on you," he replied, voice devoid of emotion.

Alana winced. "Only two hours. That's an improvement over last time."

"Yeah, an improvement," he muttered, the first traces of anger showing in his voice.

Alana ignored the irritation she heard. He had a right to be annoyed. All things considered, she was shocked he hadn't tossed her out. "You got us home. I'm impressed considering what happened to your car. I'll pay for the damage."

Leo looked her in the eyes for the first time. She trembled in the face of his volcanic rage. "No, you will not pay for the damage to my car. Do you think I give a damn about my car right now? I could care less if it was *totaled*. We were nearly ripped apart by a thing I don't even have a name for. You've been lying here, dead to the world for two solid hours, not moving an inch. I checked every fifteen minutes to see if you were breathing. And I still have no idea what happened or how we got out alive."

Alana's lips trembled, but she refused to break down. She wrapped her arms around her chest, steeling herself to face his hatred. "You deserve an explanation."

"Damn right I do," Leo muttered as he reached for a blanket lying on the floor. He tucked it around Alana's shoulders before settling in next to her.

A small piece of her heart melted. He didn't hate her. Yet. She gripped the edges of the blanket, pulling it tight. "The creature that attacked us was the same one you saw before, the one after Amber."

Leo nodded, but sat silent, his face unreadable.

Alana cleared her throat before continuing. "It's called a cearb, the Killing One. They inhabit areas of Scotland."

"Las Vegas is a far cry from Scotland," Leo commented, his dry tone giving Alana no clue as to his thoughts or feelings.

She nodded, fidgeting more with the edge of the blanket, sliding the seam between her fingers. "True. It had to be sent here."

Leo perked up, a slow, evil smile spreading across his face. "You mean a person is responsible for this."

"Yes," she replied, afraid of where this was going.

"Tell me who and I'll see he's brought in. I can't charge him for sending magical creatures out to kill people, but if he did this there's bound to be normal crimes I can connect to him."

"That won't be necessary," Alana replied, voice cracking at the thought of what she had done.

Leo waved her words away. "I know you think you have this whole mystical protection thing going, but I'm a cop. I know how to handle bad guys."

Alana reached out, running her hand along his cheek, enjoying the rough texture of his unshaven skin. "I believe you, but after tonight, I doubt there's much left to arrest."

When Leo started to argue, she placed her fingers against his lips. "I sent the cearb back to his master. You heard me. I sent back his wrath, three times three. I doubt the creature left more of its master than a few smears."

Leo pulled away from her and leaped to his feet to pace in front of the fireplace. "I can't trust that. Until I hear of a weird missing person case, I have to assume this freak is out there. That's it, I'm getting you out of here, taking you someplace I have more control over."

"More than your own house?"

The look Leo gave her was less than pleased. "I want a more secure environment. Too much is left to chance here. There are too many variables to take account of. It's impossible to protect you while surrounded by so many people. I need a place I can close down if I have to, a place that no one else should be going to, unless they're our killer. Someplace I can control all the variables."

"And where is this mystical safe haven?" Alana couldn't help the sarcasm from slipping into her voice.

Leo stared off into space for a moment, a small, malicious smile twisting his lips again. "I think I have the place. I need to give Gabe a quick ring first, make sure it's okay and to have him set it up with the department. But I think it will be perfect." He shook himself to stare at Alana once more. "Pack up your things. We're headed out of town."

"Where and for how long?" she asked his retreating figure. "I didn't pack for an extended stay anywhere."

Leo shrugged, oblivious as his mind whirled with details involved in the move. "That's okay. If you need more, I'll send Gabe out for it. As long as you have some jeans and a sturdy pair of shoes, you should be okay for the time being."

A true city girl at heart, Alana didn't like the sound of that. She dropped her blanket to the floor and leaned forward. "Where are we going?"

Leo's foot began tapping as he answered her. "The department's got a cabin tucked away up in the Mount Charleston area that we use as a safe house. It's off the beaten trail, takes a jeep to get up there. It's small, surrounded by a large amount of privately owned land, bordered by parkland. It should be perfect. We'll stop and grab some groceries on the way. After that, we'll be safe and secluded for the time being. If anyone other than Gabe shows up, we'll know to be on our guard."

Alana gave a mental prayer of thanks that she'd had the foresight to fill her purse with the bare magical necessities before leaving her house. If the place was as small as he said, it should be easy enough to put up an effective ward with the things she had stowed away. And her leaving town might be what was needed to drag her stalker out of hiding before any Otherworldly intervention.

"Okay, you call Gabe and I'll start packing," Alana replied, dragging herself off the couch and stumbled to her room.

"That's my girl."

Alana froze for a moment, letting that soft-spoken phrase flow over her. She'd never liked being referred to as a girl. At her height, few people identified her as a child, and any who did were taunting her. But she liked the sound of it coming from Leo. Maybe this little retreat would have added bonuses that she hadn't considered.

Secluded in her guest room, Alana pulled out Rick's cell and dialed Fiona's number. This would be her last bit of complete privacy for some time. She'd better take advantage of it. Holding the phone with her chin as she threw her clothes back in her suitcase, she listened to the ringing.

"Bell, Book, and Candle. How may I help you?" a breathless voice answered.

"It's me again, Sis," Alana replied as she tried to zip up her bulging bag. "Have you found out anything yet?"

Fiona's worry was almost palpable, even over the extreme distance. "I'm glad you called, Alana. I don't like the feelings I'm getting from all this. You need to be careful out there."

"Anything more concrete than feelings, though?" Alana asked, eyes staring at the door, willing Leo to take his time with his own calls.

Fiona snorted. "I wish. It would make me feel better if I had something concrete to tell you. I'm too drained to get anything clear. All I can say is that it's a man with a major hate on for you. It's personal with him. You've managed to piss him off."

A bitter smile glided across Alana's face. "Well, that's nice to know. I'd hate to think I'm the only angry party in all this. But can't you tell me anything more than what he's feeling?"

"I wish I could." Alana could hear Fiona gritting her teeth. "I don't have enough umph to get a clearer fix. If you can give me a few days, I'll try again. But that's all I can tell you for now."

Alana collapsed on the bed, looking up at the blank ceiling, trying to picture her sister's face. Fiona might be the youngest, but she'd always had such a calming presence. Alana missed her, especially at a time like this. "Well, thanks anyway," she tried to reassure Fiona. "And do keep trying. The powers that be aren't happy with the situation. Bad mojo is going to come crashing down on Las Vegas if I don't end this thing soon."

Fiona's voice tightened with strain. Fear for her sister's safety echoed in her every word. "Maybe you should call Dad, or track down Adain. It sounds like you could use all the magical help you can get. If the Otherworld has decided to become involved, there's no telling what the carnage will be."

Alana's face hardened, determination gleaming in her eyes. "Not yet. I can't go running back to Daddy the first time things start getting rough. I have to be able to deal with this on my own."

Fiona made disagreeable noises. Alana continued before Fiona could state all her many logical objections. "If it gets down to the wire, I promise to ask for help. Until then, I'll work at it on my own."

Fiona gave a long-suffering sigh. "Alright, I'll leave you to it. I'll keep trying to see more, something that could help you. If I get anything, I'll call."

Hearing movement in the rooms beyond, Alana knew it was time to close this conversation and find a place to stash her phone. "You'll have to leave a message on Rick's cell. I'll have to turn it off from now on. Detective Grady and I are going into hiding for the time being, and I don't think he'll take kindly to me holding out on him. Especially if it's over some kind of contact with the outside world, when he's trying to protect me from it."

Fiona chuckled. "Trying to keep you out of trouble, is he? I wish him luck. Knowing you, he'll need it."

Alana rolled her eyes as she pulled herself out of the bed's tempting embrace. "Thanks a lot, Sis."

Fiona ignored the obvious sarcasm in Alana's reply, having heard that 'big sister' tone too many times to count. "You just promise to take care of yourself."

Alana laughed. "Don't worry. Today isn't a good day to die."

"Heaven forbid." For a moment, Fiona paused. Alana wondered if she saw something she didn't want to share. "I love you, Alana. I'd hate to be the only girl left in the Devlin clan."

There was no laughter in her voice as Alana replied, "I love you too, Fiona. And I promise to be extra careful."

Chapter Eighteen

The darkness became a physical presence by the time they reached the cabin, deep and murky. The barest sliver of a moon gave light to the area, all hint of civilization left far behind. Were it not for the jeep's headlights, Alana would have missed the cabin. As they bounced and jarred to a stop at the end of the rutted path, Max catapulted out of the back, intent on exploring his new surroundings.

Leo sat staring out the window, hand lying across the gearshift of Gabe's jeep. "Well, here we are. Hopefully it won't be as stark inside as it looks out here."

The small, log cabin sent a feeling of foreboding rising through Alana. It would end here, for better or for worse. Even though vision was not her gift, she knew that this was a place for endings. She kept her voice calm as she replied, "From the looks of things, I rather doubt it'll have red velvet curtains, satin sheets, and mirrors on the ceilings."

Leo chuckled at the image. "At least that would be colorful."

Leo looked over at Alana. Her milky skin looked paler in the weak light, her features tense. He noticed her hands twisting together. Without thought, he reached over and pulled her into his arms. "Don't worry," he muttered, holding her head to his shoulder and smoothing her fiery curls. "I won't let anything happen to you, I promise. I know I gave you a hard time before, with you disappearing and all. You worried me. But I won't let my guard down. I'll take care of you, I promise."

Leo felt her lips curve into a smile against his neck. He squeezed her shoulders before moving her away. "Now you go on up, I'll grab the bags."

Alana nodded, sliding out of her seat and stumbling towards the cabin. She couldn't help but be touched by Leo's caring gesture, even if it meant more to her than it meant to him. She felt guilty that she hadn't been worrying about herself, as he thought. Alana couldn't help thinking about what would happen to Las Vegas if she didn't catch the killer soon.

If the Otherworld sent the Wild Hunt into Las Vegas to seek vengeance against the killer, confusion and disappearances would break out across the city. While Herne and his people would not stop until they found the killer, they were not above taking any mortal who fell within their reach. Any who did not lock themselves in their homes at the mere sound of the baying hounds and charging steeds would be swept along with the Hunt. Herne and his followers would see this as a chance for sadistic play with paltry mortals. With luck, people would think they were delusional as the green clad faeries rode wildly down the Strip. But the result would still be the same. Utter havoc.

But the Hunt might be the best-case scenario. If the Sluagh came, the consequences would be dire. So many different types of faerie existed in that group, dark, Unseelie fey. Mischief, murder, and mayhem would rule until they were called off. Not much would be left of the city, possibly even the state. The killer would be punished, but the number of innocents paying right along side would be astronomical.

And God forbid if the Otherworld released the Morrigna

on the city. The triple war goddess of the Tuatha de Danann would leave no mortal alive. Badb, delighting in slaughter, would incite open fighting on the streets, raising fury in all she encountered. Macha would raise those battles into an all-out street war while Morrigan bathed in the blood of the dead.

Alana forced her thoughts away from the possible horrors. She couldn't let it happen, that was all. Instead she concentrated on the cabin, planing the best way to defend it. As luck would have it, the building was small, cozy. It wouldn't be hard to ward. Not with only two rooms and one entrance.

A living room with an attached kitchen took most of the cabin's floor space. A wood-burning fireplace stood at one end while a gas stove sat against the other wall. Spartan would be a kind way to describe the furnishings. The kitchen had a small, dusty table with two chairs, doubling for both a preparation and eating area. One old, battered couch sat alone in the living area, facing the fireplace. A woven, Navajo rug covered most of the scarred hardwood flooring.

Alana wandered into the only other room of the cabin, wondering who would have to sleep on the couch. She was surprised to find a set of bunk beds as the main feature. Alana fought a grin at the image of Leo trying to fit his huge form into one of the tiny bunks as he walked in behind her, tossing the bags on the floor.

Leo's shoulders sagged in relief at the room's bedding options, causing Alana to give a self-deprecating smile. "I hope you don't mind sharing the room. I gave the couch a test and there's no way anyone could get a decent night's sleep on it. It feels like something straight out of the Flintstones. I'll take the bottom bunk."

Alana fought back the sudden speeding of her heart. The thought of Leo sleeping in the same room with her forced a flush to creep over her skin, even with the innocent bed arrangements. She glanced about for something to distract herself. "I hope there's a bathroom in here. I don't look forward to visiting with the creatures of the night while answering the call of nature."

Leo gestured to a small door at the back of the room that Alana had assumed was a closet. "There's a toilet in there. No shower. Hopefully we won't be here long enough for the smell to become a problem."

Alana raised a brow, hands at her hips and foot tapping. "You had better not be referring to me. Oh, and don't worry, Detective. I'll be sure to let you know as soon as you become *too* offensive."

Leo snorted as he pulled a pair of blue sweats out of his duffel bag. "I'm sure you will, sweetheart," he replied as he moved toward the bathroom.

Alana pulled out her own nightclothes, a pair of loose cut-offs that had once belonged to Adain and an oversized UNLV T-shirt. She rummaged in her purse for a few other, more esoteric necessities. She glanced at the bathroom door and prayed that Leo would take his sweet time getting ready. Luckily stage one of her plan shouldn't take too long.

First, she put a light dusting of dried cowslip beneath Leo's pillow while muttering a short incantation. She would have made a tea out of it for him, but she didn't want to raise any type of suspicions if he slept too deeply. It wouldn't do for him to accuse her of drugging him or hexing him. But she needed Leo to sleep soundly if she was to have time to ward the cabin. She wanted to keep Leo out of this small habitual magic. He dealt well with what he had been exposed to so far, but she didn't want to push his limits, not over something as minor as a warding.

As it was, Alana barely had time to stash the container of cowslip back in her purse before Leo came back into the room, stretching and yawning. "I don't know about you, but I'm going to enjoy a good night's sleep tonight."

More than you know. "I agree," Alana replied, gathering up her clothes. She gave a self-conscious chuckle as she danced around him, trying to reach the bathroom in the close quarters. "It'll be nice sleeping somewhere I know I'll be safe. It should take him at least a day to track us down, right?"

Leo shrugged, pulling down the covers on the bottom bunk. Alana took great pleasure in watching the well-worn material of Leo's sweats pull tight, outlining a fine specimen of male buttocks. "It should. No one in the department except Gabe and the chief will know where we are until tomorrow morning." Leo glanced down at his watch. "Or I should say this morning. I didn't realize how late was. You go on and change, and we'll call it a night. Hopefully, we'll catch the bastard soon."

One way or another, you're right. "It'll only take me a second," Alana promised, eyes glued to his shoulders as he pulled off his T-shirt.

Leo didn't notice, or chose to ignore, her preoccupation. "Take all the time you need. Don't be surprised if I'm asleep when you get back."

Believe me, I won't be. Alana kept her thoughts to herself as she closed the bathroom door. There was less room to maneuver here, the toilet and small sink taking up the bulk of the closet sized room. But with running water, she'd be able to wipe off while roughing it.

Waiting several minutes for Leo to doze off, Alana crept out into the room. At the squeak of the door's ancient hinges, Leo murmured and tossed on his bunk. Alana eased towards him, chanting to herself, pulling her energies to her then surrounding Leo with a pale blue light. All the tension eased out of his body as he sagged into the bed.

Satisfied that he would be out of commission for long enough, Alana grabbed her purse and headed outside, patting Max's head as she scooted by the couch he'd claimed. In the near complete darkness outside, she pulled out a box of salt. Chanting in an ancient tongue, she began pouring it on the ground. Ignoring the cooling mountain air that sent goose bumps down her arms, her steps traced a complete circle around the cabin three times. The circle complete, Alana went back and retraced the area in front of the door as well as pouring more salt on each of the windowsills.

Satisfied that the first step was complete, with the help of a compass, she placed a small egg shaped piece of onyx at each of the cardinal directions, burying them in the ground, so as not to be visible to Leo. She then poured a bit of salt on top of each, making certain that no part of the circle was broken.

Stepping back, she considered her work. After checking that the physical parts of her ward were properly placed, she began the ritual. Pulling out her athame, she petitioned the four guardians, invoking their powers once more. Each area above the onyx began pulsing with different colored spectral light as, one by one, the guardians responded.

Finally, she called upon the gods and goddesses of old. Under normal circumstances, she would have included a petition to Morrigan for protection as well, but thought it not a good idea all things considered. Instead, her voice rang out, "Oh Brigit, Triple Goddess, I call to thee for wisdom and power to guard those who dwell within my circle. Oh Cerridwen, Mother Goddess, giver and taker of life, I call to thee for protection against all who seek to harm those within my circle. Oh Cernunnos, Horned God of nature and the underworld, I call to you for protection against creatures of both the mortal and astral plane. Oh Lugh, Celtic God of Light and Chief of the Tuatha de Danann, I call to you for the strength needed to protect myself and all those who dwell within my circle."

She then touched the tip of the athame to the circle of salt. Her eyes went up to the sliver of moon showing in the sky as she gathered her magics around herself. "Guard the circle, traced by three. As I will, so mote it be."

From the point of contact, a silver shimmer started outward, flaring when it made contact with the lights already glowing above the onyx. When the circle was complete, a dome of pure white energy flared around the cabin before fading from physical sight.

Reaching out with one hand, Alana could feel the throbbing of power. Any creature, mortal or immortal, that crossed the barrier with evil intent would immediately alert Alana. With more power pumped into the ward, she could restrain or even destroy the person, but the constant pull on her energies would leave her too weak. An early warning was the best she could do if she wished to keep the ward up for any extended period of time, especially as weak as she was.

Satisfied with her work, Alana gathered up her materials and went to bed. She would enjoy what rest she could get this night. It might be the last peace she had for some time.

Chapter Nineteen

Alana's mouth watered as she awoke to the crackling and smell of bacon. At first she laid still, soaking in the peaceful feeling of waking to someone else cooking breakfast for her. She couldn't remember the last time someone had done something that simple for her. Other people didn't take care of her. She took care of them. She let herself float in that carefree sensation for a moment, refusing to open her eyes.

Her stomach rumbled, reminding her of what little she'd eaten the day before. Alana arched her back and stretched, throwing her hands above her head and rapping her knuckles on the ceiling. With a mild curse, she sucked on her scraped flesh. She took a quick moment to orient herself, surprised that Leo hadn't woken her as he got out of bed and dressed. It wasn't like her to be so comfortable with someone else's presence.

Alana slipped out of the top bunk and pulled her clothes from the small bag she'd thrown together the night before. In the cramped bathroom, she made do wiping off with a washcloth and cold water, freshening up as much as possible before pulling on her jeans and T-shirt.

After tying her sneakers, she stepped out of the bedroom, avoiding tripping over Max by inches, before sliding into one of the two wooden chairs that formed the kitchen area. "Something smells good," she commented, reaching down to Max's head. The dog whined, his large, puppy eyes pleading, deserting her as Leo tossed him a burnt piece of bacon.

Leo smiled as he slipped a heaping plate of eggs on the center of the table in front of Alana. "I hope you like scrambled. I tried to fry them, but I don't know why I waste my time. They always end up scrambled." He turned for another plate filled with crisp bacon, missing Alana's quick grin. "I would have made toast, but doing it without a toaster is beyond me. I like my modern kitchen gadgets. So, plain bread will have to do."

It was clear to Alana that Leo meant this as a peace offering of sorts. She felt guilty for having put him through the worry and work of tracking her down yesterday. Even though she'd do it again, if the circumstances were the same, she still felt sorry for what he must have felt. It was good of him to try to put them back on even footing this morning.

Alana met his timid look with a smile and nodded towards the opposite chair. "I'm sure the eggs will be fine. Now sit down, you're making me nervous hovering around like a masculine June Cleaver."

The wooden chair groaned and creaked, the legs parting under Leo as he lowered himself down. He grimaced at the plaintive sound, clutching the seat. "The department needs to look into redecorating this place. Any more time passing, and I think some of this stuff will disintegrate."

Alana tossed back her head, her musical laughter dancing off the walls. "I don't know," she struggled to say between giggles, "I think the couch will end up being like Twinkies or non-fat cheese. When mankind goes into extinction, they alone will survive as a testament to our presence on this planet."

Leo's answering laugh sent strange, happy shivers down

Alana's spine. "Now that's a cheerful thought. Whoever comes next will know exactly what kind of losers the human race was. I can see it now, a museum display showing Homo Couchpotatus, sitting on the couch snarfing down Twinkies sprinkled with non-fat cheese. Very appealing."

Alana burst out laughing again in pure delight, causing a child-like grin to slide across Leo's face. He reached out to place his hand on hers. "It's good to hear you laugh. Things have been rough, I know. But it's nice to know that you still have the ability to laugh. Too many other people would have lost that by now."

Alana pulled her hand away and used her fork to swirl her eggs around her plate. She wasn't certain how to explain her way of looking at things to Leo, but it was important to her that he understood her. "I'd be lying if I said I wasn't scared. I'd also be a fool. But, for better or worse, this situation will pass, and I'll go on from there. Until then, I plan on enjoying life as I always have. No man will ruin that for me."

Leo stared at her for a moment, questioning, probing, before nodding in agreement. "I'm glad to hear it. I see too many people who, once something horrible happens to them, can't seem to find their way beyond being a victim. They get trapped in that moment, those feelings. In the end, the survivors allow the criminals to win by changing their lives because of fear. I'm glad you won't let Burke win."

Alana looked down at her scattered and congealing eggs, her appetite disappearing. Giving up, she sat her fork down. "Speaking of which, how much time do you think we have before he finds us?"

Leo sipped his coffee and stared into space, as if uncertain how blunt to be. "I give it until the afternoon," he answered. "By then, the leak in the department will have given Burke the information that we're at the cabin, and he'll have time to look through public records to find where that is. We should be safe until then."

Alana nodded, running her hands up and down her arms, feeling closed in. Trapped. "Do you think we could go for a short hike this morning, then? I know I'll be safest if I stay inside after that, and I'd like to enjoy a little freedom before I'm completely cooped up."

Leo's own face darkened at the distress crossing Alana's, who flinched when he slammed down his coffee mug. His voice softened. "I don't see a problem with that. But we'll stay close to the cabin. And we'll take Max. He's not the best protection in the world, more likely to lick an attacker to death than to fight him off, but he's a good early warning system."

Alana gave Leo a weak grin. "Sounds like a plan to me."

The day was warm and bright, not a cloud in the sky. A cool breeze offset the usual high temperature, something Alana was thankful for as she struggled to keep up with the ground-crunching pace Leo set. Leo made it a point to keep the conversation light and cheerful as they climbed up the narrow path. It was hard to imagine that someone was hunting her, trying to kill her in these peaceful woods. Alana lost herself in the fantasy that she was out on a weekend escape with a nice young man she was getting to know. Someone she liked, maybe more than like.

It was a nice fantasy.

And Leo made an excellent guide. While he had never been to the cabin before, he visited the Mount Charleston area whenever he could. He shared amusing little stories about his own misadventures with Alana, surprising her.

She lived for moments like these, ones she could tuck away and remember in the distant future.

She wished that this one moment would never end.

"Here's where the trail gets harder. It's worth it, though. Watch your step," Leo warned as the incline grew and the path began to switchback. Alana watched Max bound up past both humans, stopping to dash back to his master, his entire back-end wiggling. Alana gritted her teeth. *If the dog can do it,* she thought as she bent her knees and took smaller steps, but resorted to grabbing trees and hauling herself around several curves. She watched the ground for treacherous roots and slick rocks waiting to send her sliding down the mountain on her butt, looking up only when she paused for air. When Leo asked if she was all right, she told him that she just wanted to take a moment to absorb her surroundings.

Leo reached back a hand to help her during one of her sightseeing breaks, but she waved him off. "I may not be academy trained, but I can hold my own in a hike."

Leo shrugged and turned back, snagging a branch and throwing it to Max. Alana was glad that he couldn't see how her heart pounded against the wall of her chest, trying to escape from the unfamiliar amount of work. As physically demanding as her show was, she'd slacked since her dancing days. Martial arts and aerobics, she was looking into those two as soon as they got back to civilization.

Alana glanced up and groaned as she saw the rock steps set into the path on the last ten yards of the hike. She watched Billy-goat Leo hop up with no problems. She stuck her tongue out at his back before all but crawling those last feet.

Leo stood at the edge of the overlook, legs braced and hands at his hips. His shoulders arched back as he took a deep breath. "This is my favorite place in the world," he said, gesturing forward as Alana sidled up to him, trying to disguise her panting as slow, cleansing breaths.

Had Alana had any breath left, it would have caught in her throat. In the pure silence of the crisp mountain morning, the entire valley spread out before her, shades of interlacing browns and greens. Rugged mountains rose out of soft desert grounds. Shallow creeks wound in between the two, waiting for the melted snowfall of spring to fill its banks. The city itself looked magical, rising up in the distance like a fairyland, with castles, spires, and towers dotting the horizon. The haze of construction dust blanketing Las Vegas added to the illusion, appearing like a mist, shimmering around the mystic buildings.

Leo glanced down at Alana, her red hair clinging to her face and neck as she gasped for breath. "You should have told me you needed a rest. We could have stopped for a break," he scolded before finding a large pine tree twisting out of the rocks to sit under. He gave her drinks from his canteen then unpacked the fruit she had grabbed before they left the cabin. Alana couldn't wipe the happy smile from her face, sitting with Leo, enjoying a picnic while watching Max dash about, chasing grasshoppers.

When Leo stretched out to look at the sky, Alana found it natural to offer him her lap for his head. Mumbling that he couldn't believe he was tired after the incredible night's sleep he'd had, Leo slipped into unconsciousness.

Alana smiled to herself as she looked down at Leo. It was her fault that he was so tired. He was fighting off the effects of the spell she'd cast last night. She should have taken the time to remove any last remnants from him, but had been too caught up in the pleasure of the morning to think of it.

But she couldn't help being pleased with the end results. With his harsh features softened by sleep, Leo was handsome in a rugged, I-can-take-anything-you-throw-at-me, kind of way. His dark hair curled against his smooth brow. His normally worry-thinned lips curved up in a tender smile. Even the crook in his nose added to his endearing appeal. Having a kind, handsome man lying asleep in her lap wasn't a great hardship. For a few moments, Alana leaned over him and ran her fingers through his hair, enjoying the contentment that filled her.

Alana sat as still as possible, absorbing the feel of the moment, until her back began to ache from the slouched position.

Alana stretched out beside Leo, trying not to wake him as she moved his head, then turned on her side to get a better look at this new, peaceful facet of him. The light breeze stirred his mussed, dark hair across his forehead. Alana reached out to smooth it back into place.

Once her fingers touched his face, she couldn't pull herself away. She let her hand slide down his cheek, the rough texture of his whisker-roughened skin tickling her palm. With the edge of her thumb, she traced his bottom lip, remembering the taste of him. Craving it.

Leo mumbled in his sleep and rubbed his cheek into her cupped hand. Remembering the kiss he'd given her, Alana leaned forward, placing a gentle kiss on Leo's lips.

Leo's arm snaked around Alana's shoulders, pulling her closer. His mouth softened under hers, tempting her to deeper contact. She inhaled the masculine scent of his cologne as she moved her lips against his, parting them, snuggling closer for a more intimate taste. His hands slid down her back as her fingers laced through his hair, and the kiss began in earnest.

Alana knew when Leo awoke. For the briefest moment, his lips hardened against hers, and he started to pull back. Alana would have none of that. Wrapping herself in the taste of the fruit he'd eaten and that other taste that was purely Leo, Alana lost herself to sensation. Whimpering, she rolled atop him, trapping his body with her own. Leo moaned in response, holding her even tighter.

Alana's hands skittered over Leo, feeling his hard, exercise-warmed muscles contracting under the thin cotton of his T-shirt and the rough denim of his jeans. A groan vibrated deep in his chest, sending sharp shivers of response throughout Alana's body. She melted into him, her entire body pouring over his.

The feel of her body covering him triggered something in Leo, something Alana hadn't expected. In a sudden whirl, Alana found herself on her back, mouth still locked on Leo's, but now looking up into his blazing gray eyes. She let her lids flutter closed and gave over control to Leo.

Leo chewed on her full bottom lip, pulling at it before licking the same spot. He nibbled at her one moment, thrusting his tongue deep in her mouth the next. Alana whimpered at the building need coursing through her, setting fire to every part of her being. Her hands clutched at whatever part of his body she came in contact with as she arched and writhed beneath him. She yanked his shirt from his jeans, sliding her hands up his heated back, raking a path down with her nails.

The urge to feel her bare skin against his raged, the warm ache controlling Alana growing hotter. She wiggled away and pulled her shirt from her jeans. She whipped it over her head, breaking the kiss for a split second and baring her bra-covered torso to Leo's heated gaze.

Leo started down at her. A deep, primal hunger blazed

in his eyes, sending shivers of both fear and arousal racing to every erogenous zone Alana ever imagined having.

Alana watched as a look of shock replaced the hunger in Leo's eyes, turning them from heated flames to searing ice. He pushed away, whistling for Max while grabbing for Alana's T-shirt. He tossed the shirt to her without even glancing her way. "We can't do this. I can't do this. Not now."

Shame flooded her, a blush spreading from her cheeks down her neck. Alana fought to keep the hurt from her voice as she clutched the cloth to her heated chest. "It looked as though we had no problems doing this a moment ago."

Leo leapt to his feet as Max gamboled towards him, the look on his face causing the poor dog to skid to a stop, whimpering. "You know what I mean," he replied, voice grim. "It's my job to protect you, not jump you like some randy teenager who just discovered hormones."

Alana pulled her shirt over her head, but stayed sitting under the tree. "What if I have something to say about your little pronouncement? What if I decide to jump you?"

Leo shoved his hands in his pockets, refusing to look back at Alana. "Save it. For now, there's nothing to talk about."

Leo stalked off, a confused looking Max slinking behind him.

Alana stared at his retreating back, shocked and not a little insulted at how he'd turned away from her. Then her features hardened. No way Leo could dismiss what had happened between them. He wanted her as much as she wanted him. She remembered the feel of his hardened flesh pressed against her. It's not like he could hide it. No way was she letting him get away with discarding those feelings.

Things weren't finished here by a long shot.

Life was a precious gift, but a short one. Much too short to waste time when you knew what you wanted.

For better or for worse, Alana Devlin wanted Leo Grady. And if, God forbid, she had only nine days left on this earth, she was damn well going to enjoy every one of them.

Leo had better watch his back for more than Charles Burke. Alana intended to knock him off his feet the first chance she got.

Chapter Twenty

When Alana stumbled in the cabin, Leo was nowhere to be seen, but Max lay panting in the middle of the Navajo rug in front of the couch. She squatted down and pulled Max's head on her lap to scratch his ears. She heard movement and cursing coming from the bedroom. She started to scramble to her feet, but thought better of it. Staring at the door as another curse echoed, she decided it might be best to let him cool off before engaging in the next battle.

And Alana *was* expecting a battle.

She knew Leo was disturbed by the feelings developing between them. She knew that he didn't want to take things further. He would list all types of reasons why they shouldn't risk becoming any closer, reasons she would dismiss as she had no intention of letting things stay as they were.

She needed time to plan out a strategy, or at least time to let him stew before going on to the next step. So, she started a small fire in the fireplace, more for something to do to occupy her time than anything else, and settled in to wait on the lumpy couch, Max curled up beside her.

Alana sat, Max curled at her feet, a few minutes collecting her thoughts, before the bedroom door flew open, banging against the wall beside it. Max ran and cowered underneath the kitchen table as Leo stormed into the room. Alana felt the aura of the room take a decided dive into darker emotions. But she sat still, staring into the fire. Waiting for him to come to her.

Leo stalked forward until he stood looming down at her, staring with blank eyes the color of a storm at sea. "We need to get a few things straight."

Alana gazed up at him, measuring his every expression. "Such as?"

Leo sighed in exasperation, running one hand through his hair before sitting down beside her. He scooted back before turning to face her. "Don't act stupid. It's one thing I'd never accuse you of being. You know what I'm talking about. We have to talk about happened out there and what we need to do to prevent it from happening again."

Again, Alana stared at him as she replied, "What if I want it to happen again?"

Leo turned away from her to stare into the fire. A minute passed in utter silence before he managed to make a reply. "It can't happen again, at least not now. Your emotions are in turmoil. You've been placed in a frightening situation, and I represent safety to you. Any kind of relationship started under those circumstances is doomed from the start."

Alana leaned back against the arm of the couch, her own arms crossed against her chest. An angry sneer slid across her mouth. "Thank you so very much, Dr. Freud. I don't know what I'd do without you explaining my feelings to me. I wouldn't know where to start, being the weak-minded little female that I am." Her voice dropped an octave as she continued. "Give me some credit, Detective. I'm a twenty-eight year old woman, not some little thing living on her own for the first time. I think I can decide what my emotions mean and act accordingly without any help from you."

Leo's jaw clenched at the rebuke, but he nodded in

agreement. "I'll give you that much. But if you don't believe what I'm telling you, and I have been placed in enough of these situations to know how twisted our emotions can get, there are other things we have to consider. Getting close to you, attached to you, makes my job of protecting you that much harder. I can't risk making a mistake with your life because of my feelings for you."

Seeing the stark fear hiding beneath his words, Alana reached out and cupped his chin with one hand. She turned his head to face her. "And you think letting this relationship cross the line into the physical will change how you feel?" She gave him a sad smile, shaking her head as she slid her fingers across his cheek. "I hate to be the one to tell you this, but your emotions are already involved. At least I hope so, since I know that mine are. Can you look me straight in the eye and tell me that you feel nothing for me, with or without us doing anything else?"

Leo's eyes dropped from hers for a moment. Alana watched as he struggled with himself, fought against what he felt. Then his eyes swept upward again, to meet hers, defeat reflected deep within them. "No, I can't say that, even if I should. I know that feeling like this isn't right, could put you in greater danger, but I can't say that I don't care about you."

"Then there's nothing more to say, is there?" Alana asked, leaning forward.

Leo reached up and took her hand from his face, placing it on her lap before backing away from her. "But I don't have to make it any worse. If I had any sense, I'd turn over the job of protecting you to Gabe and concentrate on putting Burke behind bars."

Alana moved closer to him, using his discomfort with her presence to her advantage, keeping him off balance.

"Then why haven't you?"

Leo shifted back a bit more, trying to give himself the space he needed. "Because if anything happened to you, and I wasn't there to stop it, something inside me would die."

Hearing the stark need echoed in his voice, Alana leaned even closer. "But why? Why would it matter that something happened to me?"

Without warning, Leo closed the distance between them, fingers digging into her arms. He shook her, before thrusting her away. "Because I care too damn much, alright! I care about you, more than I should, more than I have a right to. And that could put you in danger. Don't you understand? It could slow my reflexes if it came to a confrontation between Burke and me. You could end up dead. I don't know if I can handle that. Is that what you wanted to know? Is that what you had to hear from me?"

"Yes," Alana whispered, crawling forward and leaning into his mouth. "Because I care more than I should about you, too."

When Alana's lips met Leo's, all his carefully constructed control vanished. His wild moan of defeat echoed in Alana's mouth as he dragged her across his body, lowering himself to lie across the couch with her body covering his. Alana's knees straddled his lower body as she put every pent-up emotion into her kiss.

Alana's fingers tore at Leo's clothing, wanting to touch him. Needing that physical contact. Leo's hands dove into her hair, forcing her mouth to fuse with his own, making it even harder for Alana's hands to explore his body.

Frustrated with not being able to reach his bare skin, Alana pulled Leo off the couch, never breaking the kiss. Pushing him onto his back on the Navajo rug, she pulled at his shirt, throwing it across the room. Leo groaned and twisted beneath her as she dug her fingers into his back, rubbing herself against his hard chest, nipping at his chin. Her hands roamed across his bare skin, paying particular attention to the small circle of puckered scar tissue at his shoulder, soothing it. Her tongue ran along a jagged strip that laced his collarbone, wondering at the pain such a wound must have caused.

Leo's mouth glided across Alana's face, down to her neck. Shivers of pleasure pulsed through Alana's body as he nibbled at the area her neck and shoulder joined, his whisker-roughened cheek adding to the sensation. A soft moan spilled from her, and Leo murmured in approval.

Leo's hands pulled Alana's T-shirt out of her jeans and over her head. Alana tossed her hair back from her face, a fiery cascade of silk. She arched to deal with the back clasp of her bra, the sight causing Leo to growl. He slid his hands over the skin of the stomach and up her ribs, enjoying the view her arched back gave him. "God, you're beautiful," he managed to gasp before she lay back atop him, her flaming curls cutting off all view of the outside world, enwrapping them in a silken cocoon.

Alana whimpered with building need caused by the feel of Leo's naked chest rubbing against her own. The rough texture of his coarse hair scraping against her breasts tightened her muscles from stomach to toes. She pulled back, laying her forehead against his chest. She panted as she struggled for control.

Leo was having none of that. He flipped Alana on her back, bringing them closer to the fireplace, his body wedged between her thighs. He stared down at her with a savage hunger. "You have no idea how I've dreamed of seeing you like this, spread naked beneath me, your hair flowing out like a curtain of flames around you, your body begging to be mine. God help me, but I've dreamed of this."

Alana's mouth curved into a smile as she peered up at him through heavy eyes. She reached up and pulled his mouth back down to hers, back into the one spell that was older than time itself.

Leo's hands skimmed down her sides to tease her skin above the waist of her jeans. Never breaking contact with her mouth, he worked the stiff material free, pulling back only long enough to jerk the offending garment from her body.

Alana laid before him naked and unashamed, this beautiful woman, filled with courage, lying there waiting for him. Leo took one split second to thank whoever sent him this blessing, before dealing with the last of his own clothes and joining her.

Alana basked in the peaceful feeling of Leo cuddling her close to his side, the fire at her back heating her naked skin. Perfect silence filled the little cabin. The wooden floor was hard and the Navajo rug scratched her delicate skin, but Alana wouldn't trade the moment for anything. It was wonderful to lie in Leo's arms, soaking up the warmth and comfort of his body.

"I could get used to this," Leo said as he pulled Alana a bit closer, slipping a knee between her thighs. "Even if it is a bad idea."

Alana flinched at his words. She used one finger to make whirls in his chest hair. "Oh, I wouldn't agree with that. I think it's a *very* good idea, an excellent idea. A wonderful idea, even if the rug burns keep me from sitting down for a while."

The purr in Alana's voice, along with her words, caused

Leo to give a self-satisfied chuckle while running a hand down her back. "I guess it's too late to back out now."

Alana burrowed closer, feeling as though she could crawl underneath his skin and be happy. She placed a wet kiss on the side of Leo's neck. "Mmmm, much too late."

Leo took a moment to soak in the idea, the thought of having her next to him for longer than one night, smiling to himself as he kissed the top of her head. He reached up to free a few strands of her hair caught in his whiskers, twirling them between his fingers before smoothing the curl back beside her face. "I can't say I'm unhappy with that. This might not have been the smartest thing I could do, but it was by far the most satisfying."

Alana leaned back on her elbows, causing his eyes to widen at the sight of her magnificent breasts so close to him. She gave him a mischievous, lascivious grin. "We aim to please."

Leo forced his gaze up from the marvelous view to look deep into her eyes, willing her to understand his feelings without him having to come out and say it. He knew it was much too early to tell her how much he felt for her. He wanted her to understand his commitment without having to say the words. Those three little words made everything much more permanent, and he wasn't ready for that. "I want you to know, I don't plan on disappearing after this is over. I want to have a relationship with you. So you'd better get used to having me around."

Alana felt the underlying seriousness in his voice. For all his words, Leo still looked rattled, like a man who'd been hit full on by a freight train and didn't understand what had happened to him. She decided humor was her best way of responding without scaring him. "I intend on getting used to *having* you. I plan on *having* you as often as I can. And you'd better not disappear. That's my line of work, so I'd be sure to find you. And believe me, you wouldn't like what I'd do to you after I found you."

Leo reached down and gave her behind a playful squeeze, causing her to squeal. "Are you sure? I've liked everything you've done so far."

Alana scowled down, her face set in mock severity as she tapped one finger against his chin. "Oh, I can be dangerous when I put my mind to it."

Taking her by complete surprise, Leo flipped Alana on her back. Smiling down at her scowling face, he slid his hands down her body. "Oh really? Funny, I wouldn't have guessed that."

Alana giggled and writhed as Leo began tickling her naked sides. She gasped for breath, hands pushing against his to no avail. She squirmed against his body, but could not break the contact.

Watching her in this moment of pure enjoyment, Leo was struck by how happy being with her made him. His smiling face turned serious. He took his hands away, staring hard at her, trying to impress her every feature, every nuance, into his memory. "You are so perfect. I can't believe you're here with me."

Alana's heart ached at the pure hunger and need reflected in his expression. She reached up to pull her face closer to his own. "I *am* here, and I'm here to stay. Remember that."

Leo kissed her and pressed his forehead to her own. "I'll try to. But so much is happening in your life. I want to be with you, to stay with you. I just have a hard time looking past this whole thing with Burke. I worry that you won't want to be here with me afterward. I might become a reminder of all the horror you've gone through."

Alana lifted his head away from her own, forcing him to look at her. She slid her fingers through his thick black hair as she shook her head. "That will never happen. I *will* be here with you. You're the only good thing to come out of this mess. Burke doesn't matter to me, not in the long run. I won't let him matter. *You* matter."

Leo's worry-filled eyes looked down into hers, searching for any sign of doubt. "And how much do I matter? I know what you mean to me, Alana. More than I can say, more than I want to admit. This isn't just sex for me, but I wonder about you. Where do you see us after all this is over?"

Alana stared up past his shoulder, her eyes clouding over as she tried to look into the future. She couldn't tell if what she saw was truth or wishful thinking, as vision wasn't her gift. But either way, she shared it. "I see you with me. I see us together. I see us getting closer, developing a relationship. I see the look on my father's face when he meets you for the first time. I see my brother giving us a hard time at Christmas dinner. I see you lying beside me in my bedroom, curled around my body. But mostly, I see you sharing my life."

Her eyes cleared, a soft blush rising up her face. "I hope that doesn't scare you."

Leo continued staring down at her, not certain how to respond. The images she created sent a shot of pain and pleasure straight to his heart. He so wanted to belong in that picture. As frightening as the thought of getting that close to a woman again was, the idea of being with Alana drew him. Even the thought of meeting her family and becoming part of it, weird as they might be, attracted him. He could close his eyes and see it. Her family and his, gathered around the dinner table, celebrating some holiday together.

A wistful smile crossed his lips at the image. "I know my parents will love you. They'll be surprised by you, but they'll love you."

Alana's brow wrinkled with concern. "Why surprised?"

Leo shook his head to clear it, collapsing on his side and staring at the ceiling. His stomach clenched at the thought of his parents, as it always did. "It'll surprise them because of what I told them I wanted for my life. I went on about how I was going to make a normal life for myself. I'd get a normal, steady job, find a normal wife, settle down and raise a normal family, in a normal neighborhood. You were right when you said my house looked like something out of a Norman Rockwell painting. That was what I was looking for. I don't think you fit the whole image I painted for my family."

Alana turned towards him, feeling exposed, feeling the weight of her nakedness for the first time. She found herself wishing they'd made it to the bedroom, so she'd have a sheet to tug around her as she asked her next question. "Then why paint that image for them? Why do you need things to be so normal?"

Leo gave a self-deprecating shrug. He didn't want to get into all this, not the first time they were together. But there were things that the person you slept with, that you wanted to develop a relationship with, would normally already know. He hated talking about his past, but Alana deserved to understand what kind of a family she could be getting into.

He lay in silence for a moment, deciding how to proceed. He sighed and settled for laying everything out in the open. "You'd have to know my parents," he answered, not looking at her. "They were both part of the hippie generation, *really* part of it, to the point that both sets of my very

Irish Catholic grandparents washed their hands of them before I was born. Both my parents are struggling artists. My father makes pottery while Mom paints these ethereal portraits of people she meets. Lovely stuff, in a spooky, Otherworldly kind of way."

He stopped, his mind going back in time, back to all the childhood anger and insecurities. Alana took his hand, encouraging him to continue. He gave her hand a small squeeze in return. "We never lived in one place for more than a year, never put down any roots. The closest we ever came was the ten months we spent living in a commune in Arizona. But even that didn't give me a chance to make friends, being home schooled. Not many kids want to go out in the middle of nowhere to hang out with someone they barely knew, and parents didn't want to let their kids go out into the middle of the desert with a bunch of nuts. I hated all the moving, the isolation. I hated not having a home, not belonging anywhere. That's why I told them I wanted a 'normal' life. Somehow, I don't think a girlfriend who's a stage magician, much less one who's a fairy with magical powers, will fit that picture."

"Why me then?" Alana asked, almost afraid of the answer.

Puzzlement etched Leo's expression as he looked back at her, sensing the underlying insecurities in her question. "Why not you? You're beautiful, caring, and courageous as hell, maybe too much so at times. So you're not the typical housewife type. Maybe I'm not cut out for that type of woman anyway."

There was something in the way he said it, some tiny bit of pain in his words, that caught Alana's attention. "Why not? I'd hate to think you'd settled on me."

Leo let a single red lock of her hair curl around his

finger, clinging to his skin like molten silk. The wildflower scent he always associated with her rose up from that single strand. "Never think that. I don't think I knew what the perfect woman was for me until I met you."

Alana tugged her hair from his hand and sat up, arms crossing against her stomach. "You didn't answer my question. Why don't you think you're cut out for a 'normal' type of woman?"

Leo's brows came together as he watched her withdraw into herself. He didn't understand what she could be thinking. She couldn't think she wasn't good enough for him. That was a laugh. "I'm a cop," he said. "It's not an easy job. Not for me and not for the woman in my life. A woman has to have a certain kind of strength to her to be able to survive being a cop's wife. *You* have that. Not many other women do."

"And you have experience with that, I presume." Her voice had a hard, chilled edge, but Alana moved closer, dropping her arms.

Again, Leo found himself going back to a time of pain and heartache. But Alana needed to understand all the baggage she'd be getting if she stuck with him. "I was engaged once, back when I was in uniform. A domestic dispute was called in. The guy opened fire as soon as he saw the squad car then charged my partner and me with a knife. My partner didn't make it. I was wounded, not badly, but I was in the hospital for a while and went through months of physical therapy to get my shoulder working right. Healed up as good as new and went back to work. I get a twinge when the weather changes, that's all. Tina left me before I ever got out of the hospital."

Alana looked at the scar tissue on his shoulder and understood the fear that the other woman must have felt. But she would never leave this man, not over something like that and not at a time when he needed her. "Then it was her loss."

Leo smiled and pulled Alana back down to his side. She held herself stiff for a moment, before melting into him. The lump of fear that had been growing in Leo's chest as he confronted his past for her began to ease. "I thought you'd say something like that. It's one of the things I . . . like most about you." Leo caught himself before saying a much stronger L word. It wasn't time for that yet.

Alana snuggled deeper into his embrace, but couldn't keep the doubt from rising within her. The vision of Jack's face the last time she saw him, twisted with disgust, fear, and hatred, filled her mind. The words he'd hurled at her that last time echoed in her mind, tearing at old wounds she'd thought had healed long ago. She could only hope that Leo would be more tolerant. After all, he'd taken everything in stride so far.

For the moment, hope was all she had.

Leo leaned over, placing a gentle, nibbling kiss on her mouth. A heavy tension began to build through her body, pooling low and hot. She turned into his arms to enjoy him once again.

Suddenly, Max began barking outside. With a sharp curse, Leo jerked away from her, grabbing for his jeans. He hopped into the tight denim while making his way to where he'd left his gun on the kitchen table.

Alana watched, wide-eyed, as he raced out the door.

Chapter Twenty-one

Leo knelt on the ground underneath the kitchen window. Between his fingers he held a pinch of white crystals. He touched it to the tip of his tongue, trying to identify the familiar substance. A salty flavor filled his mouth before he spat it out. Again, he looked at the footprints, ending at the very edge of the line formed by a thin stream of salt.

His brows wrinkled as he considered the crystals. Was this Alana's doing? When had she done it and why?

Shaking off the edgy feeling, Leo knelt down again, this time concentrating on the footprint. The gritty dust didn't make for good medium for long-lasting prints. A gentle breeze would wipe away the deepest mark. The fact that there were prints here at all meant that they must be recent. The pattern didn't fit any shoe he owned, and it was too large to be Alana's.

Leo jerked as Max bounded out of the trees, still barking and wiggling for attention. When he made to leap for his master, Leo pointed a single finger at him.

"Sit!"

Immediately, if with a bit of whining, Max plopped his tail down a few feet from Leo and the print, panting and drooling. A large, doggy grin spread over his muzzle. He knew he'd done something good, and it was only a matter of time until his master rewarded him.

A soft crunch behind him had Leo whirling about, gun

raised. Alana scrambled back, hands raised above her head. "Don't shoot. I'm on your side."

"Get your sweet ass back in the cabin," Leo growled as he scanned the tree line, lowering the gun to his side, but not putting it away.

Alana refused to look at the weapon in his hand, locking her eyes to his own. "Not before you tell me what's going on or come back in yourself."

The sharp pinch of fear still gripped Leo's chest, making his voice harsher than he intended. "What's going on is someone's trying to kill you. He's started casing the cabin. And now you're standing out here, making the perfect target for him. Get your ass back in the cabin."

For a moment, Alana's expression took on a rebellious cast. But even if she didn't like how he said it, she couldn't argue with Leo's logic. She was putting herself in danger standing out here. But then, so was he.

Alana straightened to her full five foot, eleven inches. With a toss of her head, hands placed on her hips, she stared Leo down. "Okay, I'll go back. But don't forget that you make just as good a target standing out here as I do. With you out of the way, there's nothing to stop Burke from coming in and doing whatever he wants to me. It's not like 911 would get here quick enough to do any good."

Leo nodded vaguely and waved her towards the cabin again, forcing his own fear from his mind. He had a job to do. That was all there was to it. "I'll be careful. And we'll talk about your concerns in a second. But right now, I want you inside. I can take care of myself. We're not dealing with a monster, so that makes me the expert."

Alana gritted her teeth before flouncing back towards the door. Still, she couldn't keep from calling back behind her, "Fine, but don't blame me when you get shot and have to drag your bleeding carcass back inside without my help."

Leo couldn't prevent the small grin from sliding across his face at the snippy sound of her voice. But he wiped it away to concentrate on seeking evidence of their visitor.

Alana paced back and forth in front of the fireplace. She rubbed her hands up and down her arms as she stared at the pattern in the rug beneath her bare feet. Why did he have to be so stubborn? Yes, he was the cop and she was the victim, but that didn't make the man bulletproof. What was she supposed to do if something happened to him, throw rocks at Burke and pray for a good shot?

Alana lost all track of time, mind focused on horrific pictures of Leo's dead, bleeding body. How long had he been out there, anyway? What was taking so long? Maybe she should go out and check on him, see if everything was okay. It would be all right to stick her head out the door and give him a yell.

Just when she didn't think she could stand a second more of waiting, the door swung open. Alana jerked, eyes widening and body clenching, preparing for battle.

A grim-faced Leo walked in, followed by a joy-filled, prancing Max.

"What did you find?" she asked, barely managing to hide the quiver in her voice. She hated not having any control over the situation, being forced to find out what was happening secondhand.

Leo tucked his gun into the front of his pants before turning to check the bolt lock on the door. "Someone was here. He walked the perimeter of the cabin, but must have been scared off by Max barking before he tested the door. He ran off through the woods. I would have tracked him further, to where he left his jeep, but I didn't want to leave you alone for so long, in case it was both Burke and Randolph, not just the one man."

Alana nodded, fighting the urge to throw herself into his arms. Her nerves were on edge and she could use all the comfort she could get. But he was in cop mode and not an approachable hugging target. "So your plan to draw him out seems to be working. What do we do now?"

Alana shadowed Leo as he walked straight to the bedroom. He pulled out his pack, removing a second gun. "First, I'm going to put this somewhere you can get to quickly. Then I'll show you the basics of how to use it. You're right about being defenseless out here, if anything happened to me. This will help. I'm guessing you don't have much experience with firearms, so I'll take you outside and give you a quick rundown on it. But remember to use it as a last resort, and stick to close range. You don't want it taken from you, but there's no telling what kind of aim you've got. You'll be able to do some damage at close range."

Eyeing the weapon with no little suspicion, she asked, "Will I have to worry about where I hit him?"

Leo gave her a grim smile. "This is a .45 caliber. It'll jerk like hell in your hands, but if you hit him anywhere, you'll leave a *really* big hole. Big enough that he'll lose all interest in you, with the possible exception of cussing you out. Believe me, it'll be one hell of a distraction."

A sick feeling rose from the pit of her stomach at the thought of blowing a hole through someone, but if that was what she had to do to protect herself from a killer, as well as protecting Las Vegas from creatures of the Otherworld, then she'd do it. It was a hell of a lot messier than a containment spell, or any of the other castings she had used in the past to restrain supernatural foes. But on the plus side, it looked like it would work quicker.

Leo watched her, but was satisfied with what he saw as he nodded. He shoved the other gun in the front of his jeans opposite of his own while he looked around the cabin for a safe, but accessible, place to store it. Alana wondered if he ever worried about blowing off something important, carrying his guns that way.

He decided to put it in one of the kitchen cabinets, being one of the only small storage areas in the entire cabin. Once he closed the cabinet door, he leaned against the sink, taking deep breaths.

Alana walked up behind him, putting her arms around his waist and laying her cheek against his back.

Leo shuddered.

Turning around in her embrace, he pulled Alana to him. Placing soft kisses in her hair, he ran his hands up and down her back. "God, this is so much harder to deal with now that I have more to lose. Here I am, spilling my life story to you with a mad man lurking around outside. We've hardly had any time for normal conversation, a chance to get to know each other, before the outside world comes in and slaps us in the face. I don't know what I would do if something happened to you, if it was my fault."

Alana burrowed further into his clasp, soaking up his heat and the feeling of safety in his embrace. "Nothing's going to happen to me. I trust you. You won't let anything happen. And don't forget, I might not be the biggest kick ass woman around, but I can protect myself. I survived the first attack before I even met you, using my own little tricks. One way or the other, things will work out as they should. You'll see."

Leo tilted her face up and placed a gentle kiss on her lips before hugging her even tighter. "I hope you're right. I hope to God you're right."

With the daylight beginning to fade, Leo watched as Alana sat staring blank faced into the dancing flames of the fireplace. His lips pursed and his chest clenched as Alana's fingers twisted in her lap. The haunted look on her face pulled at every protective instinct Leo had. Slowly, as if on its own accord, one of Leo's hands rose to slide beneath her hair and across her shoulder. Alana murmured, rubbing her cheek against the back of his hand before jerking away. He stood with arms hanging at his side as she scurried into the kitchen and began pulling out various pots and pans.

Leo forced himself to turn from Alana's frantic movements. He grabbed his cell phone and headed out the door, dialing Gabe's number as he stalked outside. There would be time enough to comfort Alana after he finished protecting her. Time enough to confront their relationship once she was safe.

Giving his partner no time to even say hello, the moment the phone stopped ringing, Leo began snarling into the mouthpiece. "Damned if I wasn't right. It looks like we have a leak. Burke took the bait. Someone's already been down here, casing the place. How are things on your end?"

"Everything *looks* peaceful." Leo's brow wrinkled at the strained note echoing in his partner's voice. "But something's up at Hands of Brotherhood."

Leo gripped the phone tighter, face tensing. "What do you mean?" he growled.

It wasn't difficult to make out the worry in Gabe's reply, his cheerful voice grating. "I'm starting to hear things from other departments. Burke is involved in something, but I'm getting rumblings, innuendoes, nothing specific. Whatever's going down, it's being kept very hush, hush."

Leo cursed, then plopped down on the cabin's wooden steps, wincing as a stray splinter bit through his jeans. "Which departments are talking about him?"

Gabe cleared his throat before admitting his ignorance. "I'm not certain. I'm hearing things secondhand. Nobody will tell me anything directly. And believe me, I've asked around. I don't like this any more than you do."

Leo glared out at the surrounding trees, a helpless feeling overwhelming him, increasing his fury at his powerlessness. "Damn it, don't they know Burke's a chief suspect in these murders? It's a serial killer case, damn it. All information involving the chief suspect should be coming to me first. How do they expect me to wrap this case if they're keeping key info on Burke from me? And the D.A. had better not be cutting him any deals." Leo paused for a moment, taking deep breaths, reeling in his anger. "You keep on it, Gabe. Let me know the second anything breaks. No one's been brought in yet?"

Gabe sighed, not certain how to continue. "No," he answered. "But you're not going to like this part."

Leo gave a humorless chuckle. "As if I've liked anything you've said so far."

"Yeah, but this could be really bad." Gabe paused for a moment, before breaking the news. "Randolph's dropped out of sight."

Leo's voice lowered, a false serenity coating it. "What do you mean 'dropped out of sight'? You were supposed to make sure they were *both* kept under constant surveillance."

"Yeah, I know it was my responsibility, but Randolph slipped away somehow. I haven't figured out how he left the Mission without the other unit or me seeing him. He's probably the one giving you trouble out there, so watch yourself. If it were me, I'd rather tangle with Burke."

Leo grimaced, eyes scanning the tree line. "You're telling me. Randolph reeks of experience. He's a professional. I'm not sure how he got hooked up with Burke, but you can be certain that I'll remember to keep my head down with him on the loose. What about our leak, have you tracked him down yet?"

Gabe gave a frustrated sigh. "No, but it shouldn't take long. Few people knew about you moving out there. I should have a name by the end of the day. I hate the thought of one of our own turning on us like this."

Leo's eyes narrowed at the thought of someone he worked with, maybe even trusted with his life, selling info. Or worse yet, one being so taken with the charismatic religious leader that he was passing information along to Burke for free. "That's something at least. I want that hole sealed as soon as possible. But back to our visitor, I have one good footprint out here. I brought some of my gear, so I'll be able to make a cast of it. But I'll need you to drop by tonight to take it in to be analyzed. I want all the evidence I can get my hands on laid out nice and neat, connecting those two crooks to these murders. They're not getting away this time."

"You got it." Suddenly, Gabe's voice switched to a more concerned tone. "How are things going out there otherwise?"

"Meaning?" Leo asked, menace dripping from his own voice. No way was he ready to share his budding relationship with Alana, not with anyone in the outside world, not even his partner.

But Gabe refused to take the hint, his grim voice prying for more information. "Meaning I'm not blind, and the woman's a complete knockout. Being that you're not brain-dead, I figure even you can see that. And there you are, trapped all alone with her, in a romantic little get-away. You're not doing anything up there that I would do, are you?"

Trying to imagine the department's pitiful excuse for a cabin cast in the roll of romantic get-away, Leo snorted. "If I were, do you think I'd tell you?"

The tone of Gabe's voice sent a chill down Leo's spine. "Just watch yourself, partner. Things can get rough if you let your emotions get in the way. And I'd hate to see you get burned on this. I'd turn you in myself if it came down to that."

"Warning noted, now butt out," Leo growled before punching the button on his phone, ending the call.

He placed the phone on the floor at his side while staring out into the woods. As right as Gabe was, Leo knew his partner's warning came too late. It had been too late from the moment Leo set eyes on Alana. There was something about her, something more than her good looks. He had to accept that he cared too much, and go from there. Because no way was he letting anyone else handle this part of the case. No way was he placing Alana's safety in anyone else's hands.

Leo reached back and heaved himself up, standing and dusting the seat of his pants. Looking one last time out into the distance, trying to catch even the slightest glimpse of Randolph or Burke, he put his hands on his lower back and stretched. It wouldn't be long now. Soon, they'd put all this behind them. They'd drive off this mountain and out into a life together. At least, that's what he wanted.

But a small voice in the back of his head wondered if that was what Alana wanted, because while she'd given her body to him, she hadn't given much of herself.

He'd been the one to lie there, spilling his guts, telling

her all about his sordid past. Alana hadn't said a word about herself, about her past or her feelings. Maybe if there'd been more time, maybe if they hadn't been interrupted when they had, she would have had a chance to open up more, to let him in.

And then again, maybe she wouldn't have.

Leo stared at the door, a tiny seed of doubt finding root. Everything had fallen together so smoothly, too smoothly. Maybe things were more one-sided than he had first thought. But Alana had to feel the same closeness to him that he felt to her, the same pull, the same connection, same emotion that colored his judgement.

Love.

That was what bothered him, what frightened him. He knew the name of this feeling building inside of him. Love.

Love.

He hadn't allowed himself to love another woman since Tina, and here he was, in love again. But did Alana feel the same way, or was he just someone she could hold on to during what must be the most terrifying time in her life?

Did Alana love *him?*

Leo opened the door, feet heavy on the threshold. The luscious scent of well-seasoned beef greeted him. And there, standing in front of the stove, whistling off-key, was the most beautiful sight he'd ever seen.

Alana, the woman he loved.

He walked up behind her, wrapping his arms around her waist, tucking her head under his chin. His heart warmed and danced in his chest as he listened to her chuckle.

"What?" he asked, a contented smile sliding across his face.

Alana shrugged, reaching over to put a lid on the pan in front of her. "You, this. I think you're the only person besides my dad and brother to ever make me feel small, feminine. When a woman gets to be my height, feeling petite and delicate isn't all that easy."

Leo placed a kiss on the crown of her head. "When you get to be my height, very few people *wouldn't* qualify as petite. But I'd never accuse you of being delicate. You might hurt me." Leo tightened his hold on Alana's waist, keeping her from turning. "Now what's this wonderful smell that has my mouth watering and my taste buds begging for attention?"

Alana shrugged, pulling the lid back off the pan to let him take a peek. "Steak a la Alana, my specialty, or at least as close as I can get to it with what I could find here. To be honest, I'm not even certain if it's beef. It looked enough like beef to risk it. We're just lucky there was anything decent in the freezer. That anything survived in that pitiful excuse for a refrigerator at all is a minor miracle."

Leo laughed at the blatant incredulity in Alana's voice. "No, the miracle is that you could make whatever it is smell so damn good. If it tastes half as wonderful as it smells, I may have to keep you."

Leo felt Alana stiffen in his arms for an instant, causing his tiny seed of doubt to plant itself deeper. He clutched her in his arms, burying his face in her curls, thrusting his concern as far back as possible. He had to make her see how much she meant to him, but he couldn't bring himself to say the words, those three little words that could change everything.

Instead, he fell back on that perfect picture that he'd drawn as a child of what his life would be like. He tried to show Alana how well she fit into that image. "I could get used to this, the normalcy of it, the rightness and comfort. I love the feel of you in my arms. I love coming in here to find you waiting for me. The thought of someone else caring enough to take time out of her own life and make me dinner means more than I can tell you. I could get used to all of this, the way you fit so perfectly beside me. This is what I've always wanted in life."

Leo didn't see the shadow pass over Alana's face as the word *normalcy* struck deep into her heart, twisting like a dagger. She winced at each passing phrase, especially the thought of her being perfect for anyone. There was no way she could ever be perfect. Her college sweetheart had proven that to her far too well.

But Leo couldn't see how his words sliced her, how she went pale in his arms. All he could envision was the wonderful life that stood before the two of them.

Chapter Twenty-two

The warmth of the fire seeped into Leo's bones as he lay face down on the Navajo rug. The dancing flames brightened the twilight filled room as the popping and crackling of the fire joined the cicadas' song to provide calming music.

Leo purred. Alana's fingers dug into his tired, aching back muscles, turning his flesh to jelly. "God, that feels wonderful. Where have you been all my life?" he whispered, resisting the urge to drool.

"Shh," she murmured as her hands moved down his naked spine, eliciting a groan, "be quiet and enjoy."

Leo closed his eyes and melted into the floor. Time ceased as Alana worked on his back, producing feelings he swore must be magic. He couldn't hold on to a single thought as she rubbed, pounded, and rolled every last ounce of his stress away. From the tips of his fingers to the pads of his feet, Alana left no muscle untouched.

He lay replete, breathing deep and even in her arms when the annoying beep from his cell phone dragged him out of his personal nirvana. Leo grunted, pulling out of her embrace. Alana gave a wolf whistle as he stood and stretched his naked, sweat-covered body.

He winked in return.

But his contented mood didn't last long. Reaching his phone, he cursed as he read the number for his captain blinking on the display. He closed his eyes and leaned against the side of the couch before punching the receiver button.

"Grady, what the hell is going on up there?" Captain Erikson's voice boomed in his ear.

Leo looked down at the rug where Alana lay, arms thrown above her head, back arched. "I'm not certain I understand sir," he replied, voice lowering as she rolled to her side, facing him.

"You know what I mean," Erikson growled. "I've spent the better part of the morning speaking with Detective Hunter. He's concerned that you're getting emotionally involved with your witness, that it's affecting your objectivity. Tell me he's wrong."

Leo watched the flickering firelight caress Alana's face. He pictured himself lifting her off the floor, carrying her to the bunk beds and inspecting every inch of her, from the crown of her head to the tips of her toes. His chest tightened, along with other parts of his anatomy. "My personal feelings have no bearing on this case."

"Bullshit! Personal feelings always have a bearing on a case if they affect how you pursue it."

Alana scooted closer to Leo, her gaze concerned. Leo smiled reassuringly, running a hand through her curls. "My feelings never change the way I pursue a case. If anything, they make me more determined. You know that."

"But we're not talking about those kinds of feelings, are we? Having sympathy for a victim and being romantically involved with her are two different things. Damn it, Grady! You're the best detective I have. I don't want to pull you off this case, but you're not giving me a hell of a lot of choice here."

Leo turned away from Alana, a quick stab of panic

shooting through him. Alana would be defenseless if the captain had his way. Damn Gabe. Why couldn't he mind his own business? He should be tracking down a killer, not running off at the mouth to the captain like a school kid tattling to the teacher.

"You can't pull me. I have too much time put into this," he tried to rationalize.

Erikson snorted before delivering his ultimatum. "You turn the Devlin woman over to Hunter and work the case from here, or I pull you off completely, put you on leave and file this in your permanent record. It's your career. You decide. Either way, Hunter will be there within the hour."

The phone clicked in Leo's ear. He dropped it on the couch, mind racing. There had to be a solution. He couldn't leave Alana here alone, with only Gabe as protection. The man was a good officer, but Leo trusted no one as much as himself with Alana's life.

"He's pulling you because of me," Alana whispered beside him.

Leo looked down at Alana, who sat with her knees to her chest, collapsing into herself. Leo knelt, wrapping his arms around her. "It isn't your fault. I went into this with my eyes open. I knew the risks."

Alana shook her head, gaze locked on the floor. "But I wouldn't let you listen to your better judgement."

Leo smirked, forcing her chin from its perch on her knees. He rubbed circles between her shoulder blades, soothing away the guilt perched there. "Funny, I could swear I outweigh you by a hundred pounds at least. I don't see how you could force me to do anything."

Alana jerked from him, lips pursed. "You know what I mean."

"Yes," he answered, leaning away to look her up and

231

down, leering, pausing at all the scenic areas. His eyes twinkled as they locked on her face. "You're a wicked little tramp who seduced me with her lascivious body."

Alana shoved him away from her, but he saw her frown before her curls swung forward to curtain her expression.

Leo reached out to push her hair back, wanting to see her face. "Sweetheart," he said, the endearment falling from his lips without thought, "I refuse to place blame. The important thing is to decide where to go to from here."

"There's nothing to decide," Alana snapped. "You're going back. I'm not letting you risk your job."

Leo gritted his teeth, eyes narrowing. Didn't she understand he had to keep her safe, that it was more than a job to him. *She* meant more. "And I refuse to let you risk your life. So what if it goes on my record? I'll have to deal with some disciplinary action, but I'm not going to be fired. Which do you see as more important, a job or a life?"

Alana reminded Leo of an angry cat, spitting with claws extended as she rounded on him. "That's a stupid question. Nothing is more important than life. We both know that all too well. But you're assuming that you're irreplaceable, that without you here, I'm a dead woman. Don't you think I can take care of myself? Don't you trust Gabe to protect me if I can't?"

Leo felt his temper flare at the thought of the woman magnet of his precinct, Gabe, being isolated in the cabin with Alana for an indefinite period of time. He restrained the growl that rattled in the back of his throat, clenching his fists. He relaxed only after Alana placed a comforting hand on his shoulder, resting her cheek by his. "You trust your partner. You know you do."

"Want rid of me already?" he couldn't help but sneer.

Alana smiled, pulling back to place a soft kiss on his lips.

"You know that isn't true. I care about you. I want you here with me, but I don't need you to keep me safe. If things are going to work out between us, you need to understand that. My life is dangerous. Your life is dangerous. We have to trust that we can take care of ourselves without help. Now, go back and nail Burke so I don't have to be stuck out here without you for long."

Leo thought about it, unhappy to find nothing in her argument to refute. She was right. There wasn't much difference between what she did and being a cop, not when it came to the amount of worry your significant other went through. He hated knowing that when she faced creatures like the cearb, he was powerless to help her. Here was someone he could fight for her, protect her from, and he was being pulled. He didn't like it.

He didn't have a choice.

Leo stood, hoisting her up with him. "I'm not leaving you completely unprotected, and I'm not talking about Gabe. We've got less than an hour until he gets here. We're using that time for you to practice with the .45."

Alana gave him a doubtful look. "I suspect it would take longer than an hour to teach anyone how to shoot, much less someone who's never done well on first person shooter games or even with water guns."

It surprised Leo to find himself chuckling. His fingers speared through his hair as he shook his head in mock despair. "I'm not expecting to turn you into Calamity Jane. I'm hoping to raise your comfort level enough that if it comes down to it, you won't be too afraid of what happens when you pull the trigger."

And God willing, you'll never have to use it.

Forty-five minutes later, Leo heard the crunch and

scrape of metal against rock. Gabe made better time than he'd expected, probably left before Leo got called to the carpet. He winced and smiled as a particularly loud screech of metal filled the air. With any luck, considering the way he drove, a good-sized rock would take out Gabe's oil pan.

Traitor deserved it, turning on his partner.

As another crash filled the air, Leo glanced at the closed bedroom door. He'd sent an exhausted Alana to bed early, promising to wake her before he left. It was a promise he had no intention of keeping. He'd never be able to leave her if he had to see the expression on her face. Knowing he wouldn't be there for her when she needed him most tore at him, burning a hole in his gut.

The noise outside stopped, followed by the slamming of a car door. Leo stepped out of the cabin with his gun in hand. Pulling himself to his full height, he glared down at his partner as Gabe slung his bag over his shoulder and walked up the gravel path to the cabin.

"I know what you're going to say," Gabe began as he approached Leo with his free hand raised in peace. "I'm a turncoat. I'm a traitor. I'm trying to steal the case from you, take the credit. I'm your partner and I deliberately made you look bad to the captain. Does that about cover it?"

Leo's eyes narrowed. "Just about," he growled, standing in the doorway and refusing to let Gabe into the cabin.

Gabe dropped his bag and faced Leo, arms crossed. "I did it for your own good. I don't know if you're sleeping with her yet, and I don't want to know. But it doesn't take a detective to figure out it's only a matter of time until you do."

"And how is that your business?" Leo asked, voice calm but body trembling with the need to pound Gabe into the dirt.

Shock crossed Gabe's face. He dropped his arms and took a step forward. "You're my partner, and I'd like to keep it that way. It's my job to watch your back. I'm not letting you toss your career out the door over a quick tumble with a gorgeous redhead."

Leo's smile never reached his eyes. "So, it's better for you, the precinct womanizer, to be up here alone with her? You're better at keeping your pants on than I am? You're the perfect choice for her protection?"

Gabe's eyes widened. He took another step closer to Leo, well within strangling range Leo noted. "That's what all this glowering is about? You think I'm going to cut in on your action? Christ, Leo, if it weren't for the case I'd be taking you out for beers to celebrate your return to the living. But this is a case, and some guy's out there killing people. I don't want the next body we find to be yours."

Leo wasn't certain if he should be insulted or relieved with Gabe's explanation. He chose insulted. "You think I'll be sloppy."

Gabe nodded, brow creasing with worry. "I saw how you reacted when this was about you not predicting that he'd come after the girl in the hospital. She was someone you didn't even know, but you felt responsible for what happened to her. If the killer comes after someone you care about personally, you won't think twice about your own safety."

"Isn't that what a good cop does, put his own life at risk for other people?" Leo asked, shoulders relaxing as he slid his gun back in its shoulder holster.

"A dead cop can't help anyone," Gabe replied, stepping back. "You'll do more good in the city than here. Something's happening with Burke, and I can't get a fix. No one's talking to me. One the other hand, you can get people to talk. Find out what's happening and wrap this up. You can get this settled without anyone coming up here to make a play for your little magician."

Leo rubbed his temples, looking skyward for inspiration. All the work Alana had put into his muscles disappeared, leaving him with sharp, jabbing pains in his shoulders and lower back. "That easy, after all the time we've already put in?"

Gabe shrugged, walking back to where he'd dropped his bag, Leo trailing him. "I have faith in you, or at least in your desire to get me as far from your woman as possible. You'll move heaven and earth to do that."

Leo grunted, but snagged Gabe's bag before he could and led him into the cabin. "You do know that if anything happens to her, I'm taking you apart a piece at a time."

Gabe gave his patented boyish grin, slapping Leo on his sore back. "I would expect no less. But don't worry, I'll take care of her."

"Don't take too good a care of her. That'll get you ripped apart quicker." Leo muttered as he dropped the bags in the main room, scratching his dog's ears before straightening. "I'm leaving Max here with Alana."

Gabe gave the drooling mutt a skeptical look. "You don't have to do that. I'm not sure if he'll be worth anything beyond comfort for Devlin. Where is she, by the way?"

"Taking a nap. She didn't get much sleep last night." Leo cast a yearning look at the closed door. He could take a quick peek in before he left. He didn't have to wake her. But if he did, would he be able to leave?

Gabe smirked.

Leo felt a blush rising up his neck to stain his cheeks. "Get your mind out of the gutter. If you do or say anything to embarrass her, you'll answer to me."

Gabe rolled his eyes. "Yeah, yeah, ripped apart, I remember." He fell into the couch, Max padding over to slobber on his shiny, black leather shoes. He shoved the dog off, then waved Leo towards the door. "Get out of here already and catch the bad guy. You don't want him coming here and giving me all the credit for his capture."

Leo gave the bedroom door one last, lingering look before picking up his own bag and stomping out the door.

Chapter Twenty-three

The bright, cheery morning sun had no effect on Alana the next morning, nor did the joyful chirping of young birds beneath the bedroom's only window. It was the lack of sound in the cabin that dragged her out of a deep sleep. Leo woke long before she did, but not this morning. No sound came from the bunk below her, or the bathroom. No smell of bacon wafted in the room, beckoning her to the breakfast table. Alana opened her eyes and began counting the different knotholes in the beams above her head while trying to collect her sleep-scattered thoughts.

Then she remembered.

She'd stayed up for several hours the night before, lying in bed, tormented by personal demons as she waited for Leo to come back inside to say goodbye. It didn't take long for her to realize that he wasn't coming back, not that she could blame him. She'd been selfish, thinking of only her own wants and needs. She hadn't considered the ramifications for Leo, how her actions would affect him. She had decided that she wanted the relationship to go further and plowed ahead.

Now Leo was gone, his career in jeopardy. Worse, he didn't trust that she would be all right without him. He didn't even know her well enough to know she could handle herself.

Truth be told, that bothered her the most. Leo didn't

believe that she could take care of herself. She never wanted to take up the mantel of Protector. It wasn't a job, like Leo being a cop. When the time came, she didn't have much choice, not unless she wanted to stand by and watch people being hurt or worse without doing anything to stop it.

But once she'd accepted her fate, she'd worked hard. She'd faced demons and monsters. She'd battled sorcerers. She had even managed to pull off a couple of healing rituals without calling Fiona for help. Alana took pride in her ability to cope with a difficult situation, to rise to any occasion. She'd survived the last few years without Leo's help.

It stung, knowing Leo didn't trust that she could protect herself.

A cabinet door slammed in the next room, jarring Alana back to reality.

With a self-pitying groan, she rolled over on her side, into a fetal position, staring down at the floor. She should get up, she thought to herself as she pulled the covers up to her chin. No matter how she felt, she couldn't sit around and mope all day. With any luck, this could be the last day of her captivity. This could be the day when the trap was sprung. Unless she wanted to depend on Gabe, she needed to prepare herself. Trusting Leo with knowing how to keep her safe from a killer was one thing, trusting Gabe was something entirely different.

A last, heartfelt sigh fell from her lips. Alana sat up, head narrowly missing the ceiling. She slid out of bed, knees creaking, and rummaged in her small bag of clothes, looking for something comfortable, but not too dreary. She had a long day ahead of her. She might as well get started.

With her jeans and Nikes, she pulled on a T-shirt with the words "Because nice matters" emblazoned across the chest, surrounded by Celtic knots. She felt off balance, off center. Something nagged at the edges of her mind. A compulsion pulled at her, one she'd learned long ago from Fiona never to fight. She rummaged through her bag for a silk satchel and a small, leather pouch that could be worn around the neck. In the satchel, Alana kept her favorite stones.

She sat on the lower bunk and spilled a rainbow of stones in front of her. Carefully she began selecting what to place in her pouch. First, she chose a small garnet and a flat bit of red jasper for courage. She felt the coming storm, today or tomorrow at the latest, the end neared. She would need all her wits about her.

To that end she placed a bit of amber for clarity of mind, followed by a shard of amethyst, purple for protection. Last, she chose a bead of lapis lazuli, blue harmony.

She pulled the drawstring closed on the pouch, looping it around her neck as she scooped her other stones up to spill back in their satchel. A last, teardrop shaped bit of rose quartz lay warm in her hand—love and healing. It called to her.

Without thought, she slipped this last stone in the pouch.

When Alana stepped out of the bedroom, walking past a contented Max curled in front of the fireplace, Gabe was already munching on cereal. Alana could smell the sweet scent of milk mixed with corn and sugar. She glanced down at the table, her eyes catching at the gun lying by his bowl. "Feeling a little nervous are we?" she asked, staring at the gun and wondering if he could feel the end coming, so close that even a fey blood without any talent for seeing could feel it.

Gabe sat his spoon in the bowl, rocking his chair back on two legs. It surprised Alana that the ancient wood didn't shatter under his weight. "The holster bothers me when I'm eating. But I didn't feel comfortable with it being too far from me. I may need to get it quickly."

"Never seemed to bother Leo. He just slung it on the chair behind him before he sat down."

Gabe smirked, the humor sliding across his mouth not reaching his eyes. "Well, we all know Leo's made of steel and can take down a tank single-handed, or at least thinks he can. Some of us are mere humans. We have to compensate."

Alana smiled, shoulders relaxing. She didn't like having such a visible reminder of her situation staring her in the face over her morning meal, but she could understand his feelings. She had her talismans, and Gabe had his.

She walked around the table to open the cabinet above the cast-iron stove. "I can make you something more substantial than corn puffs if you want," she offered, needing something to do with the time of waiting that stretched out endless before her. "I'm pretty sure I saw some oatmeal in here. Not exactly a good Irish breakfast, but it'll stick with you better than that glorified bowl of milk and sugar."

Gabe rocked his chair forward to sit on all four legs and slurped the last few ounces of milk from his bowl. He wiped his upper lip clean with the back of his hand. Alana's lip curled and she wondered what other women saw in this man beyond his looks. It certainly wasn't his table manners. "Don't bother," Gabe replied. "Make some for yourself though. You'll want to keep your energy up."

Alana closed the cupboard. The thought of food made her insides twist. Gabe was right about the need for energy, but worry filled her stomach, leaving little room for food. Instead, she started a pot of water boiling and reached for a jar of instant coffee. She rarely drank the stuff, but felt the need for a good jolt to the system.

"Not hungry, huh?" Gabe asked, scooting his chair back and turning to watch her.

Alana shook her head, staring down at the pot, willing it to boil.

Gabe snorted. He stood and walked over to her, laying a hand between her shoulders. "Yeah, these kinds of situations can get to a person."

"Right, these situations," Alana replied, denial clear in her voice.

Gabe grimaced, staring down at the crown of her head. "It's not that is it?" he pushed. "It's about Leo."

"Psychic are we?" she asked as she turned to get a cup out of the cabinet.

Gabe gave her a dark look. "No, but I've never seen him afraid to face anything. I saw how he looked at your door last night before he left. He was afraid to go in. What did you do to him?"

"What did I do to him? What did he do to me?" Alana slammed the cup on the counter, causing Max to run under the table. Until that moment, she hadn't realized how angry she was—at the situation, at Leo for not saying goodbye, at Gabe for telling Leo's captain about them, at everything. And Gabe was an easy target for all the rage burning in her gut. "You know what happened. You're the one who went running to your captain. You're the reason Leo's not here now," she sneered.

Gabe took her hands and led her back to the table. He sat her in the seat across from his and stepped back. "I didn't believe things had gone that far with the two of you, not until I saw his face." He picked his shoulder holster up from the counter, slipping it on. He then picked the gun off the table, checked the safety, and slid it in place. "I knew he was close to falling, but I gave him credit for being stronger than that."

Alana glared across the table, temper riding her, heating her skin. "Leo did nothing wrong. I am not a criminal. He can have a relationship with me if he wants to."

Gabe turned on her. "And it looks like he wants to, doesn't it?" he scoffed. "Leo didn't even say goodbye last night, did he? That's what the attitude this morning is really about, he left without even saying goodbye. Stings, doesn't it?"

"You're here to protect me, not analyze me," Alana snapped.

"No, I'm here because you fucked my partner, literally and figuratively." Gabe walked over to stand above her, glaring down with fists clenched at his sides. "Let's get one thing clear. You're the reason I'm here instead of Leo. He's been my partner for two years now. I respect the man. He's a damn good cop. Now all that's in jeopardy because of you."

Alana froze at the venom in his voice. Max whined under the table, pushing his head in her lap, nudging her hand for comfort. She rubbed his ears, collecting her thoughts before replying. "Don't take this wrong, Hunter, but at the moment I'm less than confident in your dedication to protecting me."

Gabe took a step back, taking deep breaths. "Anything happens to you, it'll hurt Leo," he said, voice emotionless.

"And anything happens to Leo, it'll hurt me." Alana stood, reigning in her anger. Gabe was worried about his friend. She could understand that. She was worried about Leo, too. Alana walked past Gabe to take the boiling pot off the stove and pour the water into her cup. She took a deep drink of the coffee, letting the steam play over her face. The warmth relaxed the tightened muscles of her cheeks and eyes. "I care about Leo, and I hate that this whole mess is going to hurt a career he's spent years building. I wonder if a relationship will even work out between us, after all the sacrifice." She stopped for a moment and gave Gabe a weak smile. "Can you see a cop dating a magician?"

"No, I can't," he answered, mouth twisting with disdain.

His reply surprised her. While she hadn't expected glowing support, she didn't expect the pure dislike she heard. "What do you mean? Isn't this the place where you give me all kinds of reasons why the two of us should be together? Give encouragement?"

Gabe's face turned icy cold, colder than Leo's cop face. "No, this is the place where I say I think Leo made a lucky escape. I don't blame Leo one bit for leaving you. You two don't belong together, not any further than a convenient screw anyway. I can't begrudge the man that. But personally, I wouldn't touch you for love or money."

Alana's eyes widened at the hatred that radiated from Gabe, even before she registered his next words. "You and your kind disgust me."

Chapter Twenty-four

Alana froze as her heart gave an uneven thump before leaping in her throat. She held her coffee midway to her mouth, unable to move those last inches. Something was very wrong here, something more than her feelings about Leo, more than Gabe being worried about his partner. The look on Gabe's face, the contempt in his voice sent mad shivers racing down her spine. For the slightest instant, he didn't even look human, the repugnance changing his aspect to something far more primal.

Worse yet, that revulsion seemed personal, directed at Alana, not the anger of a man concerned about his partner. It had the dangerous, bitter taste of undiluted hatred.

"I'm not sure I understand what you're getting at," she managed to whisper above the sudden clutching pressure in her throat as she stepped back a pace, hot coffee sloshing to spill heedlessly down the back of her hand.

Gabe smirked at the caution and beginnings of fear reflected on her face. He stepped closer, crowding her. She could feel his breath sliding across her skin as he spoke. "I'm sure you don't understand. People like you aren't the brightest in the world. All you know how to do is lie and deceive. You're just like my ex-wife. Leo's lucky he came to his senses before you got your claws into him."

Alana stared at him, inhaling the sharp alcoholic smell of his cologne, her mind fighting against the realization lurking beneath the surface. The vehemence in his voice clashed with the character of the man she'd thought of as a laid-back playboy. Her stomach twisted at his mere presence. A warning sounded deep within her, her powers pulling to her, preparing for attack.

Gabe continued, ignoring the way Alana began drawing into herself, backing away from him. His eyes took on the glassy look of someone watching a movie that he'd seen one too many times. His voice dropped to a deep monotone. "Yeah, Linda thought she was something special too, with all of her strange beliefs."

Alana began inching sideways, trying to gain some room, but Gabe's hand snaked out, grabbing her shoulder, forcing her stillness. Without pausing, he continued. "Even in college Linda used to read about the occult and different mythologies. Then she started making more and more weird friends. You know the type. You see them everywhere these days. The kind of people who were either so flighty you wondered how they remembered to breathe, or they looked like they'd just stepped out of some old Vincent Price movie. But I put up with it. I put up with a lot, because I loved her. I told myself that she'd grow out of it, that it was one of those rebellious stages people go through. Linda was only eighteen when we got married. She still had a lot of growing up to do."

Alana wished that she hadn't wasted so much power over the last few days. She found herself faced with the cause of all her problems, the root of all her fears, and she wasn't certain she had enough juice left to take him down. Her eyes locked on the cabinet behind Gabe, where Leo put the gun last night. It was so close, her fingers itched to lunge for it, but she knew Gabe would stop her long before she managed to open it.

As Alana watched, weighing her options, darkness crossed Gabe's handsome features, contorting his pretty-boy face. "Then Linda started in on my baby girl," he whispered.

Gabe's face softened at the mention of his child, but the harshness of his previous expression had etched itself in Alana's mind. A monster lurked behind the shallow surface the likes of which she'd never seen before. Human monsters held an evil no Otherworldly being could hope to reach, evil with a soul behind it.

"Breanne was beautiful," he said, his voice falling calm as tears came to his eyes. "Perfect in every way. She looked like a little angel sent down from heaven especially for me to take care of. I loved her more than anything, more than my job, more than Linda."

Suddenly, his grip tightened on Alana's shoulder, his knuckles turning white as his fingers dug into her flesh. She winced, drawing in a hissing breath, but could tell that he didn't even notice he was hurting her. Gabe's voice cracked as he continued talking, his pain echoing in every word. "When things got bad between Linda and me, I couldn't believe the courts let her take my little girl away, even if it was for just half the year. Didn't they realize what kind of a person Linda was?"

Gabe focused in on Alana again, accusation flashing in his eyes. Alana forced herself to stay silent, afraid to say anything that might provoke him before she had a chance to figure out what to do. She knew that he was willing her to understand, wanted her agreement in some way. But she feared that she already knew what the ending to his story would be. She couldn't find it in herself to feign agreement if what she suspected about his daughter was true.

"I tried to explain to them," he continued, ignoring her

silence while staring into her eyes, "but they wouldn't listen. They didn't want to *discriminate* against Linda because of her religion, as long as she proved to be a good mother."

His eyes stayed locked on Alana's as he sneered, spittle spraying her face with each syllable. *"Religion!* Can you believe that they called that mumbo jumbo she did a religion? Lighting candles and praying to the lord and lady. Saying that God was as much woman as man. Professing that one could control the elements, fate, and even other people's emotions if you just knew how to ask, what chant to say. Believing we have that much command of the universe, more power than God."

He stopped for a moment, wrapping his rage around himself before glaring at Alana once more. Even without the sensitivity of her sister Fiona, Alana could feel the anger coming off of him in waves. "Can you believe they thought she could be a good mother when she practiced witchcraft?"

Not waiting for a response, Gabe shook his head. His hand fell from her shoulder, and he took a step back. The distance should have relieved Alana. Instead, she wondered what he planned for her that needed the separation.

"Then I found out that Linda was taking Breanne to some of those gatherings of hers, those coven meetings." Gabe looked down at his hands. Alana noticed the tiny tremor running through them, his nerve pulled so tight he couldn't control it. "People run around naked and do God knows what else at those things. And the bitch was taking my little girl, my precious little angel, with her. I couldn't let it happen. I couldn't let my baby be exposed to that kind of filth."

Gabe pulled a gun from his shoulder holster, staring down at the cold metal. He ran his fingers up and down the smooth barrel, a lover's caress. In a flash, Alana pictured her life torn from her, the silver cord broken by the cold metal he so lovingly stroked.

Gabe petted the dark metal with a single finger as he whispered, "I never meant for Breanne to be hurt." His bleak eyes begged Alana to understand him, to understand his pain. "I just had to take Linda out of the picture. It was the only way. The law wouldn't help me, so I was forced to help myself."

Tears streamed down his cheeks when he lifted his head. Had circumstances been different, Alana knew she would have reached out to comfort him. The loss of a child had to be devastating, something no one should live with. But she couldn't bring herself to pity him, not after all the lives he had ended, not when faced with his cold brutality.

Gabe laughed, no humor in the sound, as he reached away from the gun to dash the tears from his eyes with the back of one hand. "It was easier than I thought. I hot-wired a beat-up old junk heap and drove out to her work. I never thought Breanne would be with her. It never occurred to me that she would be there. Linda usually left Breanne in day care, abandoning her with strangers while she went to work. She never gave the child enough attention. But for some reason, Breanne was in the car that day."

With Gabe's attention focused on his past, Alana took one careful step toward the cabinet with Leo's gun. If she could reach it before he realized what she was doing . . .

Gabe spun to face Alana, pinning her with his stare. Alana froze, cursing silently that she hadn't used the opportunity to make a run for it. Like she'd be able to get the gun and hold him off until the cavalry arrived. The cavalry didn't even know she was in trouble. That might have been the only chance he would give her. Now she'd have to make her own chances. She was alone.

She wanted to prove to Leo that she could take care of herself. Be careful what you wish for.

Gabe's eyes gleamed, his face earnest, compelling Alana to listen to his every word. "I never meant to hurt my little girl. I swear to God above that I never meant to hurt her. But Linda had her in the car, and I didn't see her. Not until it was over. Not until I was called in to ID the bodies."

For a moment, he looked as though he was going to be ill at the thought of what he'd seen that day. But he pulled himself back together, standing a bit straighter, his hand rising to caress his gun again.

"You'll never know how I felt," he whispered, his fingers running back and forth across the cold steel. "No one could. But I swore that day that I would do everything in my power to prevent anyone else from feeling that same pain. I swore I would do whatever needed to be done in order to stop the spread of the crap Linda was into. From anyone else finding themselves in the position of having to take a life to protect their child."

"So you went out and started killing other people you thought held the same beliefs of your ex-wife," Alana replied, eyes glued to his face, heart racing. She forced herself to take deep breaths, try to find her center. Calm, she had to find the eye of the storm, the calm. If she panicked, she had no chance of survival.

Gabe nodded at Alana's bald statement. "Or those that helped convince others, especially children, that witchcraft was real. People like you."

"If you didn't want other people to feel the way you did, how could you have killed?" Alana asked, trying to reason with him, knowing that her chance of success was minimal. But every second she kept him talking gave her more time to plan, more time to decide how best to survive the situation she found herself in. And she was determined to survive. "Each of those people had families. Those families had to go down into that same morgue to identify their own loved ones. And you were the cause of their pain, their heartache. How can you possibly justify that?"

Gabe grinned as he shook his head, amazed at her obvious ignorance. He rocked back and forth on his heels, fingernails clicking against the butt of the gun as he tried to explain it to her. "They brought it on to themselves, don't you see? It was their sins that brought them to me, to my judgement. I will admit that I wished that those who loved them didn't have to suffer as well. But I would rather a few people suffer than watch those monsters cause so many other people pain. It had to be done, and I don't feel sorry for doing it."

A sickeningly sweet smile crossed his face as his hand gripped the gun. "Just as I won't feel sorry about you. I will hate to see Leo go through the anguish your death will cause him. I hated watching his pain when he lost the one in the hospital, and your death will be much harder on him. But he seems to be realizing the folly of entangling himself with you already. That will soften the blow."

"You've been watching us. You were the one that Max chased off," Alana said, her voice emotionless. Max whined at the sound of his name. Alana glanced down to see the agitation building in Leo's dog, and the beginnings of an idea tickled the edges of her mind. She tilted her head, her expression going cold. Gabe wouldn't keep talking much longer. Time was about to run out. She hoped that her powers and skills would be enough to save her, to save them all, because if she failed, all of Las Vegas would pay the price. The Otherworld would see to it. "And if you kill me here, how do you expect to get away with it? Leo will know what happened. He's good at what he does. You're his partner. You should know that."

Gabe laughed as he raised the gun, pointing it straight at her chest. "I plan on having a fight with a masked man, one wearing the same clothing you described the man who broke into your house wearing. The fight will be close enough that any powder burns on my clothing will be explained. I'm afraid I'll have to be wounded in the struggle, something enough to take me out of the immediate action, but not career threatening. You, on the other hand, won't be so lucky."

Alana's hands went behind her back, looking as though she was fidgeting with fear. Her fingers etched intricate designs while she chanted ancient charms in her mind. But her voice remained calm, trying to delay Gabe long enough to complete her last ditch effort. She prayed that the people-loving Max felt close enough to her, protective enough of her, to play his part. "And if Leo doesn't believe you, if he figures out what really happened?"

Gabe shrugged, unconcerned. "I'm willing to sacrifice one honest cop for the greater good."

Her spell close to completion, Alana prayed that he wouldn't notice the scent of flowers that was beginning to fill the air. She had to keep talking to cover the faint sound of chimes rising around her. A few seconds more, and it would be over, one way or the other. "You know you're insane, right?"

Gabe laughed at the audacity of her comment. He had the gun, and she was trying to insult him. "Maybe, maybe not. I shouldn't matter either way to you. You've been as good as dead since I was first put on this case. You just didn't know it until now."

Chapter Twenty-five

"Arrested?" Leo growled into his cell phone while pawing through his cupboard for his instant coffee. After his late night drive, Leo collapsed into bed, falling into a deep sleep. He'd planned on working in his home office, looking over the files on the killer for something they missed, anything to help connect Burke. He had to have made a mistake somewhere. The man was slick but not a genius. But he needed rest to get a fresh look, a new eye. The ringing phone jarred him awake after only three hours' sleep. Leo's eyes were still unfocused and filled with grit as he prepared his precious caffeine.

"What do you mean they've both been arrested?" he growled, running his hand over a whisker-roughened cheek. "How did that happen? And why wasn't I notified? They're the top two suspects for the serial killings that I'm investigating, and no one tells me that they've been arrested!"

"Messages were left for your partner," the offending officer all but whispered. "I guess he didn't get them."

"You guess he didn't get them," Leo repeated back, enunciating each syllable. He fought against the urge to reach through the phone lines and deck the guy. He had to remind himself that it wasn't this little weasel's fault, and killing the messenger wasn't his style. But he damn well intended on finding out whose fault it was. Time to go to the top.

"Is the chief in?"

"Yes, I can forward your call to him right now if you want to speak with him." The officer put Leo on hold without waiting for an answer.

Leo's lips curled, the image of a snarling wolf. "Oh you better believe that I want to speak to him," Leo muttered, taking a deep drink of his bitter brew while waiting for the connection to be made.

"Want to find out about Burke and his flunky, I take it?" the chief asked without preamble.

"Why else?" Leo asked in reply, looking out the kitchen window, eyes straining in the early morning light. "I don't suppose you can let me in on what's going on now?"

Chief Erikson didn't respond to the accusing tone in Leo's voice. "I'm sorry I couldn't tell you anything sooner. I know those two were on the top of your list of suspects, but it looks like you're going to need to search elsewhere. It's certain that they had nothing to do with the killings."

At the utter confidence in the chief's voice, Leo felt a weight falling on his shoulders. And he thought things couldn't get any worse. It was too damn early to deal with this kind of shit. "How certain are you? What *exactly* is going on?"

Erikson cleared his throat before making his reply. "It seems that the DEA has had the entire work force of Hands of Brotherhood Mission under surveillance for the last several months."

Leo felt his stomach drop. If Burke's been watched for that long, how could he or Randolph be involved with the murders? And if he wasn't involved in the killings, what had Burke been up to?

"The DEA? You've got to be kidding." Leo's voice sounded strained even to himself, but it couldn't be helped.

He just didn't know what to think. "Tell me you're kidding."

Erikson grunted. "Afraid not. Seems your gut feelings about Burke were right. He wasn't all that he seemed and he *was* up to his neck in crime. But not murder."

Leo still couldn't wrap his mind around what he was being told. He'd been so certain that Burke was his killer. He didn't know how to react. The rug had been pulled completely out from under him. It was a feeling that he'd been getting a lot lately. "You're sure?" he asked one more time, hoping his case wasn't falling apart around his ears.

Erikson's voice crackled, sounding even more ancient than his sixty years. "He's been laundering money for a major drug trafficker. The DEA has been keeping close tabs on him and all his employees. If Burke had anything to do with your murders, they would have caught him on tape."

Leo gritted his teeth and shook his head in exasperation. How could he have missed something like that? It should have been obvious. There must have been clues to Burke's criminal involvement that he'd overlooked, while trying to fit Burke into the role of his murderer. "Money laundering, Burke's been money laundering. No murders, just drugs and dirty money. Damn."

"Yeah, seems like with all the donations coming in and the cover of a non-profit organization, it was pretty simple. Took the DEA two years to figure out. Hell, it's embarrassing he wasn't caught earlier. When Burke was dealing in antiques, he was smuggling the stuff into the country for one of the major players. The Feds are hoping he rolls on his boss."

Leo ran his fingers through his hair as all the ramifications began sinking in, his stomach sinking as he thought of

Alana. "Shit, I'm back at square one again. The killer could be anyone."

"I'm sorry I couldn't tell you sooner and kept you from wasting so much time. I didn't know Burke was under any type of investigation until last night, after I'd already talked to you. The arrest didn't happen until a few hours ago. I left messages for Gabe, but he must not have gotten them before he left for the safe house."

Leo wheeled around, slamming his mug on the table. "Damn, I'm going to have to pull what we have and start looking for more connections, start at the beginning and look for what we missed."

"We're running out of time here. The media is going to find out about things soon, and the mayor's getting antsy. I'm giving you two more days to come up with another viable suspect before I look at turning this over to someone else."

That shocked Leo. Since making detective, he'd never had a case taken away from him. "Someone else?"

The chief cleared his throat. "I've been getting pressure to turn this whole mess over to the Feds. I need you to show me that there's no reason to do that, understand?"

"Yes sir. I'll get right on it."

"You do that," Chief Erikson replied before hanging up.

Leo went straight to his home office, shoving aside miscellaneous papers stacked on his desk before pulling all the files on each of the victims and fanning them out in front of him. He stared down at the different faces looking up from the pictures of the victims before the attacks that were clipped to the front of each folder. Something had to be here. The victims couldn't be random. There had to be a thread, a connection, something to lead him to the killer.

But damned if he knew what it was. He and Gabe had

been over this a million times it seemed. The only connection other than Burke was the victims' apparent connection with the occult. And even that felt flimsy to him now. Of course, that could just be his mixed feelings about the subject coming into play, messing with his instincts.

Leo pitched the last folder onto the floor with a disgusted grunt, both hands sliding through his hair. He couldn't remember ever being this frustrated, this confused. His temples throbbed and a tic twitched just beneath his right eye. He was no closer to the identity of the killer than he had been at the very beginning of the case. All he *did* know was that if he looked at the pictures of the victims one more time, he'd go stark raving mad.

Maybe he had worked so long in homicide, he was developing an affinity for the dead.

He stood, fingers running yet again through his disheveled hair. His mind was still on the case as he walked into the connecting bathroom, but his reactions were still sharp as the door slammed to a close behind him. He spun, hands raised ready to strike. A beautiful woman stood before him, a picture of pride in misery. Her skin was a milky pale, almost translucent, reminding Leo of a mother-of-pearl necklace his father had carved for his mother.

The woman was tall, meeting his eyes with ease, but so dainty that she seemed much smaller than her true height. Her face was long and delicate with a pointed chin and red-rimmed, swollen eyes. Her cupid-bow lips quivered. Long streams of tears flowed unchecked down her pale cheeks. But it was her green hair, hanging well below her knees and complementing her flowing green and blue dress that caught and held Leo's attention.

"Who are you?" he asked, almost afraid of the answer. He might be new to all this supernatural stuff, but even he could recognize someone not quite human.

The woman looked into his eyes, her grief becoming a tangible thing, flowing off of her in waves. Leo ached along with her pain, fighting against the urge to reach out and offer comfort. He watched the long, glittery material of her sleeve dangle from her wrist as her thin, pale hand reached forward to trace his temple. He flinched at the frigid feel of her skin sliding against his own.

"Who are you?" he asked again, shocked to hear the tremor in his own voice. Deep in the recesses of his memories, a suspicion grew. The hairs on the back of his neck stood at attention as he considered the possibilities of her identity.

Her voice echoed back at him, as hollow as her eyes, the sound more poignant than a dirge. "You will be my last, the last whom I shall watch over, L. E. O'Grady. When you are gone, all is finished for me. I will have none to stand over, and too many to mourn. My portion of the O'Grady line shall end with you. What shall become of me then?" She glided forward, reaching out to embrace him.

Leo stumbled backward, putting as many steps between them as the miniscule room would allow, wedging his body between the bathtub and the sink.

The woman's lips arched upward into a smile filled with melancholy and ancient sadness. "You have nothing to fear of me, young O'Grady. I come not to take you from this life. I am the messenger, the one to warn you, to grieve for those who belong to your family."

With that, her head tilted up, staring into the flickering fluorescent lights. Her mouth opened wide as her eyes closed. A soul-wrenching wail erupted from the very depths to echo from her throat, ringing against the walls.

Leo clamped his hands on his ears, trying to shut out the

shrieking sound, or at least muffle it so it wouldn't deafen him. Still, his eyes welled up with tears at the pure, unadulterated pain saturating the woman's cry.

As abruptly as it had begun, the sound stopped. The woman fell to her knees, sobbing into her hands, rocking back and forth.

Leo glanced at the door, amazed that none of his neighbors burst in to see what was making such an ear-piercing noise, or at least that the cops hadn't been called. He stared down at the woman at his feet. The rate of her sobs seemed to be increasing, with no sign of stopping. Another shriek began to build within her broken cries.

"*What* are you?" he whispered, trying to fight off the feelings of sympathy that her obvious grief dragged from him.

The woman dropped her hands, tears still streaming. Her red eyes narrowed in disbelief. One finger tucked a long stream of green hair behind a pointed ear. "Haven't you guessed yet, dear boy? Don't you know? Did your family tell you nothing of the old ways?"

A chill ran down his spine as he remembered the stories that his father loved to tell him, stories that he discounted as more weirdness spouted by his unconventional parents, stories he'd recently began wondering about the truth of.

"Banshee. You're a Banshee," he whispered, as if by giving voice to the name made it more real.

Tears flowed down her face. The woman smiled up through the streams at him and inclined her head. "Yes, I am Bean Sidhe. I have followed your branch of the family O'Grady for time without end. And yet, with you it shall end."

"You've come to predict my death," he stated with a calm he didn't feel, the skin of his face tightening.

Her smile fell as she shook her head. The Bean Sidhe stared down at her hands twisting the cloth of her outer skirt between her fingers. "No, not your death. You shall be the last to whom I will come, the last of whom I shall mourn. But not for many a year will you die."

Leo swallowed the lump forming in his throat and licked his dry lips. "Then I don't understand."

More tears welled up in her eyes as she looked back up at him, pity etched in every feature. " 'Tis for your child that I mourn. The girl child who shall never be born, as her mother will not live to see the sun fall on this day."

It would have been kinder for her to punch him in the gut. The action would have been less shocking. "What are you talking about?" he managed to choke out as he pushed away from the wall, stepping closer to her.

"The young Protector, the Devlin woman," she answered in her sorrow-filled voice. "She holds your girl child beneath her heart, a heart that will beat its last before the moon rises, bathing night in its cooling light."

The blood drained from Leo's face as the foundation he believed his life to be built on fell away beneath his feet. "A child? That can't be true."

A grim chuckle escaped the lips of the Bean Sidhe. She sat back, pulling her knees into her chest. "One night is all it takes, human. You must know that. I thought every mortal boy was taught that in his youth, even in this misbegotten age."

Leo shook his head, ignoring her sarcastic comment, still grasping the idea of being a father, of he and Alana having created a child together, a little girl—a little girl destined never to live to see the world.

Leo's hands clenched at his sides. "Gabe is there to watch out for her. She knows to stick close to him, to stay safe. What's happening?"

The Bean Sidhe bowed her head, her tears pouring down her cheeks. "She stands in a secluded cabin, plotting her escape from the mortal killer. He speaks to her, explains the necessity of her death. The battle for survival begins soon, and no earthly power will enable you to get to her in time. She will put up a great struggle, her parents taught her well to protect against the mystical. But it will only be a matter of time until she fails. And then you will be the last O'Grady. The guilt will keep you from ever forming a lasting relationship with another woman, having a family. My reason for existence will be no more."

Images of Gabe dead or disabled, lying on the floor unable to help as Alana struggled against the superior strength of the killer haunted Leo. His expression darkened, the determination that made him one of the best detectives in the homicide unit coming to the forefront. "There has to be a way. I have to get there, be with her."

He looked down again at the woman still sitting in a heap at his feet. No earthly way to get to Alana on time, but what about the unearthly? He couldn't believe what he was considering, but if it was the only way . . . "You, you're magical. You could get me there in time, couldn't you?"

The Bean Sidhe shook her head, tears splashing on her knees. "I am but a messenger. It is not my place to interfere with the natural order of things."

Leo clenched his jaw and fought against the urge to drag the creature to her feet. But if he laid his hands on her, he wasn't certain what he'd do. The frustration caused his entire body to shake. She would help him, no matter what he had to do. "This is not a natural death, and you know it. And what will happen to you if you're right? Alana dies, my unborn daughter dies, and where will you be? You'll wait until my parents and I die, and then there will be nothing for you. No one to watch over, nothing left to do in the mortal world. No reason to exist."

If it were possible for her to sound even more grief stricken, the Bean Sidhe's voice dripped misery. "I will fade. I will be no more."

Leo unclenched his hands and placed a gentle palm on the sidhe woman's shoulder. The tone of his voice dropped, comforting. Thankfully she couldn't see the rage etching his face. "That doesn't have to happen. You could help me to get there in time to save them both. Then you will have my daughter to watch over, perhaps even other children, and eventually their children as well. The O'Grady line that you have been tied to for all these years, the family you have stood sentinel over for so long, will go on. But you'll have to help me get there in time to save them."

The Bean Sidhe stared up at him, her hollowed and reddened eyes taking on a lively glow. Leo wondered if this wasn't why she came here in the first place. Why else would she come to warn him so early? According to what his father told him, the banshee came to cry over a death that had already occurred, not to give a warning about one about to happen.

Never trust the wee folk.

"Done," she answered, leaping to her feet. She reached out, wrapping both arms around his body, pulling Leo to her, while giving him no time to change his mind. "You may wish to close your eyes, mortal. We will travel in the places between, slipping through the lands of time and shadow. The very sight could be enough to break your mind were you to witness it. Are you certain you wish to risk all for your love?"

Leo nodded, clenching his eyes closed. "Do it."

Chapter Twenty-six

Alana and Gabe stood in a frozen tableau, eyes locked. Alana felt each thump of her heart pushing blood through her veins as time slowed, every second lasting hours. Each beat of her heart pounded against her ribs. Each breath tightened her lungs. Alana's senses snapped into an acute state. Colors and shapes zoomed into sharp focus. She could count the individual motes of dust floating in the air. Even with the few feet of distance between them, she could smell the sweet, mint scent of Gabe's warm breath under the overpowering aroma of his cologne. She heard two birds chirping and swooping outside the cabin, the air beating under their wings. She heard Max's soft whimpers coming from under the table as he felt the tension between the two humans. She could feel every one of the eighty degrees pressing in on her skin.

Each and every muscle of her body screamed for her to run.

But that wasn't an option. The slightest movement she made could end in her death. He was too close. The gun was too close. Gabe could squeeze the trigger quicker than she could leap out of the way. The only advantage Alana had was that Gabe didn't know she really was what he would call a witch, that she could do magic. That skill was all that stood between her and death.

Alana realized that she couldn't form one of her illusions

263

too quickly, not with Gabe so close, with the gun pointed directly at her. Nothing must startle him. With his finger poised on the trigger, Alana couldn't risk Gabe getting off a lucky shot before she could move out of his way. So instead of more dramatic illusions, she began changing little things in their surroundings. Inside the cabin, she changed the size of the furniture, making the table seem smaller, while the couch grew a few inches. She put up obstacles where there hadn't been anything before.

Outside, where he couldn't see, she made more drastic changes. She brought the trees closer, disguising roots, rocks, and holes that might trip a pursuer. She added to the foliage, darkening the surroundings. Beads of sweat dotted her brow from the stress, but she did anything she could think of to give her an advantage when she made her break.

She had no choice but to run for it.

"Why the claddagh? That, I still don't understand," she asked, trying to buy a few precious seconds more, time to plot out the course of her escape. If she could make it out of the cabin and to the line of trees, she could turn the entire mountain into a jungle that Gabe could never escape.

Gabe seemed distracted, sniffing at the air. Alana tensed for a brief moment, but then relaxed as he shrugged off the wildflower scent of her magic. His gun hand stayed still, barrel pointed between her eyes, as he answered her question. "It's because of my wife, of course. She wanted her wedding ring to be etched with a claddagh. She was one of those wanna be Irish fanatics. You know the type, wearing Celtic crosses and knots, decorating their homes with pictures from the book of Kells. I thought the claddagh would be a fitting symbol for my crusade."

Thinking of his wife, and of what she had caused to happen to their daughter, Gabe's eyes glazed over. Alana seized the opportunity, realizing that it might be her last. With a quick prayer to whatever god was listening, she ducked and grabbed the coffee pot off the stove. She barely noticed the heat of the glass scorching her fingers. She pitched what was left of the scalding liquid straight at Gabe's face.

Gabe screamed, but kept his grip on the gun, pulling the trigger. Two bullets slammed into the cabinet behind her, sending splinters of wood showering down around her. Alana ignored the scratches. She spun around, lunging for the door.

Gabe grabbed a hunk of her hair, yanking her back to him. "Fucking bitch!" he spat as he hauled her closer. Tears clouded Alana's eyes as she struggled to wrench loose, blocking the pain.

A growl erupted from beneath the table as over a hundred pounds of golden furred fury launched itself at Gabe. Max's jaws locked down on the fist Gabe had wrapped around Alana's curls, snapping his head back and forth. Gabe cursed in pain as the fangs ripped through his skin and sank deep into his flesh.

Alana didn't wait to see what happened next. Even as she heard two more shots explode behind her and Max's high-pitched yelp, she tore open the cabin door, stumbling down the steps.

Alana sprinted for the trees, adrenaline pumping energy into her legs, leaving her light-headed. Gravel crunched beneath her feet, sliding with each step. Alana focused on keeping moving, keeping her feet under her. Images from every horror movie she'd ever seen danced in her mind. She had to keep on her feet. If she fell, that was when Gabe would get her. That's how it worked, if you fell, you died.

Sparing a moment to kick Max in the head, Gabe scrambled after her, tripping over furniture that he couldn't see and dodging around furniture that wasn't there.

Those few seconds that Gabe wasted gave Alana the narrow lead she needed as she made it to the tree line. Focusing all the energies she could spare as she ran, Alana threw a massive illusion over the woods. False darkness fell across the land, the sun's rays blotted out by an immense shadow. The trees grew taller, denser. The underbrush sprang up, blocking most of the space between the trees.

Alana ran through the illusionary background, ignoring the glamour that she had created. She prayed the trees she ran straight for were of her own creation, prayed that she wouldn't knock herself out slamming into the real thing. Her lungs burned. Her body shook. Her mouth was so dry it felt as though fur sprung up in the back of her throat. Her mind blanked out any thought not integral to her survival. It took intense concentration to run without slipping while ignoring the look of her surroundings.

But she had a chance at living, however slim.

Alana's heart raced from the exertion of holding together so much magic while trying to put as much distance as possible between her and Gabe. Blood pounded in her head, her temples aching. Her stomach twisted from the pain, threatening to wrack her with dry heaves. But Alana gritted her teeth and kept running and casting. Vines sprung up, twisting under her feet. Grass and shrubs spread out in plush, green carpeting. Tree branches thickened and moved without a whisper of sound.

Alana listened to the crashes and curses behind her as Gabe stumbled over hidden roots and ran into disguised branches. Her plan was working so far. Still, he sounded much too close for Alana's comfort. She had to find someplace to hide. She could only run for so long before she ran herself into the ground. Already her legs trembled as the rush of adrenaline wore off. If she kept running with no plan, other than to pray that Leo figured everything out and rescued her, she might as well turn around and give herself up.

As things stood, without Leo, Gabe would kill her.

She needed a place of seclusion, a place to sit, think, and take some time to figure out her next move. It was difficult enough running and casting spells at the same time. She couldn't think and plan at the same time too.

Drawing a little extra erg of energy, she drew her glamour away from her eyes. Where before, she'd allowed herself to see her illusions as shimmering shapes, she blocked them from her sight. It took precious strength and focus to do so, but now she could search for a place to rest in relative safety. She needed a place where she didn't have to depend on her illusions for protection.

After several more chest-constricting minutes of running, she spotted one large, flat stone fallen atop another, creating a small shelter. She fell to her knees on the moist ground and scooted into the tiny space, throwing up an illusionary wall of brush over the opening.

Then she waited. The smell of damp earth and rotting leaves filled her nostrils, the rich scent calming her ragged nerves. She listened as the sound of cracking wood and feet sliding against rock thundered closer. She curled herself up in a tight ball, arms around her knees, trying her best to disappear into herself.

A short time passed before Gabe dashed by, not even glancing down at Alana's hiding place. She breathed a sigh of relief, scooting further back against the clammy sandstone. The aching in her temples became a sharp pain stabbing at the area behind her eyes, the strain of controlling such a massive illusion beginning to take its toll. Her stomach rolled, gorge rising. She raised her hands in front of her face and watched them tremble, unable to keep even one finger steady. All Alana could hope for was that Gabe got himself lost before she was forced to drop the glamour.

Minutes passed, feeling like days as Alana's pain intensified, jagged bolts beating at the inside of her skull. Her fingernails cut crescent circles in her palms as she clenched her fists, fighting against the rising agony.

Finally, the strain became too much for her to take. The pain transformed from agony into total anguish. Tears flowed freely down her pale cheeks. Alana was faced with the choice of dropping her glamour voluntarily, or losing consciousness and dropping it anyway—no difficult decision there. Fingers crossed, she began stripping away layer after layer of illusion from her surroundings, saving the brush that covered her hiding place for last.

She held her breath, a whisper of a prayer on her lips, waiting for any sound of her pursuer.

The crackle of brush served as warning. Tears of pain became tears of hopelessness falling from Alana's eyes. After all this, Gabe couldn't find her now, when she was too weak to defend herself.

Please let him keep walking. Don't let him look down. Don't let him see me. God, please.

Alana jerked, suppressing a frightened whimper as Gabe called out, "Come out, come out wherever you are. You can't hide forever, witch. I don't know how you're doing all this, but I know you can't hide forever. It's just you and me out here. You're only delaying the inevitable."

His word were sharp and clear, his voice much too near.

Alana lowered her head and peeked out of the small

space, her eyes locking with his shoes, scant inches from her nose.

Though later she would swear that she hadn't moved, Alana must have made some sound. Abruptly Gabe stopped, dropped to his knees, peering into her hiding place.

A dark smile slid across his face, turning his boyish features demonic. "So there you are, little witch. Did you honestly think you could stay hidden down there until Leo comes back for you? I'm so sorry that I have to disappoint you, but it's the end of the road. Face it. I win. Game over. Come out, little one. I don't want to shoot you where you lay. I like having a body to serve as a warning to all the others lurking out there, and I don't fancy having to crawl in that hole and drag your stinking corpse out. Dead weight is a bitch to handle."

Alana shivered, fighting back a weak snivel, but dragged herself out. He was right. He could kill her where she lay crouched. Nothing stood in his way. Maybe out in the open she'd have another chance at escape.

But she doubted it.

She stood in front of him, her hands clasped above her head, trying to look as unthreatening as possible. But she stood straight and tall. There may be nothing left that she could do to protect herself, but she'd face him on her feet.

Gabe's triumphant smile grew at her obvious defeat. It was clear that she had been the greatest challenge he had faced in his self-proclaimed quest for the purification of Las Vegas. But he had won in the end. "Now you know," he all but laughed, celebrating his final victory. "I am stronger than any of your kind. I will wipe the city clean of your filth. Nothing can stop me."

Alana watched as he steadied the gun. She could see the muscles in his wrist twitch and his hand tightening as his finger began pulling back on the trigger. She had an instant to realize that nothing she did could save her. This is how she would die. She wished that she'd listened to her father and Rick. She wished that she'd taken martial arts and target practice instead of dance—anything that could save her life now.

But most of all she wished she could see Leo one last time. They could have worked out their problems. She could be more understanding of his doubts and give him time to adjust to her and her lifestyle. He hadn't screamed at her like Jack had. He hadn't left her. Leo still loved her. As long as that was true, the rest would work out.

Too bad she realized all this too late.

Suddenly a large body appeared out of nowhere and hurled itself forward, shoving Gabe's gun hand to the side. The gun went off with a loud pop. Alana felt a sharp sting slice her arm as she dropped to the ground, rolling away through the fallen leaves, away from the two combatants.

The sound of flesh striking flesh rang in her ears, coupled with curses and groans and grunts of pain. When she looked up, Alana watched in amazement as Leo, snarling and muttering obscenities, shoved Gabe to the ground, slamming his gun hand against a rock until it finally loosened its grip.

Alana scrambled to her knees, holding her injured arm against her side as Leo shoved his knees into his partner's gut, pumping his fist repeatedly in Gabe's face. Blood spouted from Gabe's nose, pouring into his eyes. But he managed to twist under Leo, bucking free and scrambling for his gun.

Leo grabbed his ankle, dragging Gabe back. Gabe kicked

out, catching Leo in his bad shoulder and climbed to his feet.

Spinning back to face Leo as his partner rose to his knees, Gabe lashed out at Leo's head with a vicious kick. Alana gasped as it caught Leo in the temple. He fell back with a grunt.

Alana hurtled forward, wrapping her arms and legs around Gabe's back. Hissing, she sank her fingers into his cheeks, feeling for his eyes. She clawed deep furrows down both sides of his face before Gabe shoved himself back against a tree.

Alana's vision was reduced to sparkles as the rough wood slammed into the back of her head. She slumped to the ground, panting, but she slung the hair out of her eyes and prepared to lunge back into the fray.

But Leo got to Gabe first. He pulled his fist back and smashed it into Gabe's face one last time, spinning his partner around. His second punch aimed for Gabe's windpipe. Gabe fell to his knees, gagging and gasping for breath.

"Not bad, for a mortal," a voice behind Alana stated.

Alana whirled around to see the Bean Sidhe leaning against a tree with an uncharacteristic smile twisting her lush lips, the beauty of a true immortal glowing through her usual misery. The woman stepped forward, her footsteps disturbing not a single twig, pulling Leo off Gabe. "I'll handle things from here, O'Grady."

"I have to take him into custody," Leo replied, wiping blood off his lip with the back of one hand as he looked at the bruises forming on Alana's face. "He has to pay for what he did."

The Bean Sidhe shoved him back from Gabe, stepping between the two. Alana was amazed at how easily the Sidhe was able to move a man Leo's size. She sent up thanks that it hadn't come to a battle over Las Vegas between herself and the Otherworld.

The Bean Sidhe placed a gentle restraining hand on Leo's shoulder. "And he will. Believe me, he will. But it is to my people that he must pay. The lives he took were ours. We shall deal with him."

The Bean Sidhe shook her head when Leo seemed about to argue. "You have no way of keeping this man. You are strong and honorable for a mortal, but you cannot stop one of my kind. It can be a fight, if you want, but you wouldn't win."

Alana scrambled forward, putting her hand on Leo's other shoulder. She ignored the pain in her arm as she cuddled herself closer to Leo, hoping her presence would keep him from doing anything stupid. She didn't know why the Sidhe was here, but it wouldn't do to anger her. Still, Alana would do what she could to help Leo. "As the Protector of Las Vegas, it is my duty to see this man punished," she whispered. "It was a charge put upon me by those of your kind."

The Bean Sidhe stared down at her, expression unchanged.

Alana pressed on. "If you and yours find our mortal punishment unsatisfactory, you have my permission to take things into your own hands. But for the sake of the man who risked his life to capture this murderer, I ask you to give us this boon."

"For his sake?" the Bean Sidhe asked, directing her attention back to Leo.

Alana nodded, pulling herself to her full height while staying tucked as close as she could to Leo. "He will have to answer to his superiors if Gabriel Hunter disappears. Let us take him first, I beg you most humbly."

The Bean Sidhe pondered this for a moment before nodding her head once. "I will agree. This mortal has given me reason to exist. I can do this much for him in repayment. But know this, if we feel the mortal's punishment is not enough, we will do whatever we will."

Alana glanced down at Gabe, pity swelling in her heart. As much pain as he had put her and others through, as much damage as he had done, she would not wish his fate on any being, human or other. None knew the true meaning of torture and torment as those who'd had centuries to perfect the art. If Alana knew anything about the creatures of the Otherworld, she knew Gabe would wish for a quick death by the time they finished with him. Nothing the humans did to him would be enough for the Otherworld.

"Even when I take him, you will punish him as well," Leo put words to Alana's fears for Gabe, resignation filling his voice.

"Most likely," the Bean Sidhe replied, unconcerned. "His fate was decided with the first murder of one of our people. Kin killing is a dread crime. Ask your woman what would have happened to your city had he not been found and you'll understand how seriously the Otherworld takes such crimes."

Leo looked down at Alana once more. Her face was pale, and her sweat soaked hair was plastered to her forehead. But it was the pleading look in her eyes that stopped Leo from resisting any further. "So be it. Just give us first chance at him. After that, he's yours."

The Bean Sidhe's lips curled back as she knelt by the prone murderer. "Since your line is now secure, I will not hold you to debt for my transporting you here. I will not see you again until your own time is upon you."

Leo nodded as he pulled Alana into his embrace, not noticing her flinch at the pressure on her arm.

With a rustle of displaced air, freezing cold in the warmth of the morning, and a low toned boom, the Bean Sidhe disappeared.

Alana looked up at Leo standing grim faced and steady. Her father would like this man. "I thought I'd never see you again."

The expression in Leo's eyes burned through Alana as he raised one hand to cup her cheek. "You don't have to worry about that. Not now, not ever."

Epilogue

The audience sat in hushed silence, shadows deepening as the spotlight focused in on the stage. The heavy, jeweled swords lay embedded in the table behind the magician, metal still quivering and singing from the impact. The scarves that formed her skirt floated around her legs in the false breeze as she spoke her closing speech. As her last words fell silent, she drew the energy to create her newest and most impressive illusion to date.

A rainbow of colors flashed up from her feet. Wind gusted, whipping the scarves around her waist and her long, fiery curls about her shoulders. Drums and cymbals crashed as the music reached its crescendo, fading into softer tones.

With no warning, a giant of a man appeared beside the magician, cloaked in chain mail. He stalked forward, sweeping her up into his arms and spinning her about in circles. Her crimson hair formed a cloak enshrouding them. Even above the pre-recorded classical music, her lilting laughter echoed through the room.

Then the image of the two lovers began to waver, like a desert mirage. The embracing couple became less and less distinct, before vanishing.

The audience surged to a standing ovation, the room thundering with applause. Backstage, Leo lowered Alana to her feet, being careful to avoid brushing her wounded arm.

Luckily, the bullet from Gabe's gun only grazed her, slicing the skin and leaving her arm with eighteen stitches but no serious damage.

The thought of how close he'd come to losing her still had the power to tie Leo's stomach in knots. Only luck, and a little supernatural help, saved her.

According to Alana, this was only the first of many brushes with the Otherworld to be expected in his new life. But no matter what they faced from here on, Leo knew that they would face it together.

Alana reached up to touch the metal mesh framing Leo's face. Clutching her hand in his, he placed a single kiss on her left palm, just below the diamond ring he'd given her the night before.

He looked deep into her eyes and said the three words that changed his whole outlook on life, opening his world to all types of magic.

"I love you."

A sniffling sound broke the romantic mood, bringing Leo's attention behind Alana. One arm in a neon green cast, Rick wiped imaginary tears from his cheek with his free hand. "Oh, you guys are just too sweet."

Alana let out a little squeal and launched herself at him, sending Rick rocking back on his heels. "I didn't know you were being released," she cried as she wrapped him in a bear hug.

"Hey now, watch the arm, and be careful of your own stitches," Rick said between chuckles. "You hurt yourself and the grizzly behind you will rip me a new one."

"Hush, Leo wouldn't hurt you," Alana replied, oblivious to the scowl Leo sent her direction.

Leo shook his head as Rick cast a disbelieving look over her shoulder. Alana didn't understand completely what she was getting into with him, but it would be fun exploring the options.

"The hospital called this afternoon," Leo said, walking forward to pry his fiancée off her best friend. "I thought it would be a nice surprise for you, so I asked one of the guys at work to give him a lift here after the show."

Alana gave Leo a quick kiss, turning back to Rick. Leo reached out, spinning her around and dipping her before locking his mouth over hers. Leo put every last ounce of emotion into his kiss, pulling Alana into a glamour more powerful than any she could create.

"Oh, give me a break," Rick whined. "Don't tell me I'm going to have to put up with this for the next fifty years. And I thought your folks were bad."

Alana pulled out of Leo's embrace to take a half-hearted swing at Rick. He laughed, catching her hand and pulling her back to him. "I'm glad you're alright, Curls," he whispered into her hair.

Alana looked up with a half smile. "Come on, Rick. Even Max came out worse than me, and he's already home gnawing on T-bones. The little scratch I got is nothing compared to some of the damage I've taken from creatures we've faced."

"But I wasn't there to help you," Rick replied, despondent. "Remember, that's my job, being a Helper."

Leo watched the pleading look cover Alana's face at the melancholy in Rick's voice. Leo stepped forward, offering Rick his hand. "And you will always be her Helper," he reassured Rick. "God knows, I'm not up to the job. Somebody who knows what they're doing needs to be there with her. Just get used to the fact that I'm going to be there too."

Rick rolled his eyes, but smiled. "Great, I get to be saddled with watching out for two gung ho types. I must have some seriously bad karma."

Rick paused for a moment, looking uncertain. "Speaking of bad karma, how's our friend doing?"

Leo shook his head, pulling the chain mail cowl off his head. "Gabe's trial isn't for a couple more weeks, but he's not looking good."

Rick raised an eyebrow.

"Bad dreams," Alana replied to his questioning gaze. "He hasn't slept in days. He says that when he sleeps, he can't wake up from the dreams."

"The D.A. thinks he's trying to build a case for the insanity plea. He keeps muttering about fairies." Leo turned his back and started tugging the chain mail shirt off. He didn't want to think about his partner, about what was happening to him already. The Otherworld had little patience, not even waiting for mortal justice to have a chance at him before beginning their work. He'd visited Gabe once in the jail. Seeing what was happening to his old partner, knowing that he could do nothing to stop it, tore at Leo. He hadn't gone back since.

Alana helped Leo tug the mail off, letting the warm metal slid through her fingers. "There's nothing else you could have done for him. He made his choices and has to face the consequences. At least you kept him here."

"But they're still torturing him," Leo whispered.

Alana turned his face towards her, holding him still with both palms. "For a single lifetime. They could have kept him alive indefinitely in their own world, a life without end filled only with pain. You spared him that. It was more than most would have done, or could have done."

Leo grimaced, not bothering to reply. He loved Alana, and he would spend his life with her. But he couldn't say that he always understood her or agreed with her. Then he smiled, laughing at himself.

Sounded like a pretty normal relationship to him.

About the Author

Jenifer Ruth holds Bachelor degrees in English and Secondary Education. She is currently working towards a Master's in Education. She has taught English for the past six years while writing, and starting a family. She lives in Las Vegas, Nevada with her husband and daughter.